Praise for DAUGHTERS OF THE AIR:

"A riveting and magical lament—for childhood, for the lost, and for the disappeared. Szilágyi has written a heartbreaking pageturner, rich in history and humanity."
—Sean Michaels, author of *Us Conductors*, winner of the Giller Prize

"Dirty—the war in Argentina. Dirty—the father's disappearance. Dirty—the mother's emotional withdrawal from her daughter. Dirty—the creaky Coney Island Wonder Wheel, the gritty New York City streets, and the polluted Gowanus Canal. Pluta, the teenage heroine of *Daughters of the Air*, flees from one dark place to others darker still, from one unfulfilled promise of escape to another. Yet in art, in opera, in the lusciousness of Anca Szilágyi's language, she soars."
—Maya Sonenberg, author of *Voices from the Blue Hotel* and *Cartographies*

"[Szilágyi's] work feels like a fairy tale—the sort of thing you'd find handwritten on a tiny scroll . . . under a mushroom in the middle of a forest on the longest day of the year."
—*Seattle Review of Books*

"Anca Szilágyi writes with an elegant economy that gives her work a moving urgency and a lushness that is uplifting. Crafting characters and moments of unexpected brilliance, Anca weaves narratives imbued with an original beauty. A pure delight."
—Chris Abani, author of *The Secret History of Las Vegas* and *Sanctificum*

D0180410

DAUGHTERS
of the
Air

A Novel

ANCA L. SZILÁGYI

LANTERNFISH PRESS
Philadelphia, PA

LANTERNFISH PRESS
399 Market Street, Suite 360
Philadelphia, PA 19106
lanternfishpress.com

COVER ART
Image: "Bird Moon" by Nichole DeMent.
Design by Michael Norcross.

EPIGRAPHS
Excerpt from "If I Were the Dark Winter," in *Artificial Respiration*, Ricardo Piglia; Daniel Balderston, translator, p. 78. Copyright © 1994, Duke University Press. All rights reserved. Republished by permission of the copyright holder. www.dukeupress.edu
Excerpt from "Sky," from *View with a Grain of Sand: Selected Poems by Wisława Szymborska*, translated from the Polish by Stanislaw Baranczak and Clare Cavanagh. Copyright © 1995 by Houghton Mifflin Harcourt Publishing Company. Copyright © 1976 Czytelnik, Warszawa. Reproduced by permission of Houghton Mifflin Harcourt Publishing Company. All rights reserved.

Printed in the United States of America.
Library of Congress Control Number: 2017944467
ISBN: 978-1-941360-11-8

"I have spoken of the theme of my story with Lisette. She asks me: Will you include a woman like me who knows how to read the future in the night flight of birds? Perhaps I will include a seer in my story, I tell her, a woman who knows, as you do, how to look where no one can see."

—RICARDO PIGLIA, *Artificial Respiration*

"The sky is everywhere
Even in the dark beneath your skin.
I eat the sky, I excrete the sky."

—WISŁAWA SZYMBORSKA, "Sky"

In memory of Beno Levi, who put a pencil in my hand, and Oscar Szilágyi, whom I never knew, source of the wanting-to-know.

DAUGHTERS
of the
Air

1. Connecticut
June 1980

A PALE BLIP dashed across the hockey field. Flitted into the shadows where the evening dew gathered, knapsack bumping against her back. Willows at the edge of the field grazed her forehead. Their branches rustled as she passed.

Her chest burned into her throat. Slipping through the tall hedges lining the Banderhock campus, she shimmied down against the dirt, breathed in the thick scent of humus, clawed at it, until finally she crawled face first into the cold of the chain-link fence beyond the shrubbery.

Tatiana laughed, a quick, self-mocking snicker. A sparrow, white breast spotted gray, clung to its perch atop the now-vibrating fence, twitching its head in the hazy evening light. It examined the girl lying in the dirt below and cheeped before pushing off in a flash of wings. With a glance over her shoulder, Tatiana pulled herself up and swung herself over the fence, thumping down with a grunt and nearly falling. Her palms ground against pebbles.

Something trickled behind her knee. A smear of blood: a little scratch, nothing more. The stragglers, the slow eaters and the dawdlers, would be filing out of the dining hall soon. Lights out would be in two hours and someone would realize she was missing. Tatiana sprinted down the back road toward New York. The gray of dusk deepened.

She didn't have an exact plan for when she got into the city, but she'd have graduated by the time she had an *exact* plan. To act at present had become her requirement. As soon as she realized this, she made the hastier plan, the I-can't-take-this-anymore-I'm-getting-the-fuck-out plan. How could she stay here? She'd turned possibilities over and upside down, again and again, until something inside her burst—and with it the ridiculous hope that her father, for two years thought dead, would come get her (tomorrow or next week or on the seventh day of the seventh month or some other mystical configuration she concocted) and regale her with incredible tales of where he'd been and what bravery he'd shown.

Now there was only the specter of that other certainty. Not yet proven but lurking, a lugubrious hobgoblin crouching heavy and low upon her insides, seeping dark juices, ready at any moment to spring: he wasn't ever coming back. (Didn't they always say *listen to your gut*? Didn't some cultures, also, read fortunes using splayed animal guts?)

There could be anywhere. *There* was away. She needed *there*; *here* was closed in, too falsely safe, too hiding of truth. For now, there was New York, sprawling and alive, big as Buenos Aires—bigger—a place to run and burst and be, unenclosed.

Sprinting faster than she had ever tried to in gym class, she felt the heat expand in her. The dark slime of her blood pooling in her ventricles, reluctantly churning. Her inner muck. After twenty or thirty minutes of this she stumbled. Vomited. Her knees shook in her clammy hands.

This won't do, she thought. Saliva dripped from her mouth. This won't do. She wiped it with the back of her hand, ran her nose along her sleeve. She should've changed out of her uniform, but changing in the woods would only cause delay. For a moment she saw herself among the trees, barefoot in her white underwear, in the glow of dull moonlight. A wet leaf stuck to one calf.

In the fog-milk of the woods, at other times, she had spied Banderhock students in furtive action. She hadn't entirely understood or taken part in that frenzied awakening of hormones: up against trees, or down in the bushes rustling. One time, a girl had seen her seeing them and smirked. Tatiana's belly had seized and quivered while her feet stayed rooted in the springtime mud. Later, by the curling steam of the cafeteria hot tables, the girl had murmured low in her ear: *perv.* But usually, no one noticed her. These sightings became a regular part of her reconnaissance missions as she searched for the best way off school grounds.

Rocking now from heel to ball, heel to ball, she braced herself to run further. Her mad hot belly compelled her. Oncoming night chilled the air, which bore the herbal scent of a fragrant bush she couldn't make out in the dark; she crushed its feathery branches, inhaling. The scent reminded her of something, of grass and of nickel, of her father or Lolo or something between her ideas of them. Crickets chirped. It was on the tip of her tongue, the name of that fragrance. It bothered her, but it shouldn't, because she should keep running. The sweat made her colder. She spat bile and then, looking up, saw

3

the high beams of an approaching car. Still bent over and clutching one knee, she put out her thumb.

The green Cadillac slowed, then stopped. The driver, a young man with a greasy brown cowlick, leaned out the window to get a better look. He wore a plaid shirt, sleeves rolled up skinny forearms roped with stringy muscles. Tatiana rose from her crouch, panting.

"Something the matter?" asked the man.

Tatiana wiped her runny nose again. "No. Can I get a ride?"

The man raised an eyebrow. He thrummed the car door with dry fingers that had remnants of motor oil sunk in their creases. He glanced down the road, over Tatiana's shoulder. "Where to?"

"New York City."

His eyes skittered over her unwashed hair tied in a knot, her disheveled blouse, and the plaid skirt she'd hiked up as she ran. She tugged the hem down as she thought, *I'm a mess, he'll say no*, but he nodded with pursed lips that seemed to say: of course. "It's where I'm headed. Hop in."

Tatiana wanted to belt out a whoop but suppressed it: her throat still burned. She jogged over to the passenger side. It would be a couple of hours to New York from northwestern Connecticut. She wondered why the man had chosen a back road, but didn't wonder too much. She could be sitting in the cold dirt trying to catch her breath, vomiting and snotting all over herself, or she could be driven into the city in some measure of style. There was something glamorous in this: two young fugitives joining forces in the woods, speeding into the big city without care. The urge to bounce against the seat passed, and she looked out the window as they turned onto another country road.

Tatiana cleared her throat. The young man handed her a slice of lemon from a small plastic container of lemon wedges nestled beside the emergency brake.

"Here," he said. "It'll make your mouth feel cleaner." She hesitated, then took the lemon and bit down on it. Its juice seared over stomach acid. "You from the school?"

She cleared her throat. "Why do you keep lemons in your car?"

"You from the school?"

"No." A shameless lie.

The man scoffed. "I'm Bobby," he said. A pause. He waited for her name.

"Pluta," she said, as clearly as she could enunciate, so that the "t" did not devolve into a "d." It was a name she'd devised for herself in early childhood, her special secret identity, cultivated almost as long as she could remember. Her parents had reluctantly consented to call her that, but when she arrived at Banderhock two years ago she'd wavered, become embarrassed for some petty adolescent reason, decided to stick with her more regal, more normal given name. But, Pluta. It had a dark ring to it that she still liked, and she would use it in the city. She hadn't yet settled on a surname that was suitable. Phantom. Fantasy. Phanta. She would have to keep thinking.

"That's an unusual name. What is it?"

Pluta—for now she was no longer Tatiana, but Pluta—coughed. Ahead lay the dark road, small patches of asphalt illuminated by the Cadillac's high beams. "Brazilian. From a place in the Amazon."

"That where you're from?"

"Yes. Well, no."

Bobby tapped the steering wheel, waiting for an explanation. The car accelerated.

5

"I am from Buenos Aires. Argentina. Do you know it?"

"Of course."

"But I have an aunt in Brazil. I stayed with her for a short time."

"So your aunt named you?" His fingers continued drumming the steering wheel. The car's speed steadied.

Not exactly. Pluta didn't care to explain. "Ye-es." Pluta, the name, had nothing to do with the Amazon, as far as she knew, because she had made it up. She was getting into trouble. Keep it simple, she told herself.

Bobby's eyes—large, brown, young—rolled. A gleaming flash of whites. He refocused on the road, accelerated again. "Your accent is kind of strange. Like, real proper, but off. I don't mean it in a bad way. Sort of British, but not. Sort of American, but not." He laughed as he changed lanes. "I'm just saying."

"Oh," she said. No one had really commented on her accent before. Not in two years at Banderhock, except early on, in the crucial first days of school when Casey had only said, demurely, "I like it," and she had muttered "Thank you" and shrunk away to make herself invisible, but then befriended Casey later, sort of. Her parents had moved her to a British school in Buenos Aires, and then her mother had moved her here, and it had changed her, made her strange. She *was* strange. It came out in her voice.

Bobby changed the subject. "I go to New York a lot. I like to drive around. See different parts. Been up north as far as Montreal, down south as far as Orlando. But I got a place in Brooklyn I'm going to stay in for now."

"Oh," said Pluta. "Why?"

"Got some business opportunities in the area that require my attendance for more than a stay on a couch. Y'know?"

Pluta shrugged.

"I'm an entrepreneur," he said with a flourish of his hand, elongating the word, taking pleasure in its sound.

"What's that?" She knew the word, but sometimes she liked to play dumb; it seemed like a tricky thing to do. Some people liked to explain things. This saved her from talking. Her father liked to explain things, but he wouldn't have liked her to play dumb.

Bobby smiled. "I'm my own businessman." The word *entrepreneur* certainly had more panache than that vague and pedestrian title, businessman. A touch of the international, the powerful. "I go where I please, do what I please."

"I see."

"And what are you going to do in New York?"

"I'm going to be an entrepreneur."

Bobby laughed. "That's good. That's good. I like that."

"So, the lemons?"

"Ah. Yeah. They keep my breath fresh."

"Oh."

Bobby sped up again, merged onto the interstate. Sharked the car across three lanes. A bottle knocked around the inside of the glove compartment, sloshing liquid against glass. He turned on the radio, fiddling with the dials.

Pluta tightened her lips into a thin line. When one of her parents had turned on the radio when she was little, the message had always been: *it is time to shut up.* Usually it had been the curt end of a "disagreement." Disagreements did not happen too often, but she still reacted this way to the sudden switching on of a radio. They rode in silence. Since Bobby did not speak, she concluded that the signal meant the same thing for him. Cars shunted alongside them. Growled. She sat back and

7

gazed at her palms, open in her lap, speckled with dirt and little scratches.

School had been a slow march toward mediocrity. Almost two years of it in the States. The prior year at the British school in Buenos Aires gave her a fine start; her father was fluent in English and helped her back then. But here, she'd resolved to speak as little as possible. Teachers walked on eggshells around her, having heard rumors of her situation. No one pushed her very hard. It was all gentle smiles and passing marks. She turned in her work on time. She seemed to try. She spent her free time alone in the library, reading books at random: anthropology, botany, capital punishment, disease. Mostly she looked at the pictures, which had a lot to say. This bookishness kept her from being labeled "at risk." Kept them from watching her too closely. Classmates, at first, had been enchanted by the international student who received care packages from Brazil. But since she didn't speak, she soon receded into the background, where it was comfortable. Often in her room or in her classes she plunged even deeper out of sight: into a notebook, drawing whatever came to mind. Stars, wings, and eyes, mostly.

Toward the spring of her first year, she warmed up to another outcast, Casey, a girl with stringy blond hair combed halfway over her face and a tangle of mouth metal. They sat together at meals, muttering brief exchanges, forking shriveled green beans and skinless chicken breasts, occasionally glancing down at their own emerging lumps. In June, Casey mumbled an invitation to her parents' summer house in Vermont and Tatiana's— Pluta's—mother Isabel encouraged her (nearly forced her) to accept. Pluta sensed it was all an exercise in pity.

"She doesn't want to deal with me right now," Pluta told Casey: one of the longest sentences she'd uttered that year. Vermont was pretty. Green hills, horses, ice cream. But she never warmed up to Casey's family and felt even her relationship with Casey to be odd: cold and distant, yet also too close. Their dining-hall exchanges stretched into awkward, halting conversations in which they avoided eye contact while asking elliptical questions and giving elliptical answers.

"My dad said Argentina had to clean up or something. For the World Cup." That time they were sitting cross-legged in the warm grass.

"Oh," Pluta said. She shredded some dandelions and forget-me-nots into minuscule pieces, a confetti of yellow and violet. "I don't know. I guess so."

"Like, all the attention was a good thing—for people."

"We left after the World Cup."

"Yeah. Right. Yeah." Casey looked confused; something about her confusion made Pluta feel a little better. She buried her hands beneath the small heap of torn flowers.

At Casey's mother's behest, they tried to play tennis, more often wielding the racquets like maces or bayonets. Many afternoons they spent in the basement, bathing in the television's epileptic glow. There was a lake, but they never swam, only wet their ankles. They got their periods at the same time and would heave their abdomens down on pillows on the floor to quell the roiling cramps. Casey's father walked in on this once; though he said nothing, simply offered the girls a bowl of sliced peppers and left, Pluta felt embarrassed for the rest of the summer.

Toward the end of the second school year, Isabel planned to go abroad and hoped Pluta would be invited to Casey's again. With Pluta away at Casey's that first summer, Isabel had discovered the freedom of traveling alone and wanted to repeat the experience. She even had the gall to call Casey's mother and arrange it. Casey's mother was too nice to say no. Pluta lied and said she would go.

It wasn't that she didn't want to go there again. No— it was more the prickly feeling in her gut, the something that pushed her now, the feeling that too much was hidden and she had to be alone, independent, to uncover it. Sometimes she imagined herself lifting a thin sheet off a mass of black, writhing snakes—a massive gorgon's head. But everyone around her kept tidying the sheet, smoothing it down, stretching it taut over churning lumps. It was the second-to-last day of school when, knowing Isabel was at that very moment flying across the Atlantic, Pluta ran.

Along the interstate the woods gave way to office parks, diners, strip malls. Small detached houses became small brick apartment buildings and then towering brown housing projects. Bronx. It had a certain oomph to its name that Pluta liked. She whispered it to herself. Bronx. *The* Bronx.

"We're in New York?"

"Yes," said Bobby.

"Faster than I thought."

"I'm an efficient driver. Where am I dropping you?"

Pluta twisted her mouth.

"Somewhere central, I guess." Maybe she could spend the night at Grand Central. She'd been there with Isabel when they went up to Banderhock. Perhaps she could curl up in a corner of one of its echoing marble halls; in the bustle, who would notice? She could wait tables or wash dishes at the oyster bar where they'd eaten. But that wouldn't work. Isabel would easily find her there.

The car slowed.

"You mean you don't know."

"No."

Bobby sighed. "You have nowhere to go."

"I guess not."

"That's all right." He sped up again with a lurch. "That's all right. No worries. Let's get into Brooklyn, we'll have some dinner. You'll figure your shit out. Okay?"

"Okay," she said, less ebullient than before.

Between the Manhattan and Brooklyn Bridges, along a partially cobbled street, a row of hulking warehouses squeezed against a two-story building with grayish paint flaking off its cornice. A neon sign in the window buzzed and flickered: "_arty's. Open all n_te." Bobby parked at a haphazard angle on the deserted street, one tire up on the curb. The East River glimmered in the distance, lapping at rotting docks.

Pluta smelled salt air and sewage when she got out of the car. Inside _arty's, a man leaned over a chipped Formica counter, leafing through a tabloid with thick fingers. His bald scalp was mottled yellow; crude blue sailors' tattoos of anchors, mermaids, and cryptic acronyms dotted his arms. He yawned as they entered, scratching the salt and pepper scruff on his jaw. He nodded at Bobby, who chose one of the three rickety booths.

"What'll you have?" asked the man.

"What do you want?" Bobby asked Pluta, as if to translate.

Pluta shrugged.

"Two number twos. And coffee?"

She nodded.

"And coffee."

"You got it," said the man, disappearing behind a swinging door.

"Marty used to be a longshoreman," said Bobby.

"What's that?" Pluta asked, wary; this term she did not know.

"Do you know anything?" he teased. "He carried heavy things off boats. Onto docks." Bobby mimed bearing cargo on his shoulders, bowing under its imaginary weight. A scrawny Atlas. "Get it?"

"Yes, I see."

Marty brought out hot, oval plates. Corned beef hash, potatoes oozing thin red grease. Pluta tried the coffee. Brown water. Nothing like her aunt Lolo's coffee, boiled in a copper pot from . . . where was it? Turkey? At least it was hot. She copied Bobby, pouring in copious amounts of cream and sugar. They ate quickly, without speaking. As they slowed, they sat back, expanded. Bobby belched, as if to break the silence. He held a curled-up fist to his mouth after the fact.

"What now, *chico*?"

"*Chica*," Pluta corrected with mild surprise. Not many people knew Spanish, even bad Spanish, at Banderhock. She'd taken English with a small group of international students. And French. Latin and German were the other popular options. Intermittent phone calls with Isabel brought her back to Spanish, seemed to wake up parts of her brain that were shriveling. She wondered if Lolo had felt the same way, all those years alone in Brazil. All those dictionaries she pored over.

A water bug scuttled across the black-and-white floor tiles. Pluta slid to the edge of the booth and stomped it out. The faintest of crunches.

"Atta girl!" said Marty, looking up from his paper. Pluta dragged her eyes away from the splotch. Marty came around the counter with a dustpan and swept it away.

"You can stay with me," said Bobby. "I have a couch." His second mention of a couch: Pluta wondered about this. He seemed proud to be offering it. Maybe it was a new thing for him, having a couch. In any case, she thought, sitting in Marty's until daybreak probably wouldn't work. And it was getting late, and she had no idea where she was, even if she could recognize the Brooklyn Bridge.

"Maybe," she said. She catalogued the earthly belongings in her bag: two changes of clothing, the remnants of Lolo's latest care package, her passport, some crumpled traveler's checks, and a small wad of cash, carefully accumulated over the last few months from Isabel's wired allowance. She wanted to revel in her freedom, in case it was short-lived. She chucked her chin toward Marty. "I want to get a tattoo. Well, not like his. But my own."

Bobby scoffed. "You're funny. Let me get dinner. And then you'll get your tattoo." Pluta made no pretense of resisting. She wanted to save her money for the tattoo.

They drove to Flatbush Avenue. It bustled in the night with fast food, clothing stores, barber shops. Electric light and music. It didn't feel as desolate as the place around Marty's.

Bobby said the area was called Vinegar Hill but didn't know why. Guessed they once made vinegar there. Or the people, mostly of the old, crusty dockworker type, were filled with it. They went to a storefront tattoo parlor around the corner from a Wendy's. Further down, the streetlamps illuminated elegant brownstones, tall oaks, and wide sidewalks that buckled over gnarled tree roots.

The shop smelled of hot glue and burnt plastic. The artist asked Pluta her age and she gave the required lie. Eighteen. Only four years off—not such a bad lie. The artist grunted assent, disbelieving and accepting, and nodded toward where she should sit and wait. Under a bright fluorescent buzz, Pluta flipped through a dusty album of images and glanced at another customer as the artist needled a woman's name into the flesh of his forearm.

She felt clear-eyed and sober. The needle frightened her, but she wanted to defy that fright. In some sense she saw it as training. She was becoming courageous, sometimes even scaring herself with this business of courage and defiance, which made her laugh. Following rules had stopped working. She would do whatever she wanted. That's what felt right.

And she knew what she wanted. At least at this moment. The only thing that made sense. Wings. Permanent wings along her shoulder blades. And her name between them. Pluta. She still needed the surname. Playing with the metal rings of the album binder, open and shut, open and shut, listening to the hum of the needle, thinking of the flap of wings, she arranged and rearranged letters in her mind. Phantamele. No. Tantaphele. No. Mal. Mel. Nightingales, larks, pheasants—Melpheasant. Yes. Pluta Melpheasant. She wrote it down for the artist in block letters.

When it was her turn, the artist quoted her a price much higher than she expected. She'd known it would be expensive, just not that expensive. But then, what did she know? She didn't have any information to go on. None of the girls at Banderhock had tattoos.

The artist explained that he worked by the hour and that she would have to get it done in installments anyway. First the outline, then additional layers, colors. She could pay along the way. They'd start with the outline. This first visit would make a fair dent in her cash reserves. But, she figured, she'd make more money somehow. She wouldn't back down now, so early. This was important.

In a curtained cubicle she took off her shirt and lay on a black-cushioned table. Wondered if the slight hump of her scoliosis would distort the wings. The artist draped a medical-blue paper towel beneath her shoulder blades, swabbed her skin with something cool, sterilizing. Then the needle began its buzzing, a honeybee dragging its stinger through her skin; when she made a face the vinyl cushion squidged beneath her cheek. She imagined the needle *was* a honeybee, depositing honey beneath her skin—honey made of magic pollen. Like in that dream she'd had in Brazil—the strange dark flower, the woman's eye. Then her mind played tricks on her, making the hot lines of honey on her back squirm. This irked her.

She tried to relax and visualized what she must look like from above. Her thin, pale torso, her pleated plaid skirt. Schoolgirl in a tattoo parlor. Fourteen going on eighteen. Not such a big jump.

She forced herself to lie still and found herself grinding her teeth. In her mind's eye she followed the trail of the needle's pressure. A needle, not a honeybee, she reminded herself, to prevent a recurrence of the honey-squirm. Occasionally the artist dabbed at her. *Blood?* At some point she may have fallen asleep, but she couldn't be sure for how long. And then it was done. The artist taped a sheet of clear plastic on top.

15

"You'll probably want to sleep on your belly."

Pluta nodded.

They got back in the car. Bobby didn't live far from there, five minutes. Misshapen white ziggurats, another set of housing projects, divided a bustling commercial district from a darker residential area. They drove on into the dark and parked in front of a row of squat walkups. Pluta asked the name of this neighborhood. Bobby said it was Gowanus.

A dog barked through a window barred with wrought-iron curlicues freshly painted with gobs of black. Across the street, a billboard solicited candidates for the job of New York City Corrections Officer: "Nowhere to go but up, up, up." They walked six flights to the top beneath dim, flickering lights. A pile of cigarette butts sat at the landing; burn marks dotted the wall. Shards from a broken bottle of vodka lay on the floor, scattered in a starburst.

Bobby swept aside some of the glass with his foot, clearing a wider path in the hall. Pluta shrank a little as she walked behind him past the shards. They stood before his door. It was tan, with chipped paint revealing green and brown islands. What would be on the other side? Would it be like the hallway, would it be better or worse? What was she getting herself into? He opened the top lock, the middle, the bottom. She stilled herself. The plastic on her back crinkled. Bobby swung open the door.

The apartment smelled of fresh paint and turpentine. Bobby stumbled through the darkness, finding the single floor lamp that lit up the living room.

He pointed to the sagging couch. "That's yours." He went into the bedroom, came out with a thin pillow and gray, institutional-looking blanket, dropped them on the couch. "Bathroom's there." He pointed to a dark room, from which gurgling and hissing emerged, and then toward another dark room emitting a shuddering hum. "Kitchen's there. I'm heading to bed." He waved over his shoulder. "Wake me if you need anything."

There was barely anything in the room. Some old curtains were piled on the floor. A family of dust bunnies nestled against the baseboards. A window opened onto complete darkness. She cupped her hands against the glass but couldn't see what was outside. Opening the window let in cool, stale air. Not the outside; an airshaft. A faint whistle chirred up the six-story tunnel. Her heart leapt.

Quickly, she latched the window shut, muffling the whistle. She held the latch tight, as if something in that dark shaft could force the window back open. Stepped back, eyes on the window, and then turned and made her bed. The upholstery was rough. She lay on her belly, her cheek down on the pillow, wondering if she'd made a mistake, but then chastised herself. It was only the first step. Everything would become clearer and more solid in the morning. She turned off the lamp and settled in, hoping she would sleep. At school she'd often mashed her face into the pillow, bullying herself out of the crying that inevitably followed long hours of dry-eyed blinking, wondering, questioning. No more. Little feet pitter-pattered along the wall of the room. She caught the outline of a mouse before clamping her eyes shut.

2. *Buenos Aires*
July 1978

HAIL CLATTERED OUTSIDE—jumped and bounced on the flagstones. Pluta fidgeted in the crimson leather armchair beside the fireplace, across from her father's big, messy desk, with her homework splayed across her lap: sentence diagrams. They worked quietly, Daniel with a red pencil hovering over a pile of exams. His class had a fancy name: Principles of Sociology. It sounded terribly boring. He brought a silvery *bombilla* to his lips, sucking up more maté from the gourd. A chill draft seeped through the garden doors. Pluta sniffled.

"Are you cold?" asked Daniel.

Pluta shook her head and waited for Daniel to return his attention to the exams before wiping her nose on her sleeve. Her mother would have used the invisible eyes all over her head to catch her. Her father, too, had invisible eyes, he just used them more judiciously. Pluta smiled to herself, drew squiggles in the margins of her paper, erased them, and gazed at the blue flowers and black wavy lines in the rug at her feet.

The next time Daniel looked up, he snorted. "What did you do to your face?"

Pluta scratched her head with the eraser end of her pencil and stood on the chair to glance in the mirror over the mantle; her papers scattered to the floor. Stray pencil marks streaked her cheeks. Daniel rose and came toward her. He was wearing her favorite sweater of his, a soft cable-knit one she used to rub her face on when she was just a bit younger, just a bit more willing to fall asleep on his arm when they watched old films on television. He licked his thumb and smeared the graphite off her cheek, the faint green scent of maté on his breath. She laughed, shrinking back. Had it been Isabel, it would have been a serious thing, but all she wanted to do was tug at his red, scraggly mustache. So she did.

"Oooph," he said. He puffed out his cheeks, put a hand on his hip in mock indignation. She bounced back down into the chair and gathered her papers; she knew she wasn't supposed to stand on chairs. Turning serious, he said, "Don't bounce so much, you'll break the springs."

"Is she disturbing you?" Isabel, her dark hair pulled back and gleaming, towered in the doorway. She wore the burgundy heels she liked to wear to see her friends in Recoleta. Pluta wondered if she'd been standing there long. Tightening the sash of her raincoat, Isabel turned to Pluta. "Don't you have homework?" Pluta thought it was obvious—the homework was right there in her lap. Isabel checked her lipstick in a compact before snapping it shut and waiting for a reply.

"What is the object complement of that sentence?" Daniel boomed in English, filling the silence. He pointed prophetically at a half-finished diagram. Pluta chewed on her pencil and pretended to look at her notebook. Outside, the hail came down harder, bouncing off the window panes; ice slid down the leaves of the potted ferns, cold gray-white gathering on the green.

"Well, you have to finish your homework tonight," said Isabel. "No homework tomorrow. We're going to La Rural."

"Yes, Mami, I know." Daniel patted Pluta's head and went over to give Isabel a peck goodbye. His wife pulled him into the hall; their murmuring trailed off to the front door.

"You let me know if you need help," Daniel said when he came back. Pluta pointed at the diagram she'd been staring at for the past eight minutes. Daniel smiled and crossed the room again.

The next day at the fairground, heifers and bulls swung their tails and lowed. Judges inspected the cattle, which were lined up by class, evaluating snouts, flanks, and rumps as the crowds watched from the stands or milled at the gates, moving between agricultural and livestock exhibitions. A proud rancher sprayed water on his prize-winning bull, whose ears were dotted with blue, white, and yellow ribbons; the bull flicked his wet tail, embellished with a red pom-pom. The flicking tail, in turn, sprayed the nearest spectators. Daniel stood by the gate, at the edge of the crowd, holding Pluta's hand. His other arm was linked with Isabel's. Droplets landed on them as the bull twitched and Pluta jumped back. Daniel laughed and squeezed her hand, pointing out how the pom-pom was meant to draw attention to the bull's rump. She squeezed his hand back and nodded. Thousands wandered around them.

A policeman in sunglasses patrolled the fairground and scanned the buzzing, milling crowd. His gaze seemed to rest on Daniel for too long before he moved on. Daniel squeezed Pluta's hand again, then grasped Isabel's. And then, as if his pulse had caught on something, as if he wished to smooth over this hiccup of apprehension and let his pulse resume a healthy pace, he squeezed their hands in turns, making a silly game of squelching palms until Pluta giggled and Isabel narrowed her eyes as if to say: *enough*. Daniel, relieved that the source of his wife's disturbance was his silliness and not that other thing, leaned in and laid on his wife a loud, wet kiss. Pluta, uninterested in her parents' romance, broke away to see the exhibition on birds.

Daniel and Isabel followed. A breeze rustled the leaves of low jacaranda trees. Daniel overtook Pluta and bent down to button up her sweater against the cold, pulling against the slight curve in her spine. The girl had recently had a growth spurt and now tended to hunch over. She'd inherited his slight bones and her mother's statuesque height; her body would warp painfully through the next stage of her life. There'd been talk among them about braces—for the back and also for the teeth: the lower row crowded, forcing the canines to turn askew, and the upper row with a centered gap. Isabel's large teeth (*chompers*, he liked to call them) in Daniel's small mouth.

"I'm not a baby," she said, squirming away yet seeming, also, to enjoy the attention.

Daniel laughed, chucking her chin. "Of course not," he said. Inside him something twinged. Pluta's general reticence often made what she *did* say surprising. Even if that claim—*I'm not a baby*—was valid. Just the day before, he realized, he'd condescended to her, but she hadn't said anything, simply bounced in the chair. Every day contradicted itself. Perhaps it was because they were in public. Perhaps it was because Isabel was with them. No—that wasn't right; he didn't want to think that. He would have to read more about child development. It wasn't his specialty. What research had been done on preadolescent only children in households of mixed heritage?

No. He was drifting into the comfort of detached, academic territory. He would have to speak to her more. Not only was her body at a tipping point, her mind was too. That dreadful age, its constant shifting. It was difficult without another child around, an ally, a measure of growth. Isabel worried that she didn't have close friends. He agreed, it would be nice, but he'd also had trouble as a child and had always been more comfortable around adults—intellectual adults, compassionate adults. Socializing was difficult for him even now, and he was frequently baffled at what to say. *Anything*, Isabel would sometimes snap after a family gathering or party. In his writing, words came from a separate well. He supposed Pluta was the same, would be the same. Isabel did not have their problem, seemed never to have had their problem. She of the long limbs, aquiline nose, and glinting black eyes.

The small family warmed in a shaft of afternoon sun. In wire cages lined up on tabletops and beneath the jacaranda trees, birds clucked, crowed, cooed, and ruffled their feathers: speckled hens; Japanese roosters gleaming black with white hackles twitching; slate-colored quails; drab pigeons. A peacock strutted, long neck bobbing forward as he dragged the eyes of his tail behind him on the grass. Radiant in the light, a lone pheasant preened in a bell-shaped cage.

"That is a golden pheasant," Isabel was telling Pluta. Daniel closed his eyes a moment to soak in the sun. Stuck his hands in his pockets, let the warmth flood his chest.

"Pheasant," murmured Pluta, as if it were a word in a

language lesson.

Daniel tried to make himself present in this small moment of happiness. Now they did not quarrel, now they did not disagree; they simply stood together in the sun. He tried to form a picture that he could imprint in his memory and savor.

It was fleeting, of course; it always was. At the corner of his eye, Daniel still sensed the hovering presence of the police officer patrolling the grounds with a slow, self-assured gait, arms folded behind him. A nonchalant façade covering who-knows-what intent, who-knows-what orders. Daniel felt the heat of the officer's body as he passed near them in the crowd. Sunlight passed through the officer's sunglasses, making eye contact possible; he was so close that Daniel smelled sour coffee on his breath. The officer looked away, swaggered on. Daniel tried to relax, reasoned his stiffness could not have been perceived by anyone but himself. He told himself: *He was not really looking at you. You are nothing but a family man. You are insignificant; there is nothing of interest. Those students were not close to you.* He forced his jaw to unclench. In any case, *this* would not be the place for an arrest. His heart pounded.

Lately there had been unrest not just in the university as whole but also, more intensely, in his own small, fledgling department. Of course sociologists in a public university would be skittish, but the anxiety took on a razor edge with the appointment of a new chair. The first serious trouble had come two years ago, after the coup, after the mass firings and restructuring of the curricula. *Let's be prudent,* they'd said after the firings; *let's reintensify our focus on practical training.* They'd redesigned the textbooks and picked the libraries clean, locking up prohibited books in a vault along with anything that bore the faintest whiff of subversion. A younger professor had joked: *Might as well throw in anything with a red cover, just to be sure.* He was also fired, though not officially for that comment. Daniel never saw him again.

It wasn't as if it hadn't happened before. On and off for his entire career there'd been these bouts of skittishness. He'd more or less gotten used to it. Now, though. Bitterly he laughed and bit his lip. He had tried to make alliances by taking on more work, tried to make himself indispensable. He'd tried to hide behind a sea of statistics and, taking a cue from the philosophy department, had clouded his work as much as possible with abstract, difficult rhetoric, always choosing the most arcane technical terms, writing for the narrowest, most specialized audience, writing some things only he would ever understand. He wondered whether five years from now even he would be able to make any sense of it. How long could this go on?

In the pit of his stomach, that irksome twinge sharpened: at some point, he'd grumbled to the wrong person. He didn't even know who; perhaps he'd grumbled to a few of the wrong people. When he shouldn't have grumbled at all. It wasn't even the content of the grumbling that was an issue anymore; the fact itself seemed worrisome enough. An offhand remark in the office? Perhaps after a lecture? A darkened face. He recalled a darkened face in the lecture hall. *How long can this go on?* Was that all he'd said? Had the darkened expression in the audience registered its answer: *as long as it takes*? He'd been upset about the students—the one and then the other. Was his question "suspicious" enough? Radios everywhere implored citizens to report "suspicious activity." Everything suspicious threatened "national security." How many people used those hotlines?

A wave of nausea surged. He needed to get away, wanted to regress to Barracas, to his parents' house, to his childhood, where he would be told with calm assurance what to do. But there was no one there. He and Isabel were adults alone. Maybe they'd been wrong to stay, but leaving never seemed an option, not the right option, giving up like that. He hated his hedging. Why couldn't he be more—? Goosebumps ran up his arms; in the cold, his fingertips grew slightly purple.

They'd been strolling, Isabel more or less leading. She seemed to know his mind and they had wandered off, far away from the fair. Though her eyes were soft, willing to let him have his reverie, he could tell she wanted him to come back to the present. Resting a hand on his wife's back, Daniel tried to think of something to say about the fair. He would go to the office now, get his things, work from home on Monday. He rubbed Isabel's back, swallowed.

Finally, he said, "I have to go in to the university today." It wasn't what she wanted to hear, but he would get done what he could while the office was empty—finish commenting on that paper and shove it under his colleague's door—and call in sick tomorrow. He would avoid the office, yes, only come in for lectures, and do a lot of work remotely, make himself seem wrapped up in technical matters. Perhaps tomorrow it would be cold enough to get the fireplace going. A nice quiet day by the fire.

"Now?" asked Isabel. "But it's Sunday." The happiness of the day still lingered at her mouth. This was her favorite event of the year; growing up, she had gone to La Rural countless times. For her it was not so much about the animals as about being around the thousands of people, the distinct feeling of tradition. But last year,

Daniel had not wanted to go, saying it was inappropriate, saying he didn't feel right, saying there were more important things. Yes, there had been other coups and life had gone on, but something worse than malaise had settled in. This year, Isabel insisted. She'd been upset by the previous year's disruption. And over the past few months, with all the manufactured hullabaloo about the World Cup, a sense of unity and enthusiasm had infected her, even though she didn't follow football. *Get your head out of the university,* she'd said. *It'll be good for you.* She brought it up again and again. They would go no matter what, be out and about as a family. Just for one day. So he relented. But now—he was leaving.

"I'm sorry. I forgot that I promised to do some things for tomorrow. The papers are at my office." He kissed her high cheekbone and tousled Pluta's hair.

"Don't stay late," said Isabel, as if she tasted something sour.

Tenderly, Daniel clasped the nape of her neck, rubbed her earlobe with his index finger and thumb; some of the sourness seemed to dissolve. She'd be happy tomorrow, when he stayed home. They'd spend some time together by the fire. "I'll try."

"Bye, Papi," said Pluta.

He kissed the top of her head.

As Daniel headed toward Plaza Italia, the sun angled down into late afternoon, warming the ruddy hair tufted in a sparse ring about his head, a small clump in the center bobbing gently like a feather.

"Let's go see the horses," said Isabel. Pluta grumbled, but they went. The horses were Isabel's favorite; they had to see the horses, otherwise going to the fair made no sense. Four enormous stallions, two black and two chestnut, trotted into the stadium; military men in dress uniform sat atop them. The crowd applauded. The stallions leapt over hurdles, jutting their long heads forward as boots flashed against their torsos. Isabel clasped her hands to her chest and crooned at the horses' strength and grace.

Next, a woman in an old-fashioned dress with a billowing, ruffled skirt led out a mare wreathed in flowers. She smiled at the audience with a game-show hostess's wave. A gold locket at her chest winked in the last rays of sunlight.

"Isn't that beautiful?" asked Isabel. Pluta nodded. The equestrian show continued for another twenty minutes. Pluta squirmed, kicking her legs against the seat and slouching. Isabel sighed—the child was much too old for squirming and slouching—but she tamped down an instinct to admonish, something she did not wish to do on this day. "All right, then. I suppose we've seen enough. Let's go home."

"Can we go to the park first?"

Isabel nodded. Why end the outing so early? They headed across lawns and red dirt paths toward the lake, through the eye-stinging smoke of grilled sausage and the scent of roasting nuts.

A chain of children ran through a damp open field in the park, the leaders stopping spasmodically so those on the end would snap forward, whiplike. Pluta ran to join them, the sweet eggshell ribbon of her dress fluttering behind her, and grabbed the hand of the last child; they ran forward with the snap of the whip. Isabel waited at the edge of the lawn, contemplating how her daughter might grow into a young lady. Classes in etiquette, correct posture? It would boost her confidence, knowing proper behavior for all occasions. The difficulty of being a teenager could be assuaged. There was time yet. A gush of pride spread through her chest. Yes, that would be just the thing. She liked this idea—she liked it very much. She would have to ask Mrs. Hoffman or one of the mothers at the British school. The line of children jerked forward and then heaved sideways and forward again. At the next heave, Pluta lost hold of the chain and slid face first into the mud. Isabel's hands curled into fists.

"Pluta," she shouted. She yanked the girl up by the arm. "Your dress is *ruined*." Her face grew hot as she boxed Pluta's ear and she wanted to cry, but of course she didn't. A beautiful dress, she'd bought it downtown just for the fair, and Pluta knew it. Isabel shook her head and rubbed her tingling palm against her own check-ered skirt as the heat slid from her cheeks. Her child was no angel. Why would she expect otherwise? A sim-ple, more instructive punishment occurred to her: Pluta would have to wash the dress. "We're going home."

Pluta cupped her ear with both hands. The side of her head buzzed with stinging warmth. She held back her tears and scrambled to keep up with Isabel's long strides toward their bus stop on Avenida Santa Fe. The mud chilled her front; some dripped from her chin and cheek, but she didn't dare wipe at it with her sleeve. On the curb she blinked through wet lashes as bus after bus ambled around Plaza Italia and down the middle lanes of Santa Fe. Isabel extracted a handkerchief from her purse and handed it to Pluta, who rubbed at the drying mud. Finally, the bus that would take them home to Belgrano screeched to the curb.

It was a straight shot down the wide avenue. Soon after they rumbled over the train tracks, Avenida Santa Fe became Avenida Cabildo. As it was Sunday, much of the city was quiet, with the exception of La Rural's bustle around the Plaza and a small number of Jewish neighborhoods, including the section around Cabildo to which Isabel and Pluta rode. The stretch between La Rural and Belgrano was quiet. A few people sat outside cafés, and Pluta, clutching her mother's handkerchief, regarded them as the bus careened down the avenue. She wondered if those sitting on metal chairs felt cold. It seemed as if most wore sunglasses, despite the approach of evening. She wished she could see their eyes.

Dusk's violet light tinted Isabel's skin. The street grid changed in the Belgrano area. Isabel had explained to Pluta once how it used to be its own town. She seemed to like how it still maintained a sense of separateness. For instance, no *Subte* lines came to the area—not yet, anyway. Maybe one day they would muck everything up, digging tunnels beneath the streets. Pluta's tears dried. Her ear tingled and her gut prickled; she glared at her mother. Isabel drew back, looking almost scared but also tense, ready to pounce. Pluta narrowed her eyes. With the bus's lurch, she jolted toward her mother. Waves of heat wafted off of Isabel. Pluta leaned into that heat.

Isabel rang for the next bus stop. As they debarked, she stuck out her hand to help Pluta down the steps, but Pluta ignored her, making a pretense of still wiping her hands with the filthy handkerchief. They pushed past Cabildo's busy shops and kiosks, surrounded by the rustle of shopping bags and the clatter of heels, the clangor of metal shutters being pulled down for the evening and the relaxed familial chatter of Sunday strolls. Turning onto their side street, they were soon enveloped in quiet. They passed the synagogue that they attended once or twice a year, to ring in the New Year and to atone. Townhouses squeezed together, doors shut and blinds drawn. Some were British-style Georgian red-brick houses; others were in the Spanish style, pink or yellow or whitewashed.

Pluta touched a wooden thorn spiking out of her favorite tree, the same thorn she touched every time she passed, on the sidewalk just outside the gate to their neighbor's house. At the British school, a life science teacher had called it a floss silk tree. In Spanish it was *palo borracho*—drunken stick. Pluta wanted bark like that, thick with thorns, as her skin, as armor. But the thorns were not really sharp and hard; at their core, they were filled with something like cotton. She tapped the fleshy pad of her fingertip against the speckled thorn and found something reassuring about this repeated gesture. The tap would travel down to the roots of the tree, under the soil, and tell the house of her arrival.

Yet their house, whitewashed with red trim, always seemed surprised at their arrival, as if they belonged elsewhere: long-eyed windows and a slack-jawed mouth of a door, freshly painted red, mustached with a scalloped and spotted glass marquee. It stood behind a stately wrought-iron fence that clanked primly behind them. Isabel's grandparents had bought the house when their business boomed, twenty years after their arrival from Syria. Three generations had once lived on its three floors. Now it was Isabel's and housed only the family of three. This was her preference: a study and library for Daniel, a place to entertain her friends (though more often they met out, at cafés), and ample room for Pluta to roam.

Isabel's sister, abroad in Brazil and much older, rarely visited. And the extended family had lately edged away, seeing them less and less, wary of Daniel's sociology, the

31

snobbish, weak-wristed, dangerous intellectualism of an Ashkenazi. The Professor, they called him, when he wasn't in the room.

Once he had told Isabel, in the heat of an argument, "Your people are a thousand years behind." It became a refrain she would spout back at him from time to time, shoulders high and eyes throwing spears: "How could *I* know? I'm a thousand years behind."

Sometimes, if they were in the kitchen when she said this, she would turn away and switch on the radio perched above the sink to blast the evening news, the broadcasts he hated most, and she would wash the dishes vigorously, water steaming hot. *"Allá,"* he might then say, his voice muffled by the rush of water and the static on the radio. And he'd stalk into his study and slam the door.

But sometimes, if he was quick enough, he'd catch her hand before she reached the dial, and kissing it firmly he'd ask to put an end to the latest skirmish of the Russo-Turkic war. And just like that, they would lean in for a delicate kiss, reunited in the shared, benign annoyance of being lumped together with the Russians and the Turks.

Isabel locked the heavy wooden door behind them, surprised at her sense of relief. She leaned against it and let out a long exhalation as Pluta went upstairs to change and retreat into the playroom. In the kitchen, Isabel reached for dinner pots above the stove. Her hand trembled but, she told herself, there was no reason for it. The pots clanged, their clangor disturbing the quiet of the house, disturbing her. She calmed herself with a cigarette and stared into the yard: the thick patch of mint, the jasmine shrubs whose white buds she clipped on spring mornings for the breakfast table, the flagstone path leading to the rickety *asador* they didn't use enough.

Church bells struck six and the mulberry sky darkened, pinpricked by faint stars. They waited two hours, and then three. This was not terribly unusual. Daniel often worked late and sometimes slept on the couch in his office. Stew bubbled on the stove; orange chunks of *calabaza* softened. Mother checked in on daughter, once, stood over her shoulder as she stumbled through a forgotten algebra assignment. If x equals six, then y equals . . . their stomachs grumbled. Isabel checked her watch. They ate without him, without speaking, save for the stock phrases: *is it warm enough, pass the salt, finish that last bite, fat is good for you, good for your skin.* It took Pluta a while to chew down the gristle.

After dinner, Isabel sent Pluta to bed. She washed the muddied dress herself. It was faster this way, less cumbersome than supervising Pluta through it, less of an ordeal. And something about watching her daughter endlessly chewing her meat at dinner, blank eyes staring at a meaningless spot on the floor, gave her a bad feeling. She wanted Pluta to learn, but she'd looked so pitiful sitting there in the kitchen, nothing but the hum of the refrigerator to fill the silence.

On the small armchair in Isabel's bedroom upstairs sat Daniel's brown corduroy sport coat, exactly where he'd flung it the day before. She ran her hands down the soft sleeves before slipping it onto a hanger. She gazed a moment at the jacket, hanging in the dark closet, and lifted one cuff to her nose. It smelled of coffee, tobacco, and cinnamon. He'd always smelled faintly of cinnamon, though he didn't eat inordinate amounts of it—it was simply his scent. She found herself smiling at this: so different from the cologne-splashed cheeks of the men in her youth. Down the hall, Pluta was finally brushing her teeth. Isabel was satisfied that she didn't have to remind her; it sounded as if the teeth were getting a good hard scrub.

Isabel padded to the bathroom as Pluta spit into the sink. A swirl of red in the white froth.

"You don't need to brush so hard," she said. Pluta looked at her in the mirror, said nothing, kept brushing. "Enough now. Go to bed." Pluta rinsed her mouth out, not looking at her mother. Isabel bent down, positioning herself for a minty goodnight peck. Cold nose, wet lips. She rose, dabbed at her cheek with a towel. "Good night."

"Good night," Pluta mumbled.

Before settling into bed, Isabel glanced at the clock: midnight. What was so important so late on a Sunday night? He must have promised something for first thing Monday. He worked too much. Isabel huffed and leaned against several pillows, flipping through gossip magazines. She kept a short pile on her nightstand for nights like this, when Daniel worked late. She knew he tried not to say what he thought of those magazines being in the house, and he knew she tried not to read them when he was there. The pages snapped as she turned them; she bit at one nail before catching herself and scowling.

They had a tradition, some Sunday nights. The three of them on the couch watched old classic films, Italian or Argentine. Pluta would fall asleep in the middle, head on Daniel's shoulder, and when her gentle snoring started, he'd carry her up to her bedroom. A few weeks ago, Pluta had stayed awake through most of *El ángel desnudo*; Isabel kept glancing over at her, but afterwards she and Daniel agreed it was probably okay that she'd seen a sixteen-year-old Olga Zubarry's naked back. The circumstances of the nudity in the film—a bankrupt gambler sending his daughter to pose for a sculptor, with disastrous consequences—seemed clear enough.

Isabel fell asleep with the lights on and the page open to a glossy snapshot of Susana Giménez strutting about Barrio Norte, tall, blond, tan, her chiseled face covered by enormous black sunglasses slipping down her nose.

That night, Daniel did not return.

3. *Brooklyn*
June 1980

LIGHT FROM THE AIRSHAFT grayed the room. Rumbling trucks, shouts, and the crashing of metal trash cans lurched Pluta out of slumber. Stiff-necked, she twisted herself slowly up and then rose with a start, forgetting momentarily where she was. Bobby stood in the doorway holding a brown paper bag dotted with grease spots.

"Breakfast." He moved toward the couch and she pushed aside the blanket and pillow, making space for him. "Thanks," he said. "This also happens to be the dining room."

They sank their teeth into soft egg sandwiches, salty grease dribbling down their fingers.

"I have some business today. Most of the day. You don't want to stay here all day, do you?"

What could I do here? she wondered. "No, I'll go out." She rubbed her face; a wrinkle in the pillowcase had imprinted soft grooves in her cheek. A faint bar of sunlight crept into the hall from the kitchen. She nodded to herself: she would see what she could see.

"Cool," nodded Bobby. "Come back around seven, if you want. I should be back by then." He gave her two coins with hexagonal holes in the middle. "Use that for the subway if you want. You know how to use the subway, right?"

She jingled the tokens in her palm. "Yeah. Thanks."

"I have to go pretty soon, so you better hurry up if you want to shower or anything."

Pluta grinned. She didn't have to shower if she didn't want to. "I'll only be a minute." In the bathroom, the toilet was wedged almost beneath the sink. The sink sputtered brown before the water cleared. She was glad to put off a shower in that water; in any case, she'd once heard that human hair was self-cleaning. She considered testing this theory. The scent of mold wafted from the shower stall, from its yellowish plastic curtain spotted with black. She changed into a black shirt-dress and tried to get a glimpse of the plastic-wrapped tattoo, but she couldn't see much; a glare reflected off the plastic.

She was supposed to take the bandaging off to give the skin time to breathe and wash it several times a day, but she didn't care to expose her raw skin to this air and this water. Later, she thought, when it scabbed over and was protected. Then she would take care of it.

When she was finished in the bathroom she took out her purse, leaving behind her knapsack. The raw tattoo wouldn't like the knapsack.

"Let's go, lickety-split," Bobby said from the front door.

Bobby pointed Pluta toward the subway before getting into the Cadillac. She shuffled down Third Avenue, which was wide and industrial, and squinted in the bright haze, finding in the distance the silhouette of elevated train tracks. A car honked: Bobby waved and grinned as he sped past. There was something giddy in his smile, and he was leaning forward as if leaning

38

would get him to his destination faster. The car made a sudden, wide turn down a side street. Then he was gone. Pluta half-expected him to turn up again, having simply gone for a joyride around the block, but she kept to her steady shuffle, not wanting to be caught standing slack-jawed on the corner like an idiot.

Auto shops and jackhammers clanked and drilled and stuttered. Sparrows bathed in the dust beside a thin tree stump. She imagined their tiny hearts vibrating beneath the small tufts of brown and white feathers, vibrating from the jackhammers' clatter. Above soared a cloudless sky.

Pluta lifted her arms and breathed in the noxious fumes of diesel and hot tar. But on the cross-breeze she thought she also caught a fresher scent, the salt of the not-too-distant Atlantic. She would find the beach.

Beneath the train tracks, the sunlight fell in slices. She walked until she found the entrance to a station on Fourth Avenue. Dodging the bluster of pigeons roosting in the station's crevices, she slipped a token into the slot and pushed through the wooden turnstile, painted yellow but flaking, before realizing that the map of the system, a colorful mess of tangled lines, was on the other side by the token booth. No matter. There were only two staircases to choose from, one leading up to the Manhattan-bound side, the other to the Coney Island–bound side. She would ride the Coney Island–bound train as far as it would go. Simple.

More people waited on the Manhattan-bound platform since it was the start of the work day. The skyline shimmered; it was already very warm. The Coney Island–bound train emerged from around the curve of the tracks, a long silver caterpillar. She was the only person waiting for it. It would be her private chariot.

The station shook. Wind and grit gusted past. Pluta stepped back from the tracks and held on to a wooden bench until the train hissed to a stop. Both outside and in, the train was covered in black and red graffiti squiggles that lent it a festive air. A lone passenger at the center of the car played a marimba. Pluta smiled hello. The marimba player nodded, polite but distant, as if this was not a performance but a private practice session on which she was intruding.

The swaying train was labeled the Culver Local, but on the tangled map streaked with more graffiti she couldn't make out which line it was. She could only tell it should be one of several purple lines. Adventure, she told herself. It would be all the more satisfying when she untangled it.

The train slid into a tunnel. The reflection of her crooked teeth flickered in and out of its windows. What would Isabel say when she found out she'd gone? Would she break something? Shout? Would she come find her? Kiss her cheek and cut her head off?

Well, Isabel was far, far away and would never ever find her unless she, Pluta Melpheasant (yes, she still liked the name, liked it very much), changed her mind. She didn't see herself changing her mind. Maybe stubbornness had been Isabel's best gift to her. Lips in the window grinned.

And what would Daniel say? Maybe at first he would have to disapprove. Maybe some part of him, even now, would see her as a baby, his baby. But, she thought as the grin in the window faded, if he could see her now there would also be a glimmer in his eyes, behind the disapproval, a glimmer that said what she was doing was, essentially, right.

The subterranean ride was brief; the marimba player

exited at one of the underground stops and after a few more the train reemerged outside, flying over small brick apartment buildings zigzagged with dull-green fire escapes, over large frame houses, over lines of wet laundry flapping on second-floor porches, and finally over an enormous, too-crowded cemetery, its slabs of granite so closely huddled they almost overlapped. Like her teeth. She tried to hold her breath as the train soared above the cemetery, but it was much too big and she failed with a gasp. Bad luck. She snapped her fingers, giggling at the schoolgirl superstition. The few people who had boarded glanced over at the lone laughing girl, turned away. The train slid around a bend and a large Ferris wheel labeled WONDER WHEEL came into view, its red lettering dull in the sunlit haze. Another ride appeared, a tall wooden roller coaster labeled CYCLONE. And in the distance, a tall metal flower: a parachute jump. She alighted at Neptune Avenue. Its name was very promising.

Here the scent of salt and sand grew stronger. The carnival stalls were mostly shuttered; the nearby roller coasters were dormant. The cars of the Wonder Wheel squeaked and groaned as they swayed, empty, in the breeze. Pluta kicked at some hot-dog and burger wrappers that blew past her feet. The streets were lined with such things: soda cups, beer cans, candy wrappers. It wasn't quite the Coney Island she had in mind: rainbow neon lights, raucous laughter, clowns, cream pies, and water balloons. But it was early.

She found the beach and headed barefoot toward the water, dodging the shells, bottle caps, cigarette butts, and shards of glass that littered the sand. Seagulls squawked and swooped overhead. She scanned the horizon, knowing her hopes were silly. She hoped to see: large, wise sea turtles; sea lions glistening in the sun as they barked; perhaps the distant fin of a whale. Instead, the only wildlife was the gulls, scavenging at brimming garbage cans.

But there it was: the wide, gray-blue sea. It boomed at her. It rushed.

Walking east along the water, away from the amusement park, the sand seemed cleaner; she didn't have to watch every step. A few elderly people sat on the boardwalk in folding chairs. Some even ventured to swim, their strokes steady against the tide. Pluta let the foaming water lap at her bare feet. The cold stung, distracting her from the flame at her back. After a time, her feet turned fish-white.

The tide swelled and crashed; she dug her feet in the sand and thought about Daniel. In Brazil, when Isabel first told her they weren't going back to Buenos Aires, she'd started to think of him as "the Professor" and sometimes found this name easier. So she wondered what the Professor would be doing at this moment, *if*. Would he too look at the Atlantic and wonder what *she* was doing? Or would he have locked himself away in some hut in Kathmandu, immersed in study?

Weary laughter sputtered from her. Isabel's early, fumbling lie: Pluta had, at first, believed it—she had no reason not to. Later, Isabel had been forced to admit the deception. Pluta imagined a fate for the Professor. She put him on a remote island, his reddish hair a long, scraggly tangle, dotted with tiny seashells and strands of seaweed. This was easier than the blank uncertainty or that other specter: dark, dripping dungeons; head-in-hands, moaning misery. Those were what made parts of her squirm and crumble. Those were what made her insides burst apart.

Clutching her stomach, she closed her eyes. Now she

saw him at the ocean shore, reaching an arm out to the horizon. As if he would be able to see it, she waved.

On the boardwalk, Pluta bought fried shrimp, fried clams, crinkle-cut French fries, and a can of bright green celery soda whose acidic bubbles washed down the frying grease. This seafood—brownish breading over gray flesh—was entirely different from the lobster dinners Casey's mother had prepared. Before dinner they'd watched the crustaceans scuttle uselessly in the metal basin of the kitchen sink, waiting to be boiled. Casey warned her that the lobsters screamed before they died, then dragged Pluta out of the kitchen so they couldn't hear it. But at the table, she casually handed Pluta the silver implement with which to crack the bright red shell, which had seemed so much heartier before the boiling.

They had never eaten much seafood back home, only lots of meat. A wave of nausea rolled over her; she closed her eyes against it. There was plenty of time today. Tomorrow, perhaps, she would look into finding a job. Today she needed to think. By the time she opened her eyes AstroLand had opened, and when the nausea dissipated she bought tickets to the rides. The ticket seller sneered. But said nothing of delinquency.

Ascending in the Wonder Wheel, she stared with unfocused eyes at the sea, the sky. When it brought her back near the ground, she identified shapes in negative spaces: diamonds in the fences, rectangles between the bars. *How far can I get?* she wondered.

This Bobby person bought her dinner, gave her subway tokens. Why? Did he like her? Why? No one had ever seemed to show much interest in her. What would happen when she returned? She wondered if she would be persuaded to settle there, what kind of strange relationship they would have. (How much older was he, anyway? Four years? Six?) Or maybe someday soon she would run again, further south. Inch her way back home. Hitch a ride on a train, a plane, a mail boat. Stumble upon fortune, get plastic surgery, be a famous, tragic recluse.

In the funhouse, she remembered her tattoo. Assuming the funhouse was as empty as the rest of the amusement park, she found a spot ringed with mirrors. The dimness of the space reminded her of the backstage of a theater. Theater class was one of the few things she'd enjoyed at Banderhock—but toward the end it hadn't been enough. Other people's words covered up what she couldn't express, that hot ball in her stomach that had no words. Drawing helped, a little. Maybe she would never find words.

She removed her dress. Multiple pairs of lopsided breasts stared back. In the past year, this sight hadn't ceased to surprise her, and now the surprise was amplified. She covered her front with her dress and pivoted until she found her back in the mirror, the clear plastic catching the light. She pulled the bandaging off to get a better look. The skin appeared angry, even in the dim light, but then she *had* gotten it stabbed up with a needle. At the sight of the wings, she grinned. Put her dress back on.

She allowed herself one more childish treat, a pink sugar cloud, and wandered the park letting bits of it dissolve on her tongue. She had no idea what time it was, having left her watch in her knapsack. It probably wouldn't be dark for a while. Perhaps she would walk back, save the second token for another trip. She had no idea how long it would take, but Bobby hadn't given her a key and she didn't want to return before him. She hadn't thought about what it would feel like to have no-where to go.

Before this thought could fully dawn on her, frighten her into giving up, she quashed it, pressing her lips to-gether in a thin line. This was part of the challenge. If she wanted to be independent, if she was going to do it—then do it. And wasn't it exhilarating to go where you wanted? She imagined what her tattoo would look like healed and complete. Bold lines—a beautiful thing. She should get a halter top for the occasion.

A broad parkway, lined with oak and honey-locust trees and comfortable apartment buildings, led away from the boardwalk. After finding an Avenue Z travers-ing this parkway, she thought it would be a simple task to keep walking all the way to A. This was more pleasant than walking beneath the clunking train.

Along the way, there was a synagogue and a yeshiva; her pace slowed as she approached two Orthodox Jewish girls, maybe ten or eleven, with matching navy blue dresses down to their ankles and matching faces. Twin sisters. They stared at her, scrutinized her bare legs. So she stared back. She'd had similar stare-downs in Belgrano and on the few occasions her father had taken her to Once and to Barracas. Because she didn't dress like them, they assumed she wasn't in any way like them. And maybe she wasn't, not much anyway. But they shared a fragment of something. Even if her parents had chosen to blend in and theirs had not. Here, she felt even more alien than there.

She stared harder as she got closer. In Yiddish, with hands shielding their mouths—infuriating gesture!—the girls whispered; did she hear them say *shiksa*? She want-ed to throw rocks at them. She wanted to say, *I know that word don't use that word*. Tried to scrape up Ladino words from the back of her mind, spit them out at the girls to show she knew something too, maybe something they didn't know, lots of somethings they didn't know; or at least use the words to whisper with someone, anyone, an imaginary twin. But she had no one with whom to conspire. She lowered her gaze and walked faster. Thought she heard laughter, but didn't give them the satisfaction of looking back.

Several long blocks down: a rapid, syncopated *thock-thock thock-thock thock!* A group of seven or eight children, mostly wearing jeans—prohibited at Banderhock even on weekends—bounced rubber balls in a narrow alley. The little blue balls, when thrown hard enough, ricocheted from wall to wall. At some point (she couldn't decipher what rule in the game triggered it) they all yelled, "Suicide!" One victim went belly against the wall as the rest chucked balls at his backside. The children squealed and roared. One of them, a bigger girl in a t-shirt of bright ketchup-and-mustard stripes, caught Pluta eyeing them and challenged her, glaring back with a hand on her hip.

"Yeah?" she asked.

But Pluta didn't wish to be an interloper. And she didn't want to be like the other little girls she'd just been so angry at. Cheeks hot, she moved on.

"That's right!" yelled the girl.

Pluta was too old for them anyway. She remembered her reflection in the funhouse. They were all still children. Whereas she—she was practically a woman. She straightened her shoulders, walking on. The lines of the tattoo burned.

It took an hour and a half to reach the end (the beginning) of the alphabet. Here an expressway fed into the parkway and she could no longer follow her straight line.

Side streets came in at strange angles and led to dead ends or circled back on themselves or changed names without warning. The houses were a motley assortment: brick, shingled, or stone; tall and grand or squat, cobwebbed, and sinking into the earth. She found a small horse stable, a large park (green, walled), a Distinctly Christian Kindergarten. After coming across the kindergarten twice, she decided to ask for directions.

Her questions were at first met with blank stares and shrugs. The people had not heard of Gowanus, or had not understood her, or had heard of it but did not know where, exactly, it was. Or they were simply suspicious of a teenager stopping them in the street. Finally an old man, long-limbed and towering like some kind of neighborhood guardian, asked her in a rasping voice where she wanted to go. She told him and he nodded, stroking a ruddy beard that reached down to his belly. He had small, close-set eyes shadowed beneath an old-fashioned flat cap.

"Yes, yes, Gowanus." The bridge of his nose wrinkled. "I don't know. Not so easy to walk." A long, gently gnarled finger pointed in the direction of the subway.

It was almost eight o'clock by the time Pluta reached Bobby's. Knocking on his door, she beamed with pride. She'd made it. She'd found her way. It had been a test she'd laid out for herself, and she'd passed.

"I wasn't sure you were coming back," Bobby said when he opened the door. "I was about to start snooping through your stuff, read your diary."

"I don't keep a diary," she said, pushing past him to sit on the couch, tired legs sprawled out.

"I know." He sat beside her, winked. She elbowed him in the ribs.

"Ha."

"So what'd you see? What'd ya learn?"

"I went to Coney Island. Went on some rides. Walked back."

"Geez. No wonder you're tired. Something to drink? Soda? Beer? Whiskey? I went shopping!" He strutted into the kitchen, his face flushed with a certain sense of victory.

Pluta nodded and weighed her options. Cotton candy in the morning, whiskey in the evening. She could get used to this.

"Whiskey, please."

"Really?" He poked his head back out of the kitchen. "Why not?"

"Our little girl is all grown up. How do you take your whiskey? With a healthy splash of Coca-Cola?" There was a hint of derision in his voice. "Or on the rocks?"

"Mm, no. Neat."

"Neat! Look at you. Neat."

They sipped whiskey and nibbled from a can of peanuts. At Casey's last summer they'd gotten into the liquor cabinet, so it wasn't Pluta's first time sampling spirits. Casey's parents were collectors more than drinkers. The girls had been careful not to leave too many fingerprints in the fine layer of dust covering the bottles.

"And what exactly is your business, if I may ask?" Liquid courage, Casey had called it. Pluta felt a tad more comfortable now, prying.

"Oh, y'know, this and that. Got a good deal on the Cadillac. So we can celebrate that." They clinked glasses.

"So you buy and sell cars?"

Bobby swirled his whiskey around and drained his glass. He nodded. Sniffled. "Buy you a steak dinner?"

"Sure, all right. Yeah."

They got into another car, this time a red Chevrolet.

An oversized pair of fuzzy dice hung from the rearview mirror. Bobby grabbed them and threw them out the window. He said they didn't match the car.

As they drove, Pluta asked, "Do you like me or something?"

"Are we in seventh grade?" Bobby laughed as he drove toward downtown Brooklyn. "Yeah, sure. You're a funny kid."

As with the previous car, something sloshed in the glove compartment. Pluta opened it, found a bottle of vodka. Unscrewed the top and sniffed, the sting shooting up her nose. Bobby glanced at her, eyes sharp.

"Did I say you could do that?"

Pluta guffawed, took a sip.

"Did I?" He slammed the brakes and grabbed the open bottle from her. Some drops splattered her face. "Did I?"

The back of her hand wiped off the drops. "I thought you were joking. I thought we were celebrating." Her back prickled hot.

"Yeah, yeah. Just put it away."

He glanced around and rubbed at his nose before driving on. Her shoulders had tensed, with a burn between the blades. She tried to relax. It was going to be okay. She set her eyes on the blur of wide, treeless avenue rushing past.

Dinner was in a wood-paneled, low-lit restaurant with plush burgundy booths. The lack of conversation, the slow sawing and chewing of meat, felt familiar, if not comfortable. After dinner they strolled along the promenade looking out at the Manhattan and Brooklyn bridges. Couples ambled by to gaze at the skyline and the stars. But Pluta and Bobby didn't hold hands or walk arm in arm. There was something in the air between them, a force field. Further down the East River stood huge, lit-up port cranes.

"They look like electric giraffes," said Pluta, quiet and wary of her voice because they had talked so little for such a long while. The cranes did look like giraffes. Reaching their necks, their mouths up, up. To eat the sky.

Bobby grinned and tousled her hair. "You're a funny kid. Maybe a little bit nuts."

"*Claro.*" She caught herself making her mother's gesture of triumph, eyes half-closed, chin turned up. She exhaled, opened her eyes wide, felt a sparkle in them.

"Yeah, you are. See, I don't even understand what you say." She couldn't figure out if she was trying to seduce him, if it was all a part of a game she'd devised on the Wonder Wheel: *How far can I get?* He kissed the top of her forehead, but it felt brotherly. No sparks. No skin aquiver. Just the faint ghost of warmth at the single spot of the kiss. Then they held hands like small children, palm to palm. "It's nice to have someone to celebrate with."

Driving back on the service roads under the Brooklyn–Queens Expressway, Pluta glimpsed women standing in its shadows. From time to time they would emerge into the dim light, lean down into a car idling at the curb. From time to time they got into the car. She did not have to ask what this was. A bar nearby advertised topless dancers; she remembered the funhouse. She imagined the funhouse with people instead of mirrors. Or a bar with mirrors instead of people.

Back upstairs, he said, "Fuck it. I want to drink. Let's drink." They sat in the corner of the living room, legs sprawled out, him with his back against the wall, her leaning forward, and they peeled flaking paint and laughed. With enough alcohol, the throb at Pluta's back dulled. Bobby taught her the cha-cha, the hustle. They danced without music, stomped their own beat. In his bedroom they jumped on the bed and slapped the ceiling until little bits of plaster crumbled onto them. They brushed the powder out of each other's hair.

"A grand old time," Bobby slurred.

"Grand."

They fell asleep with the lights on, holding on to each other's faces. She thought he would kiss her goodnight, she sort of wished he would, but he didn't.

Pluta woke up a couple of hours later, still woozy. Their faces were three inches away from each other, hands lax around each other's ears. Bobby stared at her. The blacks of his eyes dilated, shrank, dilated. She said his name, but he didn't respond. Warm whiskey breath puffed at her in soft, shallow gusts. He was asleep. She said his name again and his eyelid twitched.

Blood trickled out of his nose. A serious look, a frightening look, passed over his face. His lips smacked a few times; he gasped and sat up and woke. He wiped at the blood with the back of his hand, a bright red line, and groaned, nearly smearing the blood on the pillow.

"Well, party's over," he grumbled. He glanced around, disoriented, and held the back of his hand to the trickle of blood.

"Should I get you some tissue?" She sat up. The room spun.

"Are you still here?" He seemed surprised.

"What do you mean?"

"What are you still doing here?" He sniffled and coughed as he jumped out of bed toward the bathroom, where he hocked and spat into the toilet. Water

51

dropping into water made a silvery sound. He gave a guttural groan. Flushed. Over the rush of water sucked down the pipes, he shouted, "Didn't your daddy teach you anything?"

She didn't reply. Was this a joke?

"Hm?" His voice echoed from the tiled room. He returned with a furrowed brow and a wad of toilet paper against his nose. "You should go." He dabbed at the blood, looked at the expanding red splotch, dabbed again, daintily. "You shouldn't stay."

"I don't understand." She squeezed her head between her hands. "Why now?"

"Why now. Why now. Because now I say you should go." His voice did not rise in volume but it was strained. "You want me to call your little school? Your parents?" Pluta opened her mouth, then shut it. He looked at the blood on crumpled tissue. "*Shit.* Are you deaf or something?" Heat rose into her cheeks; her ears pounded.

"I—I'm going." The room went sideways as she edged off the bed, and she swayed a moment until it stopped tilting. "I'm leaving."

He stepped away from the threshold so that she could pass.

Her knapsack was in the corner of the living room where she'd left it; she picked it up with trembling fingers. Her torso shook. She'd never felt it shake before. A single hurried glance back at him, in the bedroom, hoping he'd say *wait, you don't have to go, silly, I'm joking, where would you go this time of night anyway*? But he said nothing, just stood in the doorway, a drop of blood on his white t-shirt; he wasn't even looking at her.

The front door thudded shut behind her. The hallway's flickering lights droned. Her belly quavered. Her sneakers slapped on the cracked, dirty vinyl, stamped with a hideous brown floral pattern; the echo of her steps trailed behind her down the staircase. She stumbled dry-mouthed into the street. She swallowed. To the left, south, sat long rows of darkened tenements, looking ominous now, with no one in the street, with so few lights. To the right, north, lay a bright avenue. She ran north. On the billboard across the street, the Corrections Officer grinned.

4. *Buenos Aires*
July 1978

WINTER MORNING LIGHT tinted the kitchen's white surfaces milky blue. The draft through the garden doors,
as always, made the house chilly. At the breakfast table
Pluta chewed absently on dry toast, hugging her maroon
school blazer around her. Refusing marmalade seemed
directly related to her father's empty chair, at which she
stared, only he liked marmalade even more than she did
and sometimes simply ate it with a spoon. When he did
that, with orange marmalade, or quince paste—*dulce de
membrillo*—he giggled. *Hmmhmmhmmmm*: a giggle with
mouth closed over the sweet spoon. Marmalade in the
morning, *membrillo* in the late afternoon, Daniel and
Pluta got their sugar fix together, tapping brimming
spoons together like glasses of champagne.

"Your father worked late last night," said Isabel. "So
he stayed at the office." Her eyes felt sunken into her
face; she hadn't slept well.

Pluta nodded and looked away.

They hugged their cups of *café con leche*, drained
them of liquid warmth, and sat a moment longer at the
table hanging onto empty cups. Isabel bristled at her

daughter's silence. Without Daniel there she had the urge to shout: *speak*, speak already and be a normal girl. Instead, she stood and brushed crumbs from Pluta's jumper.

"You have your piano lesson this afternoon," she said. "Don't be late."

After the gate clinked behind Pluta, Isabel sat at the kitchen table in her nightgown. Something was wrong. He would have called, at least in the morning if not the previous night. Cradling the phone's receiver in her lap, she spun the rotary dial and tried to reach him at the office. Ring after ring, he did not pick up.

She chewed her thumbnail. What had they argued about before La Rural? They'd whispered in bed. Another student had disappeared. She'd insisted that the young man must have done something, to get arrested. Daniel had only shaken his head, removed his glasses, and rested his forehead in his palms. He knew she hated to discuss these things.

Two years ago, after the coup, he'd tried. *Take those high school students in La Plata. All they wanted were subsidized bus fares.*

And she had been angry then, too. *I don't know. That doesn't sound right. That just can't be right.*

It had been said on the radio. The country was infected, and it would be cleaned. The terror and chaos in the years before the current government—the kidnappings, the bombings—had been too much. Something had to be done about it. There would be sacrifices for peace.

Yes, the first six weeks of the coup had been as terrifying as the prior chaos, with reports of missing persons and bullet-ridden bodies dumped in back alleys or along lonely waterfronts. But then the reports stopped; the clampdown on violence granted a modicum of peace and stability. Obviously, Daniel had survived the mass

56

firing of university staff considered dangerous because he wasn't dangerous. The fact that he hadn't resigned long ago, during the previous dictatorship, showed his loyalty. It should protect him.

So she had asked him never to mention the high school students in La Plata again. Ugly, inflated rumors; ugly stories. It was best not to talk about such things. He'd nodded and tried not to look frustrated.

She had meant *never, with anyone*; but what if he had understood *never, with her*? He *had* been patient with her, avoiding the topic. Except there was that one student of his in '77 and then the second, only a week ago. How could so many of them get mixed up in terrorism?

Isabel stopped biting her nail and hurried to dress.

The piano teacher, Mrs. Hoffman, waited in the hard-backed pink armchair in the front room next to the potted fern: a chair that only she ever sat in, tapping gnarled, ringed fingers on the armrest or talking about an opera she had seen at Teatro Colón. Her hair that day was especially blue and especially bouffant. Isabel knew what sorts of questions would send Mrs. Hoffman off onto long ramblings that seemed to need no listener; as the old woman spoke, Isabel kept an eye on the door, an ear pricked toward the phone.

When the front door unlatched, Isabel jumped from her teetering perch on the edge of the sofa, kissed Pluta on the forehead, and half-guided, half-pushed her to the piano. Mrs. Hoffman rose and adjusted the silk scarf tied in a knot at her throat, where it squeezed her ruddy loose flesh together. They sat side by side at the piano bench and began. It was a simple thing they'd been working on, a Bach minuet which had not given her much trouble the week before, but Mrs. Hoffman rapped misplaced fingers as the metronome ticked.

Isabel removed herself to the kitchen. The music, however wobbly, was a relief. The day had been long and muffled in silence. Daniel had not called. All morning, he had not answered the office telephone. Isabel had ridden a bus across the city, hoping she'd catch him, clasp him to her, and chastise him for making her worry. The secretary of the department had stuttered, said she didn't know; no one else had been there Sunday evening, no one had seen him. But when she barged into his office, the papers scattered upon his desk were splotched with fresh tea stains and maté leaves. The new head of the department, a tall man with a booming voice, came out of his own office adjoining the reception area to see who was bothering the secretary.

"Mrs. Spektor," he said. "Your husband did not come in today." He moved forward as if expecting Isabel, like most others, to step back. When she didn't, he gently took her by the elbow, bent low to speak in her ear. "I'm sure he'll be in touch soon."

She shivered at this, disturbed by the lack of warmth, the absence of civility. She returned home just in time to let Mrs. Hoffman in.

At the end of the lesson, Pluta clambered upstairs. Isabel came out to pay Mrs. Hoffman and receive her unsolicited progress report. This was when the teacher hoped to be offered brandy and gossip and was occasionally obliged. Isabel was torn between impulses to shoo her out and be left alone or to have her company; the prospect of more hours alone—or worse, expressing her worry to Pluta—horrified her.

"And how is your American?" asked the piano teacher, warmed by the brandy. She had an annoying habit of calling people by whatever nationality she vaguely associated with them. Daniel was the American, because he'd gone to graduate school in Texas. Isabel's sister was *la Brasilienne*—in French, for some reason—because she lived in Manaus. Mrs. Hoffman herself wouldn't have minded if people called her "the German" (even though she, like Daniel, was closer to Russian), but no one ever did. Isabel's Sephardic coloration cast her as Turkish.

Isabel glanced at the silent black phone and smiled, baring her chompers.

"He's just wonderful," she said. "You're due your pay for the month, yes?" Mrs. Hoffman hesitated, balking at the abrupt change in subject and Isabel's directness. Isabel left the room, clacking on the hardwood, and returned with a roll of bills. These rolls had thickened rapidly with the inflation of the last two years.

"Until next week," said Mrs. Hoffman. It was almost a question. It had become an awkward subject with Mrs. Hoffman, whether the lessons could continue with the cost of everything going up so quickly. Isabel never let her worry.

"Yes, yes, we'll see you then." Isabel watched her blue bouffant bob down the dusky street. The street lamps switched on. The bouffant vanished around a corner. In each direction a solitary walker in a dark coat strode home after a day's work, neither of them Daniel. Isabel locked the door.

Upstairs in the playroom, Pluta sat atop a pile of cushions reading a dog-eared and stained English translation of Hans Christian Andersen tales. Last year, before she started at the British school, her father had gotten her an English tutor who taught her grammar from books with names like *The Chicken Smells Good*. But Daniel would always take time to read the "good stuff" with her too—mythology, fairy tales—translating as necessary until she was able to read English on her own.

She heard Isabel pacing downstairs. Irregular, fitful pacing. What was she doing down there? The piano bench scraped against the floor. There was a quick playing of fingers over keys that stopped abruptly. Pluta returned to her book. The little mermaid had gotten her legs; the sensation of stabbing plagued her as she walked. Pluta closed the book and chucked it across the room, pages fluttering before the hard cover thudded against the wall.

The black hall telephone rang: a piercing shrill that froze the nervous pacing and tapping and chair scraping. Clacks hurried into the hall. Pluta edged to the top of the stairs and grabbed the railing. An airplane buzzed low in the sky.

"Where are you?" asked Isabel, voice straining. "When are you coming home?"

Pluta pretended she could hear her father's voice, tinny in the phone.

Her mother sucked in her breath, sharp. "*What?* What did you do? What does *soon* mean?" She clutched the receiver, knuckles tight. The hardwood creaked under her heels. As if the whole house were a ship, groaning and shifting in the wind, Pluta squeezed the railing to keep balance. Isabel paced; Pluta caught her biting her nails, even if she always told Pluta not to, threatened to dip her fingers in hot sauce to deter her. Isabel seemed poised to protest, lash out, interrogate further. The house tipped from side to side. But all Isabel said was, "All right. All right. All right." Unsteadily, she hung up the phone and her body stiffened into a rigid composure.

The tipping slowed. Pluta backed into the playroom.

A doll at the low tea table sat askew in its chair. She plucked it from the chair and returned to her pile of cushions. Staring into a middle distance, she popped off the doll's head and squeezed the plastic face before snapping it back on the neck and popping it off again. Maybe he'd gotten sick of her mother. Maybe he'd gone off on his own, found a woman who didn't yell. She thought of those black-and-white Italian movies with beautifully coiffed women sobbing into white Princess telephones. But then why promise to return soon? If you leave, you leave. Perhaps you write a note, with elegant penmanship. She returned the doll to its chair and smoothed its hair, tried again to read, but her eyes skimmed over the same lines again and again, taking in nothing.

In the kitchen, Isabel switched on the radio above the sink.

"*Las Locas*—" rumbled a newscaster. The Crazy Ladies, with their white bonnets. Isabel had passed their insistent march at Casa Rosada. Quickly she turned the dial. Searched the stations until she found loud, static-crackled flamenco. Took a roast out of the fridge and set it on the table, waiting for the oven to heat. Lit a cigarette with shaking fingers.

Smoke curled over the meat; ash drifted. She circled the table, tapped her heel, picked off a piece of ash that had landed on the meat. From a drawer she extracted a knife, cradled the handle in her fist, gazed a moment at the blade. She stalked up and down the kitchen, knife in hand, not taking in any of the objects around her (oven, counter, table; table, counter, oven) yet at the same time focusing intently on them, as if the familiar objects could dismantle the fears forming in her mind before they were fully articulated.

They'll release me soon, he'd said. But there was hesitation in his voice; it seemed like someone else was listening. Surely a police officer was standing by, waiting to take him back to a cell. He couldn't say exactly when he'd be released because he didn't really know, he was only trying to appease her, and he also hadn't said *where* he was being held, and there hadn't been time to ask *should I come to you.* Back and forth she paced, the phrase *it must be for something* repeating in her mind, in the tired, knowing voices of everyone she knew. When she couldn't take it anymore, she plunged the knife deep into the roast and watched its thin red juices spurt and dribble.

That week the house was taut and silent. Isabel created a field of tension around her that enveloped the place, almost calcified the air. Pluta didn't dare ask about her father, or make much noise at all; she slid across the hardwood in stocking feet. After school she eavesdropped. She held her breath and listened to her mother's side of phone conversations, accumulating a mass of meaningless clues. With friends, the subject of Daniel never came up. At times Isabel even broke into lighthearted laughter. But Pluta could tell that Isabel was pretending, her confidence thin and cracked. There was no sadness in the silence but rather a familiar fury, amplified.

"I want to confirm an appointment . . . I don't want his associate, I want the man whose name is on the door. I'll pay."

"Yes, her suit was divine. Where did she say she got it? . . . Oh, what a *bore.* . . . I'm so sorry—we won't be able to make it to your party. I'm just so overwhelmed with . . . this and that. You know how it is. I'll stop by like always. But I can't stay long. I have some appointments.

Just some silly checkups. . . . Oh no, no, nothing serious, nothing serious at all. You're a doll. *Ciao ciao ciao*."

Between calls Isabel, too, seemed to hold her breath. When she couldn't hold it any longer, she dialed again, expelling her questions in hot bursts.

"What time do you open? What time are you receiving people? . . . Only Thursdays from twelve to one? But . . . Yes, yes, I see. Are there special papers I should prepare in advance? . . . Hello?"

The windows of the house clamped shut. The television and radio remained off. Only Isabel could break the sound embargo, as needed. Pluta took to whispering to herself, but only when she was sure Isabel was as far away from her in the house as possible. It seemed Isabel was going out while Pluta was in school, seeing friends and shopping more often than usual. She always had a new bag of something. Her tense body almost hummed.

And this hum of activity, whatever it was, spoke to Pluta. She imagined the worst, even though she had no idea how bad the worst could be. She imagined him running off to the countryside on horseback to be a *gaucho*, some faceless young woman at his side. At school, in geography class, she decided that when he settled in the Pampas she would visit him and he would teach her how to ride a horse. In math, she calculated how many hours and then minutes and then seconds it had been since they'd seen him leave La Rural and extrapolated, by arbitrary calculation, when the true story might be revealed.

Late in the week, Pluta heard her mother stumble through a conversation in that strange language, Ladino. She was on the phone with her sister. Pluta sensed reluctance in her voice; she knew that Isabel disliked Aunt Lolo. At dinner that night, as they stared at leftover gristle, Isabel told Pluta that her father had gone away on a business trip. Since Isabel had broached the subject, Pluta dared to ask where. Tierra del Fuego, said Isabel. And then maybe Kathmandu. Some sort of comparative study.

Isabel did see her friends. They met in cafés at the usual times, in the usual neighborhoods: Tuesday afternoons on Olázabal, Thursday mornings in Recoleta. She'd always felt good on the north side, even had daydreams about living there had she not inherited her parents' house, or had her sister remained in Buenos Aires to claim it. Growing up, she'd imagined a tall, dark husband in a pinstriped suit and a cream-colored cashmere scarf, walking southward to work on brick-paved streets crowded with French architecture. They'd live in a stately limestone townhouse, though even an apartment in a well-appointed high-rise would have been nice, with a view of the city's vast tangle of boulevards. These were old daydreams, daydreams from before Daniel. But returning to Recoleta regularly, she wondered what she would be doing now if that had been her path.

She said nothing to her friends of what had happened. At first, she was gathering courage. Then, she was keeping up appearances. It was an embarrassment. They would cut her off, float away.

At the university they seemed to know that Daniel had done something in which they did not wish to be implicated. This made Isabel even angrier. At night she lay in bed, questions endlessly repeating. What happened? What right did he have, ruining the family, his career, her life? He was not one of those insouciant young people corrupting the country; if their ideas had rubbed off on him somehow, surely he was weak. This nighttime train of thought did make her cry. To avoid waking Pluta, she chewed on her pillow.

One night in the middle of the week, as Isabel lay in bed, a loud thumping beat the air above the house. It seeped into a dream: she was making a milkshake and dropped gleaming, slippery red fruit into the blender. She could barely grasp the fruits or make out what they were—neither raspberries nor strawberries nor plums—before they fell into the whirring milk. Instead of turning pink, the milk swirled into a deep crimson. The blender became so loud in its chopping and so terrifying that its noise roused her from the dream.

A helicopter throbbed over Belgrano. A flash of light glanced into the bedroom. The windows shuddered in their frames. Isabel slid out of bed, knelt, and clutched the curtains; with one eye she watched through the slit between them. As the helicopter hovered and then floated away, two green Ford Falcons screeched to the curb, from which several men in plain clothes emerged and marched up to a house across the street. The men banged on the front door. When no one answered, they kicked it in. A gust of wind swayed young tree branches, rustled leaves. Soon the men dragged from the house one woman and one man—Isabel did not know them by name and had only rarely seen them slink in and out of the house. Through the closed window she heard faint shouts and crouched lower. One high-pitched scream rattled through the glass. A scream that seemed to say a name, one she couldn't make out. She peeked out again. The man was gone, presumably inside one of the Falcons, which was pulling away from the curb. Wind blew hair in the woman's face, obscuring it. They shoved her into the other Falcon and drove off.

Isabel released the curtains, which had become damp

in her grasp. She rose, lightheaded and unsure what to make of what she had seen. Proof of the country's far-reaching infection? She nudged the curtain open. The dark, wet street appeared as it always had.

A rustle inside the house hardened her flesh. Jerking the curtain closed, she spun around. Pluta stood in the doorway.

"It was nothing," Isabel said. *A bad dream of bad people.* "Go back to bed."

The wood creaked beneath her daughter's hesitant, shifting weight. With the curtains drawn, Isabel could only make out the silhouette of Pluta's white nightgown and the faint gleam of her eyes. The small feet shifted and padded away down the hall. The silence resurged. Isabel could even focus, it seemed, on the sound of her daughter's sheets being pulled safely around her. Pluta would fall quickly back to sleep.

Isabel cracked open the curtain again and watched the empty street. What else would she see? Nothing, she assured herself, and yet she continued watching, her stomach trembling. At some point two men emerged from that house with some bags. So they hadn't all left together. What did they carry out with them? Evidence, she supposed. One seemed to make a joke and they both laughed as they swaggered away up the road. Isabel backed away from the window and slowly sank into bed. But she stayed awake the rest of the night in a cold sweat, wondering.

After that night, she gathered the courage to approach the police. She'd been ashamed, but what if there had been a mistake after all? To bolster her confidence—though riddled with guilt—she first went downtown to purchase a new blouse. Something that would endear her to the officers, that would in some subtle way encourage them to help her. She went to Harrods, where she picked hopefully through an array of tops, scrutinizing them for possible signals: class, respectability, an appropriate level of female authority. She bought two crisp white blouses, a black pencil skirt, and a sharp-collared sheath dress. Before and after her standing appointments with friends, she hurried from bureaucratic office to bureaucratic office, and at the end of the day arrived home loaded with yet more shopping bags.

For each attempt at entering the bureaucracy, she braced herself. No hair out of place, lipstick freshly applied. The police, both in the station near the house and the one near the university, stood behind large desks, went over lists of prisoners, and shook their heads, telling her to check with the office of this-and-that. Office of this-and-that shook heads; those officers were mistaken; it was not their jurisdiction. A lawyer with bleary, red-rimmed eyes explained a process to her and said that at most he would prepare paperwork but would not represent her. Frankly, it was not likely anyone would. She could submit the unsigned papers to a big pile of other unsigned papers that a judge might look at, or might throw out.

It didn't make sense. She returned to the stations, demanded to see higher-ups. Someone said, *you are in the wrong place.* Someone said, with bared teeth and glinting eyes, *what's a nice lady like you doing in a place like this.* Someone said, shrugging, *I don't know where he is, but maybe you're better off without him.* Someone said, *if he's not on our list, he's not on our list—stop wasting our time.*

She felt squeezed crushed twisted: hot rusted metal cranked through something that shrieked.

Compulsively, to reconstitute her shredded self, she finished each day by returning to Harrods and the nearby shops. Each time, laden with bags full of dresses and shoes wrapped in crinkling tissue paper, she stood for a moment at the corner of Florida and Córdoba, staring across at the rococo Centro Naval, its bronze door adorned with shields and arrows and tridents and the puffed cheeks of wind. Atop the door a triumphant sea god blew a conch shell. Who was higher up than that? She wracked her brain for friends, friends of friends, anyone with military connections who might be able to help, anyone discreet enough to protect their reputation.

Late that week, she called her sister in Manaus. Her sister insisted they speak in Ladino but would not explain why. Isabel did not have a good grasp of the language. "You need to practice," was all her sister would say in Spanish. At times, Isabel was so uncertain of the language that her sister might have been speaking pure Hebrew. But she did understand that her sister didn't approve of the military-connection plan and thought Isabel should keep looking for a lawyer, or try other police stations. Isabel clamped her mouth shut and listened.

The next afternoon she heard rapid knocking at the front door. She had been sitting in the kitchen with a cup of coffee that had long grown cold. A magazine was open on the table, but she hadn't been reading it. She'd been staring at the white wall and listening to the hum of the refrigerator. She hadn't yet resolved how to again approach the police, since she didn't know the appropriate station or the appropriate officer and didn't want to fumble again in this regard. The sound of the knocking did not at first register. Four quick knocks. A pause. Another four. It was after the second four that she was jostled from this state of blankness.

She swung the door open. No one was there. The sun blinded her as it sank behind her neighbors' houses. She squinted down the street in both directions: no one. Sighing, she went to shut the door, but as she glanced down at the doorstep she saw a plain navy shoebox. She knelt, touched the lid with hesitation, and felt on her brow a soft ocean breeze.

Upstairs, Pluta had heard the knocks on the door. Now she crouched at the top of the stairs, watching. Isabel whimpered and stifled a moan and scrambled to shut a box. Before Isabel turned, Pluta retreated out of her line of sight. Listened as her mother hurried to the back of the house into the garden and retched into the mint patch.

Pluta sat still in her room with the lights bright, listening for muffled activity. Isabel stayed in the garden a long time. Pluta listened to the tick of the clock. Nearly an hour passed before Isabel came inside; gradually, Pluta realized she was gripping the edge of the bed; she eased her grip and waited for Isabel to come upstairs, perhaps to explain, perhaps to offer some partial story. But Isabel did not come upstairs.

They did not eat. They did not speak.

Pluta turned out the lights and lay down above the bed covers, still in her clothes.

In the middle of night, Pluta woke to the smell of the fireplace. The ice in her limbs melted. She burst upright: had her father come home? She leapt from bed to greet him, to throw her arms around him and squeeze, to press her face into his belly and tell him never to leave again. She hurried, nearly tumbling down the stairs.

The door to her father's study stood ajar, revealing the fire's orange glow. But a strange feeling stopped her at the threshold and she swayed back on her heels. He wasn't, in fact, there, and what was going on instead baffled her. Isabel, in a bathrobe, hair in a loose braid down her back, kept moving between a wrinkled pamphlet laid open on the desk and a pile of books.

Pluta recognized the pamphlet. It had come two years ago when she was still at the public school. The Ministry of Education had published and distributed this pamphlet, to be brought home to parents: *How To Recognize Marxist Infiltration in the Schools: Key Words to Watch*. Warning words included *capitalism, socialism, structure, change, popular leader, liberation, dialogue,* and *compromise.* Daniel had read the pamphlet at the dinner table and then crumpled it, ready to throw it out. But Isabel stopped him. So he stuck it in the back of a drawer. *One day, it will be a historic artifact,* he said. *Until then, Pluta must go to a private school.* Isabel had no objection. The British school was nearby; they enrolled her at the start of the new school year.

Isabel glanced through a book, glanced at the pamphlet, murmured one of the forbidden words as if it were a curse, then tossed the book into a growing heap inside the crackling fireplace. Books at the top of the heap, their edges already charred, slipped down under the impact. Bright embers jumped as paper curled and vaporized. Half of one bookshelf was empty. The strange fumes of burning glue and ink reeked. Pluta sucked in her breath. Isabel turned; her eyes, glassy and bloodshot, bore into Pluta. Bounding up, she grabbed hold of Pluta's shoulders and glared down at her, the tip of her nose wet and reddened, her mouth a grimace.

"Go back to bed," she said. Her voice heavy, sopping. With hot, rough hands, she peeled Pluta's fingers off the edge of the door. "Now." Then she shut the door.

Pluta's eyelids fluttered. Her mother's footsteps creaked on the other side of the door. How could she— *why* would she? Her throat convulsed; her stomach shrank. Thick saliva pooled in her mouth while her insides crumbled into useless powder.

She spread her hands against the door, seeking the heat of the fire.

What was Isabel doing? Would she burn down the whole house? Was Papi coming back? If not, if not, Pluta hoped that her mother *would* burn down the house, burn the whole thing down. It would be better than only the books.

5. *Brooklyn*
June 1980

PLUTA DASHED down the bright avenue, Third Avenue, knapsack swinging in the clutch of her fist. Her breathing felt jagged—she had been stupid to trust a stranger, but he hadn't been so bad at first. Why did he kick her out like that? What would she do now? Where would she go? She knew Bobby wasn't following her, but running had just happened; her feet had done it without her. She wanted to gain distance. To be away. She imagined her sneakers hurrying ahead while the rest of her vanished.

Compared to the residential street Bobby lived on, the predawn avenue seemed brightly lit, but once she gained the distance she wanted, the yellow streetlamps grew sporadic and dim. Unsure of her direction, she slowed. She slung the knapsack on backwards, the bulk against her front, and clasped her arms around it. Maybe it was better that he'd kicked her out. She'd gotten to the city, hadn't she? She'd gotten a few meals out of it, hadn't she? She'd gotten the tattoo she wanted. That apartment with its creepy airshaft—she didn't need that. She'd wanted to be independent, and here she was. Independent. She took a deep, shuddering breath as she passed a sparse playground.

Darkened warehouses rose about her. Not as hulking as in Vinegar Hill, nor with brickwork that veered toward pretty with arches and wrought-iron stars, but simple, large, functional warehouses, smooth-walled, with barred windows high above the sidewalk—or none at all—and rooftops ringed with barbed wire, bits of plastic bags caught in it, fluttering. Adults dealt with strangers all the time. So. She would have to deal with them too. She turned up a side street.

Most of the warehouses were unmarked or had small signs with inconspicuous names that gave no hint as to what happened inside. But some advertised a fabric dyer, a box factory, a casket maker. In a fenced parking lot filled with the rusted husks of cars, a Rottweiler growled and barked, trying to wedge his dribbling snout through the fence. Her chest had been pounding, had started to slow; now it jumped to pounding again. She made a wide arc around the fence, walking in the empty street. The dog calmed, snuffling at the air as she passed. She wondered whether it could sense the remnants of her fear. Should she walk until daylight? Curl up in an inconspicuous corner? She dug through her knapsack while still walking and found her wristwatch; it was four A.M. Where were all the unsleeping people? Wasn't this the city that never? At least daylight wasn't so far off. She felt safer on her feet.

A canal, gleaming black, cut through the neighborhood, creating a dead end. The closer she came to the water, the more pungent the air became. A stench stabbed at the nose, burned the rims of the eyes, made the mouth feel gritty. This fueled her curiosity. What could possibly smell this bad?

The asphalt gave way to spots of cobblestone. Tall, pale, wild grass grew in wispy tufts at the street's end, but on the bank leading down to the water the grass was stubby, patchy, and a shade of green that seemed, even in the dark, unearthly bright. The warehouses along the canal had carefully guarded access to the waterway (more high fences, more barbed wire), but she didn't see many barges or boats. A single tugboat was moored across the water, beside what appeared to be a huge pile of scrap metal. The moon sat low in the sky, illuminating in the distance a bridge. Pluta backtracked to the avenue and walked parallel to the canal until she found the bridge in the moon's jaundiced glow. There she stood over the water, the cause of the stink. Was it worse than the Riachuelo?

The water appeared thick; on its surface opalescent bubbles of oil floated like jellyfish.

The smell of the Riachuelo, what she remembered of it, resurfaced. She'd only been there once as a little girl, maybe five years old, when Daniel had taken her to see where he'd grown up in Barracas. She recalled taking the bus, crossing through the busy center of the city, gripping his hand. Her grandparents were no longer living, but they'd walked by the houses of his childhood anyway. His loafers trod softly on the pavement and the wet leaves. Light steps on a slick street. Then they'd gone down by the river, to La Boca, because he'd heard from a shopkeeper that some crazy artist had dyed the water bright green and he needed to see it. It was a place Isabel would never have taken her. Industrial red cranes loomed over the water, like the ones she had seen on the promenade with Bobby. Large, rusty boats. And that stink. And that water clouded with an incredible green. In her mind's eye, she craned her five-year-old head up to look at her father, to gauge his reaction to this artist's daring act—he laughed and shook his head with a vague pleasure, a vague sadness. She grasped the railing of the bridge.

It was her father who had shown her things; it was her mother who hid them. She leaned in against the railing, feeling the bulk of her possessions press against her through the bag. Again she thought of the Gorgon's shrouded head, her desire to rip off that covering. She fought a yawn.

The moon was low enough to catch. To reach up and pluck it from the sky, punt it down the road. What to do next? She rubbed her eyes against her forearm. Make a nest somewhere; wandering all night was ridiculous, impossible. She headed back to the playground. There were benches there.

The playground was empty except for a tall woman pacing beyond the far corner, outside the wrought iron fence. Her arms were crossed and she kicked as she walked, as if she'd been waiting for something or someone for a very long time. Pluta slipped into the playground, careful to avoid an encounter with the woman. As the adrenaline that had come with leaving Bobby's dissipated, her limbs grew heavy and a dull strain throbbed at the backs of her eyes. The benches seemed so exposed; she wished she could make herself invisible. She couldn't bring herself to stretch out on the bench to sleep, a pose that suddenly seemed to her a signal of weakness, so she sat upright a while, trying to get her bearings.

There was a single slide, which looked more comfortable than the benches; a set of metal swings for larger children; and a set of swings for babies. What children could play in smelling distance of the canal?

She supposed they must get used to it—perhaps anyone could get used to it—and wondered how long it would take, what kind of determination. Hedges grew around the playground's perimeter and, at each corner, a short, slender tree. At some point there had been an effort, then, to make the area more inviting. In fact the hedges looked more inviting than the exposed benches. After sitting a while on the bench, fighting sleep, she contemplated curling up beneath the hedges, where she would at least feel hidden and perhaps the earth would be soft. But she couldn't bring herself to do it. She didn't want to encounter whatever little animals might be living there, didn't want to wake up to some bug, or rodent, scuttling atop her face.

Nodding off while the sky grayed, hovering between sleeping and waking, Pluta saw a single green star. It pulsated. Someone in it was trying to climb out, unburned. Long white arms emerged—first one, then the other—a well-trained contortionist. Then came the top of a bald head. No, not bald; shaven. Then the brow. What did not emerge were the eyes, still sunken in the star.

The early rumble of delivery trucks idling before the warehouses roused her as she tried, unsuccessfully, to latch onto the star, pull at the crowning head, and crack off a piece of hot green sparkle.

Scents other than diesel materialized: the cool of morning, but also the moldering of fungus. It reminded Pluta of the time in Brazil when she'd opened Lolo's freezer and was greeted with an awful, overripe smell. *Why does your freezer smell like that?* Pluta had asked. *I'm making tinctures,* Lolo explained. Nothing about the unmarked packages in the freezer indicated what a tincture might be; they sat neatly stacked, unassuming and covered with frost. Pluta didn't know, and didn't want to know, what a tincture was, as long as she didn't have to eat one. Luckily, Lolo did not cook.

Pigeons' cooing started low but rose into a garbled frenzy. A man with white hair, coarse and wild, flung shredded hunks of bread to the ground. Early June had brought a warm morning, but the man wore a thick beige sweater closed with wooden toggle buttons. Pluta set her bag to the side; she had hugged it in her lap the whole time she was sleeping. Lazily, she scratched an itch at her back. *Mustn't touch that*, she remembered. Yawned and stretched, cracked the spine. Twisted in both directions, vertebrae popping. A dull ache filled her head.

"Hullo," the man called from ten feet away. "Don't often see young people here in the morning."

Was this an accusation? *I'm older than you think*, she thought to say. But she wanted to be nice.

"Hello," she said. "I just moved here." When she spoke it felt like a metal rod was boring through her head.

"Well, isn't that something. And what brings you to our late, great neighborhood?" He gestured all around.

"Adventure," Pluta said. The rod shrunk, expanded.

"Now, now, ha ha. Very good." He shook a finger at her, raising one thick, weedy eyebrow, then finished strewing the bread. "Have you toured the canal? Just like Venice! Better, even."

"Do you know much about it?"

"Do *I*?" He patted his chest, milky eyes brightening, as if he'd waited many years for this day. "Do *I*? Come on, girlie, and I'll tell you all about it."

"Oh," said Pluta, rising and feeling a tingling down the backs of her legs. "Okay." Nothing better to do. His talk might distract her from the metal rod. Maybe after she listened to him politely he'd tell her where she

78

could make some money around here. Wash dishes, stock shelves, wait tables. Something.

"Leonard," the man said, thrusting out a large, wrinkled hand.

"Ta—Pluta," she said.

His handshake was warm, dry, firm. "Tapluta? That's an unusual name."

"Pluta. Yes, it is."

"Aha. Come on," he said, gesturing for her to follow. Pluta had to shake her fatigue to catch up. Jars of *dulce de leche* clunked against each other in her knapsack. "You carrying the world in there?" the man asked, eyeing the bag.

"Ha, no. No."

"Ah. Playing it close to the vest, are ya?"

Pluta shook her head, not knowing what he meant but bristling at the questions. Leonard led her to a bridge, a different one from the night before, and stood with authority at its midpoint.

"Take in a nice, deep breath, Pluty."

At first she thought he was joking, but he filled his own lungs with a deep inhale, slowly exhaling with guttural satisfaction.

"Go on, *iiiin—*" He gestured like an orchestra conductor. Graceful. Pluta humored him (maybe the fumes would clear her head), breathing in the foul air until she sputtered a wet cough. "That's the smell of *progress*, girlie."

Catching her breath, Pluta asked why. Instead of answering, Leonard launched into a lecture on the history of the canal; it seemed often practiced but rarely performed. As he talked, Pluta studied the water, which in daylight remained inky and thick. White spots speckled the water's surface, the white itself flecked with faint blue. Like Roquefort, thought Pluta. Revolting. And yet delicious. The thought of eating Roquefort beside the canal made her gag. She looked up and away to suppress the gag, holding a fist over her mouth. The cloud cover turned chartreuse.

"Lavender Lake is what it was called. Know why? Of course you don't. Because—see all these factories along the water? When they first got going, in the last century, see, they made this canal *lavender*. With all the chemicals, yes? And all of that eventually filtered into Buttermilk Channel. Do you like buttermilk?"

"I don't know."

"I like a glass now and then myself. Anyway, not to worry, not to worry: There is *no* buttermilk in Buttermilk Channel." He laughed at his own joke, warmly, a low *ahahahahaaa*, pounding the heel of his hand into the bridge railing. The rod in Pluta's head throbbed. "So, you see, they got a lot of gunk going into this canal, back in the good old days."

Pluta leaned on the railing, tried to stay awake. Leonard leaned beside her, shoulders hunched. They looked down into the water together.

"Now, at some point or other," said Leonard, "there was a pump, 'cause more stuff, flotsam and whatnot, kept coming into the canal and wasn't moving out to the channel fast enough, and the pump flushed out the gunk real fast. Or faster, anyway. And then, as these things go, we entered some dark times, dark times, yes, and the pump broke. Been near twenty years, they never fixed that damn pump. And the lavender water went black." An oily mallard paddled around some reeds near the bridge. Leonard dug deep into a trouser pocket, found and lit a cigarette. "Bet that damn duck dies by the end of today. How much you wanna bet?"

He grazed her arm with the back of his hand, apparently ready for a wager. A breeze rustled the reeds, rippled the water.

"So garbage is the smell of progress?"

"Well," he said, gazing into his reflection, "we all start out as bottom feeders, don't we?" Pluta's stomach growled. "Ha—you agree, you agree, then," he said. "Very good."

His urge to instruct reminded her a little of her father, only Leonard was much more excited and much odder, and she wondered whether his strangeness as a teacher had grown from a lack of practice or whether it repelled potential "students" in the first place.

"Are you a teacher or something?" she asked.

Leonard let out another cackle. "You'd think. I wish. No, no, I guess you could say I'm an archivist. Retired now. Thank god." He clucked his tongue and shook his head. "Us archivists, we get into trouble. Hoo!" Pluta's stomach growled again, the steak and baked potato of the night before a distant memory. "I think your stomach is trying to tell you something."

"I guess it thinks it's hungry."

"I'm all outta bird feed. But I got some cookies back home if you've got a hankering." From the small watchtower by the bridge, a bell clanged. Pluta resisted the urge to clutch her temples. "Ooh, your lucky day. Hold on, let's step off the bridge a minute and watch the action." They rushed to the sidewalk on the other side and the bridge retracted, making room for a passing barge. "Don't you just love boats?"

"Hey, can I have a cigarette?" asked Pluta.

Leonard sucked at his teeth and handed her one, looking smug. "Why not. Cleans the ol' windbags out, doesn't it. Nothing like a morning smoke at my favorite bridge. This is where the action is, Pluty." The bridge reconnected. Leonard nodded at the man in the control tower and gave him a thumbs up. The man nodded back, as if used to this ritual. "N'yeah, you were hungry, weren't you. I know the type, needing three meals a day. What nerve." He started walking. "Coming?"

The breeze shifted. A fat raindrop fell, then two, then multitudes: a summer storm.

They ran, skipping over growing gutter-side puddles. Their clothing soaked beneath the deluge.

Leonard stopped at a squat wooden house wedged between a pair of two-story industrial buildings, one sooty brick and the other grimy stucco, each Cyclopean with a lone small window. The wooden house, dull yellow, had chipped siding. Its rotting porch sagged. A rusted bike with a banana seat was chained to one of the porch's columns and a deflated basketball sat in the gutter of its roof. Rainwater filled the dent in the ball and spilled over, creating a waterfall they had to dodge.

"And this would be the Winter Palace," Leonard said. The step to the front door was broken. Leonard leapt over it and held out his hand to assist Pluta.

Inside, it smelled of dust and damp wool. The vestibule was cramped with stacks of boxes out of which poked the tips and corners of curling, yellowed paper. The front room, with blinds drawn over its two windows, housed floor-to-ceiling stacks of books, their cracked spines streaked with age.

"My book tomb," he said. "I can't help it. Libraries' detritus. I scoop them up when they're dumped and give them a home, but y'know, honestly, I barely read them. I never did get around to putting up some shelves." A card catalog occupied one side of the room, each drawer labeled in meticulous handwriting. "It would make more sense to put them on shelves so you could get at them and keep 'em in order. But there you have it. Tea?"

"Please." Leonard disappeared into the next room, the kitchen. The rooms were railroaded. The bedroom and bathroom were further in, beyond the kitchen. There was a leak in one of the back rooms. Drips dropped into a pan. A faucet squeaked and water rushed into a kettle; the gas stove clicked on; the ignited burner emitted a faint *woomph*.

Pluta caressed one dusty tower of books, imagining an alternate universe of discarded things. As if, once her father's books had burned, they could have reappeared here. A shiver rippled through her. Worried she might topple the tower, she turned away, pulling at the wet shoulders of her dress and letting them fall again with a dull slap.

News clippings papered the top half of the opposite wall above a couch. "Two Tons of Tapioca Spill into New York Harbor: Bring a Spoon," proclaimed one article. "Lost Whale Stuck in Gowanus Creek," lamented another. Everything had to do with New York waterways. Accidental spills; swimming and canoeing races; a Coast Guard mutiny; the small, obscure islands around the city—Blackwell's, Rat, Hog, Barren. The article on Barren Island declared its end: absorption into the rest of Brooklyn, the gap bridged by landfill. There was a place called Dead Horse Bay.

Leonard came out with a towel and a plate of tea biscuits as Pluta skimmed the articles. He set the biscuits down on the coffee table. Pluta dried her face and neck, squeezed the rain out of her hair, and dabbed at her damp shoulders.

"Yes, yes, my wall of knowledge. Was a long time ago when I decided it would be good to know something

83

about something. So I chose the water." He took the used towel and handed her a plate, and they ate standing up and looking at the articles, crumbs flying onto the couch cushions. It felt good to eat.

"Why?" said Pluta.

Leonard shrugged. "Why anything? Go with what you like, I say. What's better than water?"

"Air's pretty good."

"Yeah, you got me there. Air. Ha. Good." He peered at her, head tilted. "Would you like something dry to wear?"

A cool, slick sensation lurched behind her breastbone. "No, thanks. I'm fine."

The kettle whistled. Leonard brought out orange pekoe tea.

"This ain't the Waldorf-Astoria," he said by way of apology. "Do you want anything else? Canned sardines? Tomato soup? Macaroni?"

Leonard refilled her empty plate with the remnants of the biscuits.

"Thanks," she said, mouth full; she couldn't think of sardines. "I'm getting pretty stuffed."

Perched on the couch, they blew at still-hot tea. Little trails carved into the wood of the coffee table hinted at termites. Through pursed lips they sipped. Straight wrinkles ran vertically above Leonard's mouth. Almost like pleats. The French teacher at Banderhock had explained how French women got those wrinkles from speaking French all the time, and she wondered if he got those lines from drinking too much too-hot tea.

"So, now then. We've eaten. We've drunk. Tell me more about your little self." He sat back in the couch. Its tired metal springs groaned. "Your unusual name, for instance. What's it mean?"

84

Pluta tried to sit up straighter. She didn't have a good answer to this question. It had to do with Plutón—*Pluto*, in the English myths her father read her. Was there a girl version of the name in English, other than the one she'd made up? "I guess it's like Pluto. You know? God of the underworld."

"You've got funny parents."

"I don't have parents."

Leonard slapped at his knee. "Ha! So what is it then? Little Orphan Annie or the Pod People?"

"I don't know. I don't really know what those things are." She settled back into a slump. "Those people."

"Where are you from? What do you do?" He leaned forward with the same intensity he had given to the canal lecture. It reminded Pluta of a pigeon or a rooster. She leaned away.

"I come from no place. I do nothing." Her back itched; she scratched it, stopped.

"I see," said Leonard, tapping Pluta's knee. "I thought so. Goddess of the underworld, eh?" He took out his wallet, licked his thumb, and counted out four ten-dollar bills, placing them on the coffee table. He gave Pluta a sidelong glance. It seemed a question to which she didn't know the answer. To her silence he said, "You're right," and threw in another ten dollars. Then he pushed her down onto the couch. The springs beneath her went *pingpingping*. "I'd prefer it if you didn't move very much."

She hesitated, voice stuck mid-throat. Hot pressure beneath her, the back-itch thorny. Pressure atop her, and heavy, him leaning all his weight down as he lifted her dress. A shin on a calf, a knee on a thigh. The money on the table was for her, she realized; she heard the drip in the distant pan, the splash of a car driving through puddles outside. How far? Was this part of the game?

Or was making this part of the game something else entirely? What time was it and why did she suddenly need to know? Her eyes roved about the clockless room. The more questions she asked herself, the more she realized she would not act. Oh well, she told herself. She looked to the side. He wiggled, half-floppy. Panted. His body odor like hot wet dust. It was over; he moved away.

"Don't worry," he said over his shoulder as he headed to the bathroom. "I'm probably sterile."

Her knees wobbled as she stood to reassemble herself.

"Do you need to freshen up?" called Leonard from across the rooms. Pluta pocketed the money laid out on the table and checked his wallet for more, but there was none. When Leonard came back, she rushed into the bathroom and washed, cursorily, in the sink. Made the water scalding. Dried with balled-up toilet paper, didn't want contact with the damp towel hanging limp on the rack.

"Damn rain's gonna flood my basement again," Leonard said, half to himself.

Pluta headed straight for the front door. "Bye!" she called.

"Going so soon?" Leonard stood in the kitchen, arms dangling at his sides. "Bye-bye then."

Pluta grabbed her bag in the vestibule, slammed the door behind her, leapt over the broken step, and marched north. The rain weakened to spittle.

Inside her, the tea kettle was still whistling.

Crossing the street, taking long strides that were almost lunges, she thought of Bobby. Should she go back there? Was he safer? Would he let her? If he had been angry before (was it only because she'd opened the glove compartment?), maybe with a little time he would forget or forgive and let her stay. She would gather some distance today—such a strange day—and then try him again. She needed to clear her head. She hadn't had an exact plan when she left the school, but now even her vague plan was imploding. She felt obscure and bizarre.

The kettle screamed, piercing hot. She wouldn't go back to the school; she would never see her mother again. If she did she would bore her head into Isabel's belly: first a head-butt, taking the wind out of her, but then she would mash her face into its softness until she herself couldn't breathe. No: she could never see Isabel again; that was obviously out. Her mother would have confirmation of her badness now, would lord it over her forever and ever.

She stuck sweaty palms to her hot cheeks and stretched her face. It occurred to her that *this* was really life, and everything that came before was ... something else. There was a pile of cardboard boxes outside a corner store; she wanted to crawl among them and hide, hands tight around her head, while she thought things through. But if she did that, she thought, she might get scooped up into a dumpster, or she might never come out again. A knot of energy propelled her forward on shaky limbs.

Within a block, the buildings became regular brick rowhouses with potted geraniums and Virgin Mary statues. Turning onto a commercial street, she passed a shoe repair shop, a laundromat, a veterans' social club. Old ladies in floral-print muumuus pushed metal shopping carts down the street; the carts rattled at her. As if even the metal disapproved.

On the next corner was a pizza shop. It had only just opened for the day. Abruptly, she stopped. The pies in the steaming window did not look so unlike those of Buenos Aires. Her eyes stung. The glass door had a weak hinge and banged behind her. The man at the counter frowned at her stomping. Dry oven heat wavered against moist summer heat. The oven heat calmed her, somewhat. If she crawled inside the oven, she'd be even calmer. Her father, with a grimace and a shake of the head, shutting the oven door behind her. She jerked to attention and ordered two cheese slices. Her hands flailed spasmodically as she spoke, as she paid.

The slices came at her practically bubbling. She felt starved yet didn't want to eat and yet forced herself. She ate despite the burn of the cheese on her tongue and the roof of her mouth. With shaking hands she took too-large bites that scraped her throat and she gulped at cola, feeling the crushed ice and bubbles scrub down her insides. A long, sonorous belch followed.

"Excuse *you*," said the man behind the counter.

"Excuse me," she replied. She wiped sauce from the corners of her mouth, pocketing a handful of extra napkins. Her back burned and itched. She resisted the urge to scratch it against the wall, as the more she scratched it, the more it burned. "Excuse me."

6. Manaus, Brazil
July 1978

THE CONTENTS OF THAT BOX would be stamped on Isabel's mind forever. She would try to erase, evade, reform the memory—twist it into something that made sense in the world—but it would always resurge.

How for a moment she'd enjoyed the sea air at her brow, despite the anxiety of seeing this box left at her doorstep. Crouching, she only had to open the box a crack to see, glinting in the afternoon light, a ring. Like his ring. She didn't take the time to recognize the rest. After she had slammed the box shut—after she had clutched it to her chest and run to the garden, to the mint patch, a spot Pluta could not see from her window—after she had retched, after she had clawed through the dirt in a panic and buried that box, which had been heavy, much heavier than one might imagine—after she had washed her hands with a hard-bristled brush and rinsed and burned her mouth with the harshest antiseptic she could find—then, doubt crept in. Maybe it wasn't his ring. Or his hands. It might have been some horrible trick perpetrated by the very people the government had been warning against all along. But it was too similar; it was much too similar. Not wax, though waxen—pale, drained. She called her sister again.

Lolo, upon answering, clucked her tongue. In a hoarse whisper she again insisted they speak in Ladino, but Isabel still did not understand why. Said she'd received a very disturbing package. That it couldn't be explained.

"Does it have to do with him?" Lolo asked.

Isabel attempted to say yes but choked on the word. Her eyes closed, fingers clutching the receiver. Lolo hissed.

"Don't speak anymore," she implored. "Let me. Come here. To my home." She mumbled something about Montevideo, about what had washed up there.

"I don't see what Montevideo has to do with anything," said Isabel. She rubbed her eyes. Pinpoints of light floated before her. Perhaps Lolo, living alone all those years in Manaus, was becoming unhinged, drifting off into early senility. But she resisted the urge to get off the phone because she feared she might not call Lolo again—so rarely did they speak, once or twice a year at best. Lolo had regained the authority of her eleven-year seniority. Isabel listened: she was to pack, lock up the house, and come with Pluta to Manaus. Immediately.

In her room, Pluta could hear her mother stumbling through Ladino for what seemed a long time until she hung up and seethed a fire-breath. Her mother the marauding dragon. Or, more precisely, a war machine, serene in her work of destruction. Did her mother *hate* her father? Had she ever loved him? Slow, composed steps ascended the stairs. Isabel entered the room with bleary eyes and creaked onto Pluta's bed.

Encircling Pluta with one arm, she said, "We're going to your Auntie's. First thing tomorrow. You're to pack your things right now. Understand?"

Even through the bleariness, Isabel's eyes commanded. Pluta searched inside herself and found nothing.
Unformed words stuck at the bottom of her larynx.

"Good," said Isabel. She kissed Pluta on the forehead,
patted her head once as if to confirm, and left the room.

Pluta slipped off the bed, feet uncertain. In the space
where her mother had been, a ghost of heat. So much
askew, everything she knew upturned: her father's
"trip"—he never went on trips—then the burning of his
things, her mother mentioning Montevideo, and now
this? As if to escape her crime of incinerating his books.
What would he do when he found out? For once she
wanted to see her mother in trouble. But she didn't dare
delay. Behind that peck on the forehead her mother's
engine revved fast and hot.

A large suitcase seemed a safe choice. She dragged
it from the bottom of her closet into the middle of the
room and packed everything she could think of: holi-
day dresses and ruffled socks; a slicker, a scarf, boots,
and umbrellas (two, in case one broke—how hard did it
rain in the Amazon?); books on meteorology, fairy tales,
Greek mythology, and the peoples of Oceania; sweaters,
crayons, a compass; and, from the kitchen, jars of *dulce
de leche*. She had never met her aunt or traveled to Brazil
and didn't know what to expect. Across the hall, Isabel's
packing seemed just as fervent. The sound of a zipper
closing; a single, strangled sob.

That night, mother and daughter lay in their beds
with wide eyes blinking in the dark, waiting for the gray
of dawn, for the mercy of morning and action.

The new day began in the cool marble hall of the bank,
as Isabel withdrew cash and rifled through the family
safe-deposit box. Pluta waited in the lobby, resisting the

urge to shout and hear her voice echo. They had drawn all the curtains in the house, bolted the doors, thumped their luggage out behind them. And even as the waiting in the bank seemed interminable, that waiting was hurried. When Isabel was done she whisked Pluta into a taxi to the airport and gave her a box of biscuits. Pluta knew to eat and be quiet.

They flew to Belém and perched on their suitcases waiting for the next flight to Manaus, and then they flew to Manaus.

Late the next afternoon, their taxi sped past slums, construction sites, factories, and a high-rise-dotted downtown, finally rumbling onto the narrow streets of the historic district where Lolo lived. A horn blast behind them startled Pluta from a heavy, open-mouthed doze. The air, which had been pleasant enough as it whizzed through the open window of the speeding taxi, grew still and hot while Isabel counted out the fare.

Lolo, her wild dark curls streaked with spiraling gray, stood in the doorway in a shaft of sunlight, barefoot and picking her teeth with a large knife. The maize-colored doorway and matching shutters took on an egg-yolk glow in that light; the rest of the house appeared indigo. When the bedraggled family of two emerged from the taxi, dazed, Lolo stuck the knife in a pot of geraniums on her doorstep and welcomed them with open arms, coos, and fervent kisses. Amid this assault their eyes roved up and down the street of houses painted pink and green and red and cerulean.

"It's been too long," Lolo told Isabel, who bent her head. "Come inside."

Lolo had married an old man when she was very

young and lived in an ancient house built by her late husband's father, one of the last great rubber tycoons. And though her parents were happy with their son-in-law's economic situation (steady, despite the rubber boom having busted), they were most displeased with their eldest daughter moving into the depths of the Amazon when she had everything she could ever want right there in Buenos Aires. This displeasure was compounded by the fact that when he died only ten years later and she inherited his small fortune, she decided to stay there rather than come home and take care of her parents as an eldest daughter should. Pluta had heard rumors of this tale of betrayal and regarded her aunt with awe, as a character out of family lore whom she never thought she'd meet.

The entry hall's teak floors creaked underfoot. Where were Lolo's maids and servants, Pluta wondered? In slippered feet they'd tiptoe up the curve of the iron staircase, working magic while remaining unseen. But the house smelled dusty and felt very still, so she guessed perhaps her aunt had no servants. Lolo led them into a dark sitting room that had way too much velvet and lace for the stifling heat and brought out a honey cake which she cut with a machete, grinning with big teeth not unlike Isabel's. Isabel stared. Lolo wiped the crumbs off the blunt side of the knife and ate them while chuckling.

"Welcome to Amazonas."

Silence.

"All right, it was a joke, *cara mia*, but I see it's no time for jokes," Lolo said, putting away the knife.

Upon the coffee table sat a cut-glass bowl filled with green lozenges; dim light refracted through the bowl onto the sliced honey cake. Lolo returned from the kitchen, humming, with a tray of coffee and no machete.

She poured coffee into three cups and a bit of brandy into two of them. Isabel and Pluta leaned back into the too-soft couch to drink their coffee, but contact with the velvet immediately set their backs to sweating and they both sat up again.

Pluta reached for a slice of cake, her hand slipping into the murk of the refracted light. There she paused, angling her wrist to one side and then the other to watch the stripes of light move over it. Before Isabel could correct her, she stopped hovering and helped herself to a slice. Absently, she munched on the dense sweetness and gazed at the mantel with the grandmother clock. Beside it was a large silver vessel.

Lolo smiled. "You know who that is?"

Pluta shook her head and fought the impulse to lick golden crumbs from her plate.

"That's your uncle. He keeps me company."

Isabel took Pluta's plate out of her hands and set it on the coffee table.

"I don't mean to be rude, Lolo, but we're exhausted and due for a nap."

"Of course, of course, my loves, what was I thinking? Rest, today—rest for as long as you need. We can go for a walk in the evening and get dinner in town if you like."

"Yes, ok," murmured Isabel, her mind already collapsing toward the oblivion of sleep.

They climbed the winding iron staircase. Pluta dragged her fingers along its elaborate curlicues tipped with fleurs-de-lis. In their respective rooms, they peeled off their travel-worn clothes, put on fresh nightgowns, and slipped into bed.

In the welcome dimness of the warm room, Isabel lay atop the covers, exhausted and expecting to fall asleep immediately. But though her eyes seemed to sink into her face, though she mashed them into the surprisingly fresh pillow, it did not come. The busyness of travel had been useful: packing, bank errands, ticket purchasing, international travel, currency exchange. She could do these things with Pluta beside her (almost, at times, wanted to heave the much-too-old girl onto her hip, if only to move faster). But now, they'd arrived. Was this their final destination? How long could they stand to be with Lolo? How long could they stand to be away?

In the pit of her stomach, she remembered the box buried in the garden: but the garden, at least, was walled. Stray dogs could not come in to dig it up. She curled into a fetal position, tensed every muscle in her body. A clock on the wall ticked. Finally she dug through her purse and found what her friends liked to call their "little helpers." She chewed on a Valium and dove back into bed, holding the pillow over her face.

Pluta had more luck with her nap, a continuation of the doze in the taxi. Several hours later, she sprang up gasping. Though the windows and doors were open for a cross-breeze, the air stifled. She listened to the noises of the house: walls settling, the beat of wings in the garden, a faint murmur downstairs. She crept downstairs, following the murmur. Thin smoke curled and mingled with the warm scent of melting tallow. She expected to find her mother and aunt quietly conspiring, but in the sitting room, at a side table behind a bead curtain, Lolo sat alone in the weak light of a single candle. Her lips moved, but her eyes were closed. Her palms lay flat on the marble tabletop.

Lolo, sensing Pluta's presence, opened her eyes. "Come," she said. "I was just speaking with your uncle."

95

When Pluta hesitated, Lolo reached for her with rough-skinned hands that smelled of ginger and garlic and drew her into a seat. Her tongue clicked. "That's him," she whispered. "He's pleased to meet you."

A moment later, Isabel appeared and scowled at the sight of her sister and daughter engaging in a séance. Lolo's grasp loosened. Pluta, sensing she might be punished but not knowing why, removed her hand from Lolo's.

"Are you hungry?" said Lolo. "It should be cool out. We can get some fresh air."

"I'm not feeling well," said Isabel. "You take Pluta out. I'll stay here. I'm sure I'll sleep through the night."

"Yes, of course. We'll talk in the morning. Or if you're awake, we'll talk in the night." Cheek to cheek they kissed.

Isabel receded up the stairs and into the bedroom, relieved. At least now she had another adult for support; Lolo was her sister, after all, and Pluta's aunt. She would understand, she would have to understand. Isabel slipped back into bed, pillow over her head.

At a nearby restaurant, aunt and niece shared a river fish, fried whole, chewing silently through the crispy skin. Pluta had never seen such a fish. Lolo offered Pluta a piece of the head but Pluta demurred, preferring to watch her aunt happily suck the meat out of the skull.

The next morning, they all stood barefoot in the kitchen while coffee boiled in a copper pot on the stove.

"I'm so tired," Isabel said, scuffing her toe on the red tiles. "I think I caught something on the plane. Why don't you take Pluta out again, show her the town?"

"Of course," said Lolo. She showed Isabel her array of

medicinal teas: a whole cupboard filled with mysterious paper, wooden, and tin boxes; glass jars that held leaves and little twigs and oddly colored fuzz. Each container was labeled in a cursive both minuscule and inscrutable.

"Help yourself," said Lolo.

In the garden a large bird squawked and alighted on a tree branch with a rustle of foliage.

"I think I just need to lie down," Isabel said.

Lolo shut the cupboard. "You know what's best."

Pluta perched on the edge of a chair tying her shoes, a process that seemed interminable that morning. Something in the girl's movement reminded Lolo of a sad, slow turtle. There'd been a lonely afternoon in Buenos Aires, when Lolo was around Pluta's age, that she'd spent idly rolling a ball against the side of the house. Scratching noises had emerged from a terracotta flowerpot that had toppled and cracked the night before. (It was a large flowerpot, or maybe an old clay cistern, perhaps knocked over by a dog or a very large cat or—likely as not, she'd thought at the time—a roving tiger escaped from the zoo.) She'd crouched at the mouth of the pot. In the damp, cool dark, a turtle struggled to turn around. Lolo reached inside; the fleshy nubs of his legs grazed her fingers as they receded into his shell. She put him down on the flagstone and backed away to see if he would go happily into the mint or begin the enormous, plodding journey to the waterfront. But after a long wait (she remained very quiet), the turtle came out from his shell—only to climb back into the cistern.

Lolo thrust her hand into Pluta's and led her out of the house, leaving Isabel to its cool, dark quiet.

Manaus was no longer the playground of industrial tycoons. Lolo had not even been born yet when the city had its turn-of-the-century heyday. But from the cab she pointed out the crumbling mansions of red brick or gray stone that had belonged to her husband's acquaintances: long-defunct rubber barons. Some of the mansions had been chopped up into apartments; some were abandoned. Thick vines crept up the façades of the abandoned buildings, curled around window frames and wooden shutters, and latched onto cracks in foundations.

"Tomorrow we'll go to the Teatro Amazonas," she said. "They just renovated it a few years ago. It's really quite beautiful."

Pluta seemed both to scrutinize the abandoned buildings, reading in them some terrible import, and to be thousands of kilometers away. Probably in whatever part of her imagination she'd put the memory of her father and what had become of him.

Lolo wondered how much had been explained to the girl, if *explaining* was even the right word. The business trip lie had been her own idea, but it had its limits and its pitfalls. The other idea had been to simply tell the truth: he'd been arrested. Except why? Where was he? When would he be released? Isabel had been unable to find any answers to these questions. And then there'd been the box, which Isabel had struggled to explain but could not. Only, Lolo could tell: whatever it was, it was horrendous and a threat. Maybe Brazil wasn't far enough away.

For a long time now, the outside world—most things beyond her doorstep and her street—had disturbed Lolo. She felt lost out there: a fragment of a speck of a particle amid chaos. Over the years she'd developed certain rituals to feel sturdier. The rubber baron had been one anchor, but after his death she'd sought other things. About a month after his funeral she took to collecting dictionaries. His library already contained German-Spanish,

Spanish-Portuguese, and Yiddish-German. She added others, the more obscure the better: her favorite was Bulgarian-Uzbek. She learned the International Phonetic Alphabet and had a poster of it enlarged and laminated.

With so much free time on her hands, she set to reading at least one page of a dictionary a day, sounding out words whether she understood them or not. Sometimes she would cross-reference words from dictionary to dictionary until she discovered a meaning she could understand; sometimes she preferred to ponder only their sounds. She would do this early in the morning in her garden, when the moon paled and dew settled on the pages and into her coffee. She would close her book when the birds began to warble, and the words she had consumed would jangle in her head the rest of the day.

And this din in the head made her happy, prepared her to go out to the market, to the newsstand, to read three newspapers in the afternoon. But this monstrous thing happening to Daniel—this had unleashed a riot of barbed words that she had to battle back in order to minister to Isabel and to Pluta. The more she thought about Pluta—her disturbance and anxiety, her desperation for some anchor of understanding—the more urgent this ministering became, and Lolo could not indulge in her rituals, however much she depended on them.

The following morning Lolo woke Pluta at sunrise, leaving Isabel to sleep, realizing that this was what Isabel wanted and allowing her one more day. They went to the old public market along the Rio Negro, where she pointed out the stained-glass windows just below the arched roof and explained that they'd been modeled after those of a famous market in Paris: Les Halles.

* * *

Sunlight brightened the yellow and blue windowpanes and twinkled in a facet of Lolo's emerald ring. Pluta gazed at the jeweled colors, in the window, on the ring, the distant city of Paris lingering in her ears. She thought this was the sort of detail that (under ordinary circumstances) Isabel would find charming, but something about the notion of a distant city far across an ocean made her gut sink.

The fog of travel and of rising so early was lifting, but she shivered at the urgent wrongness of it all: rushing here, to Manaus, and being yanked about by Lolo, nice as she was. Something was happening that they weren't telling her about. Her gut trembled; she clutched at it with both hands. Lolo gave her a questioning look. Pluta let go and shook her head. As Lolo guided her to the market she tripped three times over her own feet.

Inside, nets of flopping fish were piled along white-tiled counters, slippery dark tails or rosy jaws hanging off the edges, splayed fillets exposing white flesh. Stacks of watermelon took up one stall. Green and red and yellow fruit—*pupunha*, said Lolo—took up another. In her basket Lolo gathered pineapple, bananas, lime, and star-fruit; she bought Pluta a mango on a stick, carved in the shape of a blossom. Pluta sighed and craned her head to bite it. The juices dribbled down her baby jowls. A scarlet ibis took flight from the market roof and soared over the placid Rio Negro, whose black water glittered in the sun.

"Stunning, isn't it?" asked Lolo.

Pluta wanted to ask Lolo so many questions, yet she couldn't even form them, didn't feel as if she could put the right words together to get the right answer, didn't know Lolo well enough to know if she could even begin to ask her.

Lolo peered at Pluta's cheeks, dripping with mango pulp, and produced a handkerchief. She wiped her niece's face with vigor.

Isabel lay immobile. Everything drifted in and out. Pluta was a red, wrinkled baby, imperial in her screams. Six months old, yet still red, still wrinkled, on the Night of the Long Canes.

Isabel surprised herself, remembering that name. *The Night of the Long Canes.* First only the rhythm of the phrase marched upon her tongue, then the exact words surfaced. Daniel had been shaken by it. The Onganía government cracking down on dissent in the university. Labs and libraries destroyed; faculty and students beaten. A lot of faculty, in different colleges of the university, resigning or leaving the country.

They'd had a tense conversation, trembling. Isabel with Pluta—Tatiana—in her arms. The baby had screamed and screamed, veins throbbing in her little neck. They decided Daniel would not resign. The faculty was small and had not been liquidated; he hadn't been beaten; his career had just started.

"What you do there is valuable," she said. She almost said it as a question but saved it at the last moment.

They weren't in a position to leave the country; it just didn't make sense. Nor did resignation make sense. He had considered a shift to a private university, something more autonomous. She wouldn't have minded. But instead he stayed on and on. Afraid of change, craving stability. Through dictatorship, democracy, dictatorship again. She soon lost patience with his indecision.

Isabel crushed her face into the pillow, mashing her nose flat, sucking the pillow into her mouth. She remembered holding her daughter—the infant quivering as she screamed, her dark howl the only sound of that terrible night.

Exhausted, she drifted into sleep again, woke again with a start. She dragged herself from bed and wandered her sister's house, running her hands over all manner of dusty objects. She wanted to touch everything: the wrought iron of the staircase, gilded picture frames, the rough paint of portraits, porcelain dolls, the grandmother clock, the marble table, her brother-in-law's urn. Soon a gray film coated her fingers. In the kitchen she ran hot water, found a hard-bristled brush, and scrubbed each hand raw. Her skin tingled, ached; she focused on this a moment. But when she closed her eyes she saw *his* hands, not her hands, and she leaned against the sink, thankful she hadn't eaten, for her stomach convulsed in waves. Her ribcage seemed to expand with the convulsions; she leaned harder against the sink, her throat muscles constricting. The whole-body heave eventually calmed. She focused again on the objects around her, not touching them now, looking at them but not seeing them. She found herself wandering the house again; she glanced into one of Lolo's few mirrors and saw her skin tinted greenish yellow. An urge to break the mirror rose and crumbled. She hurried away from herself into the room with the television, turned it on, and let Portuguese fill her ears.

Lolo and Pluta returned to escape the height of the day. After the heat subsided, they would go to Teatro Amazonas to buy tickets to a show. Isabel still wished to stay behind and had not bothered to change out of her nightgown. She'd spent the day glancing through rotting mystery novels and letting *telenovelas* wash over her in a long, flickering stream; Lolo nodded at this and let it be.

It was her job, for now, to distract the girl. In the plaza by the theater, Lolo explained that there hadn't been an opera company in Manaus for many, many years. When the government renovated the theater, there'd been hope of a permanent return. But not enough people were attending, and the show would soon close, the itinerant singers scattering the globe. They must snatch the rare treat.

"Music soothes the aching soul," said Lolo as they left the box office. Pluta looked away, embarrassed. "I look forward to spending time with you, Pluta." Lolo's gold tooth shone under the street lamp, which was just blinking on against the pale twilight. "I hope you'll have a good time here." She gave Pluta's shoulder a squeeze.

The next night was the show: some version of *Orpheus*. Isabel insisted they go without her and was thankful Lolo did not fight her very hard. Going to an opera seemed ridiculous when her life would never be the same. She thought of the cousins back in Buenos Aires, how they'd avoided Daniel. How could she even begin to tell them about *this*? But since she hadn't told them— when would they realize she'd left?

It seemed someone should know something of their whereabouts, before they began to worry. If they were to be abroad for a time, it would be good for someone to walk by their house from time to time, maybe even make it seem as if someone still lived there. Maybe she could say that she and Daniel had separated, so she'd gone off to her sister's for a while? No, that didn't seem quite right. Maybe just that last part. Leave the rest out.

In a corner of the square before the theater, an old woman sold bags of nuts; Lolo bought a bag for Pluta to eat as they strolled. Small plaques, worn with time, exalted local politicians who'd contributed to a small renovation here or there during the many years in which there had been no opera company in residence. The tiled dome atop the theater twinkled patriotic green and gold. A tree had grown atop the roof, been mostly removed, and appeared to be sprouting again.

Lolo told Pluta about the theatergoers of the rubber boom. Horses tipsy on champagne would bring them into town; the women would wear sleek fur coats, beneath which they dripped with diamonds and sweat. They climbed the stone steps to the main entrance and into the marble, chandeliered hall. Nearly everything, Lolo explained, had been shipped from Europe to build this theater: marble, stone, glass, gold leaf. It was extravagant, but that was what they wanted at the time. To flaunt new wealth. When the boom ended, this crowd, who'd sent off their laundry to Lisbon or Paris because the local water was considered impure, dissipated. Bankruptcy ruined some while others chased the rubber to Malay or Sri Lanka.

"Your uncle," explained Lolo, "did not care to chase wealth elsewhere. He was happy here. There was no other place he wanted to be. And when he brought me here there was no other place I wanted to be either." She said this with pride, almost with indignation.

Pluta nodded. Thought about this question of running or staying.

During wartime, Lolo continued, the stage's underbelly had stored barrels of oil. Now the opera house was of little use; from time to time it hosted fashion shows or beauty contests or graduation balls. They sat back in seats whose velvet upholstery had long since been threadbare.

Though the theater was cavernous, it was not airy and Pluta fanned herself with the brittle program. The room was half-full: elderly couples in modest dress, moving in slow, deliberate steps. A handful of grand dames in rouge, brooches flashing in the incandescent light, ornamental mustachioed gentlemen at their sides. Lolo nodded at some of these, as if she had met them once or twice some twenty years ago. They nodded back with the same vague politeness.

"Do you know them?" asked Pluta.

Lolo hesitated. "A bit. From your uncle's time. I don't go out much myself anymore." She paused a moment. Her pitch soared upward: "So it's so nice to have you!" Lolo recovered from this near-screech with a low chuckle and a pat on Pluta's cheek. They looked away from each other.

Gilded pink Cupids, fluttering about gauzy-gowned women or romping among verdant jungle ferns, adorned the ceiling. On the embroidered stage curtains, nymphs and fauns also cavorted in greenery. Pluta told Lolo she had read about Orpheus in a book of mythology once. Her eyes darted about the theater as she told the bits of the story she remembered: how he had traveled to the underworld in search of Eurydice, how he'd looked back too soon and lost her forever.

Lolo nodded. Her eyes moistened.

"You'll love this, then," she said, patting the back of Pluta's hand. "It helps to know the story."

Pluta fidgeted and unfolded her hands and played with the hem of her dress and cleared her throat and swallowed. Abruptly, she lifted her eyes to meet Lolo's gaze.

"Do you know when my father will be back from his trip?"

105

Lolo looked to the cherubim for answers. Her instinct was to pause and pause until she found the right words, but the right words would not come. The right words were impossible. Still, she could not remain silent.

"Maybe not for a while," she said.

Pluta's hands were clammy and cool even in the warm theater; Lolo rubbed warmth into them. She couldn't bring herself to say *ask your mother*, which in some sense was the right thing and in another sense a very wrong thing to say. Isabel had muddled through this so carelessly, running off without saying why. But what could you do? What could you do? Who would know what to say? She hoped Pluta would not push for more information. The girl's eyes, so often thickened by the glaze of some dream world, had a new sharpness that seemed to beg for blunt truth.

"Have I told you yet about the mermaid people?" Lolo asked.

"No?" said Pluta.

This tentative curiosity spurred Lolo on. "The mermaid people are here in Amazonas. During the day, they swim deep in the water. They look like the pink freshwater dolphins, the *boto*, if you can imagine. And at night, they emerge from the water with arms and legs and put on normal people-clothes and hats, and walk about the market looking just like us, except they are hiding their blowholes under their hats!" Lolo clapped and let out a cackle before composing herself. "And that is why if you wear a hat, no matter how pretty and fashionable it is, it is not polite to leave it on when you go inside. So people will not have to worry if you are hiding a blowhole under your hat."

Pluta half-smiled.

* * *

106

Strains of music began. The moment of potential skewering had passed. Lolo turned her attention to the parting curtains.

In the darkened theater, Pluta studied her strange relative's profile. She supposed there were no hints about her father in that mermaid story. So what was it then? *Maybe not for a while.* Was he lost? In trouble? Hiding? Or did he just run away, as she had thought before? She tried to focus on the show. *Maybe not for a while.* The music wavered, cool and eerie. A female chorus set a dark tone—almost like a horror-film score. Pluta squinted down at her program and tried to read the explanation, but it was in Portuguese. She struggled to follow; the music continued, slow, low. The warmth and darkness weighed on her and her eyelids drooped. Lolo patted a shoulder, indicating Pluta could rest her head there. Pluta wanted to see the show, but the fatigue was overwhelming. She complied with the offer, pleasantly surprised at the softness of her aunt's shoulder. Soon after, all went black, and she felt as if she was falling.

It's dusk. Dark, heavy leaves tinge the air a smoky green. I come to a bend in a river, but it's stagnant—a lagoon. Algae chokes the water, makes it soupy. Tangled in the reeds, grasped by aquatic ferns, dark hair sways gently. The dark hair, silky in the water, extends from the body of a woman, brown skin tinted violet, lavender robe on bloated flesh. Floating on her back, she looks at the sky. A black and purple flower, bulbous and oozing white, emerges from one eye. I wade into the warm water, my dress billowing up around me. Clay slides between my bare toes. I pluck a black petal speckled purple and slide it under my tongue. In the humid sky, a star wavers.

Pluta came to; the show continued. Long bolts of iridescent blue fabric stretched across the stage in the dim light, suggesting currents of a river. Broken shards of mirror hung from the rafters in a sun-shaped cluster. Orpheus, a baritone, sang gravely on the bank of the river, strumming a lyre. Maenads crept up behind him on light, quick feet. *Prestissimo*, Lolo whispered, on the edge of her seat as they pattered with malicious grins. Some began to wail. He continued his song, solemn, oblivious. They danced around him and tried to envelop and entice him, but he batted away their reaching arms.

Eventually the Maenads surrounded Orpheus completely and covered him so the audience could no longer see; a lacuna. The crowd of Maenads writhed as one churning lump and an unearthly hum pulsated out of the lump, the buzz of an enormous hive, until, piercing through their hum-buzz, Orpheus howled and slipped beneath the blue fabric, his singing head bobbing down the river. Hunched Maenads continued to churn in their lump, but a few broke away to watch Orpheus float downstream. The lights were cut.

There was anemic applause and the house lights rose. Pluta lifted her head from her aunt's arm. The final scene had left her with a sense of being exposed, as if skinned. She ran her hands along her forearms and smoothed her skirt as if to confirm that everything was still there. "I'm sorry. I didn't mean to sleep the whole way through." She wiped her mouth with the back of her hand.

Lolo fetched a handkerchief from her handbag. "That's all right, love, that's quite all right." She dabbed underneath Pluta's sleepy eyes and mouth.

Back home, Isabel stood in the center of the sitting room, adrift. Outside, crickets sang.

"I made a phone call," she said to Lolo. Lolo took her by the elbow to the kitchen.

"What do you mean? To who?"

"To cousin Claudia. Just to say—"

Lolo motioned for Pluta to go away. Pluta furrowed her brow but ran upstairs. After Lolo closed the kitchen door she crept back down to listen.

Lolo said, "I wish you hadn't. Next time, let's take you to a place in town."

"Why? You're paranoid."

"Hold on," said Lolo. She opened the door and looked at Pluta. "I'm sorry, dear, but this really isn't for you." She led Pluta into the library. "Here, you can read any book you like. If you like it, you can keep it."

The lock scraped as it turned.

Aghast, Pluta stared at the locked door. She'd never been locked in a room. It seemed to give her license to do anything; Lolo had even *told* her to take what she wanted. There was something comfortable about the library. As if its age, its book-lined walls, and Lolo's fondness for it could make up for the exposed feeling Pluta had had at the end of the opera. She ran her fingers across the crumbling spines of moldy books, imagining an outfit for herself composed entirely of open, hard-backed books, their pages against her skin and their spines facing outward as jagged armor.

Phrases of the night's strange music replayed in her mind, cool, dark, low, slow; it hadn't sounded like anything she'd ever heard before. Through the closed doors came muffled shouts. Pluta paused, thinking she caught her mother's voice; then the strained voices lowered again.

On a large mahogany desk, dictionaries of all varieties lay open. The desk had been her uncle's. A small, shriveled man looking over yellowed ledgers. Now, Lolo used it. What weird combinations: Hungarian-Finnish, Inuit-Quechua, Japanese-Tajik. A placemat of sound symbols sat beneath the dictionaries. There was some elaborate system of cross-reference. Perhaps Lolo started with a word in Spanish or Portuguese and then tried to find its equivalent in all these other languages. But why? Many more dictionaries stood on the floor-to-ceiling bookcase nearest the desk. She tried to count them but stopped after fifty.

She thought of the story Lolo told of the mermaid people, how they hid in the water during the day and walked in the streets at night, how they hid their blowholes with hats. Who were they hiding from? Perhaps they didn't want to scare regular people. Or perhaps they felt safer this way. Did their feet hurt the way the Little Mermaid's had when she grew legs? Did Orpheus hurt at the end of the opera, when his severed head still sang as it bobbed down the river? Would the hurt make his song louder, or would it muffle it?

Behind the desk, a long window and glass door looked out on a walled garden. The nighttime shapes of bushes and a large, vine-laden tree tossed. But there was no wind; Pluta could not tell if what moved the branches was birds or bats. Her fingertips went to the door, but she was afraid that if she opened it the animals would come in flapping and screeching. The woman from her dream at the opera house, with an eye replaced by a flower, resurfaced in her mind. A bird had pecked it out, that eye, had dropped a seedling in its place. Bees would make a strange honey of it. She pressed her palm against the door, trying to suction it to the glass.

A large insect with green gossamer wings bumped against the window, attracted to the lamplight. It seemed to have flown out of the world of her dream, summoned by the thought of bees. She opened the window a crack and let it float inside. It went straight to the lamp on the desk, whose shade was also green. Perhaps the bug was attracted to something like itself. Buzzing and bumping against the lampshade and then against the bulb and then against the shade again, which was not as hot as the bulb. The bug confused the two surfaces, it seemed, the light and its reflection—couldn't decide what it wanted from them. The nearest book at hand, a heavier, newly expanded dictionary, seemed ripe for the moment. When the bug hovered far enough away from the lamp—*thwack*—Pluta pressed the bug between its pages.

A spot of green ooze stuck to the inside of the dictionary. Pluta would have to tell Lolo that she wanted to keep the dictionary, but she felt it would be wrong to say why. She ran a finger through the ooze and skimmed it with her tongue. It was strangely sweet but with a bitter aftertaste, like blackberry with a tang of copper. She took another taste, if only to clean off the tip of her finger. Then the lock in the door turned and she hurried to shut the book and fold her hands behind her back. Lolo stood in the doorway. A tingle grew in Pluta's throat; she began coughing.

At first, Pluta thought she was putting on an act, and quite a convincing one, but soon the coughing became very real and difficult to stop. The veins in her neck throbbed as the muscles of her throat contracted convulsively. Lolo rushed across the room.

"What's the matter? Why are you coughing?" She hit Pluta on the back. Pluta shook her head.

Isabel came in as Pluta's face reddened, veering toward purple.

"What now? What's going on?" Isabel ran a cool

hand over Pluta's hot and sticky forehead.

Lolo shook her head. "I don't know, I don't know."

"What did you do, Pluta? What's happening?" They made her raise her arms to give the lungs more oxygen.

As she coughed, she opened the dictionary again, to the spot of ooze, now gluing the pages together and seeping through the thin leaves. "It stung me."

Lolo looked at the splotch and frowned.

"What is it?" asked Isabel.

Lolo shrugged and shook her head. "Where did it sting you?"

Through dry and violent coughs, out of fear that the lie would kill her, Pluta admitted: "In my mouth. I ate it."

With a wheezing Pluta between them, they rushed to the medicine cabinet and gave her a dose of ipecac so that she might vomit up the bug, and considered also feeding her milk, as if she had swallowed something caustic.

Late in the night, the local physician arrived, smelling of ether. His cheeks, sprouting long, dark stubble, belied the composure and expertise Isabel looked for in a doctor. But Lolo said he knew much of poisonous bugs and plants (and had, in fact, consulted her on medicinal teas). After the ipecac, Pluta had vomited a green-flecked mess, and that process was also wrought with gasping and wheezing; blood vessels popped, forming little freckles around her eyes. The women had then worried about choking, watched anxiously, but the purge seemed to help against the coughing. Now the physician felt her damp forehead and ran his fingers beneath her jaw and along her neck, checking for swelling. He requested water and gave Pluta two large white pills that took an effort to swallow without gagging. The pills calmed her fever, which had spiked during the vomiting, as well as the last gasps and wheezes. They tucked Pluta into bed and went to the kitchen.

The doctor washed his hands and asked for a cigarette. They stood smoking.

"Coffee?" offered Lolo.

"Thank you, no."

Isabel showed him the splotch of green and remnant wing in the dictionary. "Can you tell what it is?"

He shook his head. "But she should be all right. She seemed only overexcited. Just show her that you are calm and believe she is well, and she will be well."

Isabel understood how important attitude was. But she still held out the specimen.

"I can take that to a lab if you like. And of course, do bring her in to the hospital if the fever gets worse or doesn't subside in a few days." He stubbed out the cigarette and scraped the wing into a little tube in his travel case and they escorted him out.

Lolo and Isabel sat in the kitchen stirring brandy into coffee. The clink of silver on porcelain mixed with the patter of rain and wind in the garden, as if the stirring of liquid stirred the wind outside.

"He didn't seem too confident," Isabel said.

"No, he is good. How can you tell, from a smudge, what something is?"

"Maybe we should take her to the hospital, if she isn't better tomorrow."

"Maybe, maybe. But hopefully not. The hospital he speaks of is filthy, not very good. If it is serious, we should go to São Paulo."

"But isn't that far?"

"It's the best in the country! But for now we can

nurse her ourselves." She sat back and contemplated herbal remedies: raspberry teas and açai poultices, hot compresses and peppermint pastes. She sipped her coffee, somewhat excited by the prospect.

"Well," said Isabel. She couldn't stand the glint in her elder sister's eye. "Let's see how she feels tomorrow."

"And then?"

"And then I don't know."

There was a long silence marked only by idle stirring and sipping.

Isabel recalled one of her earliest memories, of the foreigner Lolo had brought home and introduced as her husband when Isabel was only five. Lolo was sixteen and had eloped with a gentleman of the outrageous age of sixty. Their father's face went from red to purple to red again—quite similar, in fact, to Pluta's face during this evening's ordeal, though without the coughing. Gradually it settled to an uneasy pallor. Playing in the space behind the hard pink sofa and potted ferns, Isabel watched the feather in the old man's fedora tremble as his voice boomed. The adults talked of things Isabel couldn't understand at the time, something to do with the end of the war. Politics and business. Her parents' tense voices softened as the hours passed, and toward the end of the visit they laughed tentatively. Later she learned that her parents were somewhat comforted by the man's possession of a fortune, but they still became tight-lipped around the extended family in light of the scandal.

For some reason Isabel remembered now the scent of his cologne, and this disturbed her, something so distant in time and distinct in memory. Not long after that meeting, her sister had moved away to Manaus. She'd visited Buenos Aires once or twice a year without her husband, who was always busy; she'd explain to them that he was diversifying his business, dipping into timber and coffee and this and that. When they'd first married, he'd profited from a brief resurgence in the rubber industry during the war. But then he'd gone back to this and that for several more years, until he died at the respectable age of seventy, leaving his young widow behind.

Isabel hadn't seen pictures of him growing up; she only held onto that memory of his fedora and crisp suit. She could not remember but supposed he also had very nice Italian shoes; she wondered if her sister kept his effects stored away somewhere in their large house. No one in the family in Buenos Aires was to talk of them; Isabel knew her cousins had snickered as children, telling each other the shocking story. As adults, those same cousins whispered in furious disapproval about Lolo's absence from Isabel's wedding—the husband was dead, the young widow should come home. No one from their family had attended the rubber baron's funeral in Manaus. And the elder daughter remained in her new home when each of their parents died—she could never travel fast enough between the news of the death and the day of the funeral, she said. The yearly visits to Buenos Aires faded into none, replaced with guilty phone calls.

Lolo sighed, poured a bit of straight brandy into her empty coffee cup, drank. "You know, I don't think it's wise for you to remain in Brazil."

"Why's that?"

"Because, my dear, no one is safe. People come here running—snip snip—change their face, and then, if they're lucky, they're across an ocean. But I don't know how many are lucky like that." She lowered her voice. "I've heard of arrests. Extraditions."

"Snip snip? What are you talking about?"

"Plastic surgery. What I'm saying is that you and Pluta would be better off far away. The farther away, the better." In Ladino she mumbled about the possibilities of Mexico, Spain, the United States.

But Isabel shook her head; she remembered her lie about Kathmandu, how it seemed both fantastic and plausible, and worried now that she had something in common with her sister. Impossible. Her eyes narrowed.

"I don't understand you." It was an effort not to shout. "You think there are people everywhere, hiding in the bushes, listening? Your dead husband tells you these things?" She tapped a finger to her temple. "My dead husband says nothing. You are crazy." She shifted in her seat. "But I agree. We will leave. As soon as Pluta is well, we will leave."

"I am glad. I'm not glad that you are upset. Of course you're upset. But I'm so glad we agree." She rose to clear the cups and stood with her back to Isabel, washing them. "I'm so, so relieved." The rush of water muffled her muttering.

Isabel stared at Lolo's meaty back and slumped shoulders before retreating into the darkened inner rooms of the house. Midway up the staircase, a thought struck that chilled her: what would she do, all alone now with Pluta? A hollow feeling spread through her. They *did* need to leave, but there had to be another way.

She clutched the banister and pulled herself up to the bedroom, glancing at the old photographs lining the walls: Tomas's ancestors sitting for stiff parlor-room portraits. The lone sepia-toned ghost of a young boy in a school uniform, standing beside an enormous horse, stopped her again. The hall light reflected off the protective glass, blurring his placid expression and the rein grasped in his little fist.

Garden light filled the kitchen late the next morning. Outside, birds sang in swooning, rococo warbles. The windows were open, the breeze warm and sweet. Lolo cleaned the stovetop that she barely used, wiping up drips of spilt coffee, mumbling in Tajik. At the sound of Isabel's creeping feet, she stopped her mumbling but tried to hold onto the words in her mind. This exercise formed a lattice there. The new words, sounds, and approximations of meaning crossed over one another and seemed to hold everything in.

"What was the name of the school your husband attended?"

Lolo turned, gauging her sister's mood. A tiny bird—it must have been perched quite near the window—chattered and peeped. "Bander . . . Bandersomething. Banderhock? Why?"

"Didn't it serve him well?"

"Yes, it was a long time ago, but yes, it did. I believe it still exists. Somewhere near New York. He did speak of it fondly."

Isabel sat at the table, slashed with a shaft of glaucous light. "Do you think they take girls, now? Would it be good for Pluta?"

Lolo sniffed and leaned against the stove. "Perhaps." From her palm, the damp rag hung. "It would give you some freedom to attend to other things."

Isabel nodded. "That's what I've been thinking."

"When she's well, you can talk to her."

"When she's well."

Lolo's voice dropped. "How much will you tell her?"

Isabel shook her head, rubbed her hands up and down her face. "I don't know. How to know? How to be sure?"

Lolo frowned and set the rag down. The small bird outside continued its peeping. Lolo went to Isabel and grasped her shoulder. Isabel stiffened, which kept Lolo at arm's length. But the sisters remained there a moment, life pulsing between them.

7. *Brooklyn*
Summer 1980

NOON LIGHT FLASHED and winked, temporarily blinding. On the roof of Pluta's mouth, the pizza burn lingered. Focusing on this hot tingle, she hurried, eyes fastened to her rushing feet; in her ears, the tea kettle keened. Her legs scissored forward, but the lower half of her body had separated from the upper half. A magician had sliced his assistant in two. She thought of guillotines and rust.

I am older than you think, she repeated to herself, a thought-shout over the whistle. This would be her defense against accusations of delinquency, in case someone stopped her: *I am older than you think.* She imagined saying it with indignant hauteur. *I have this medical problem, you see. How dare you force me to speak of it? It makes me look much younger than I am. Actually, I am twenty-six. It's true! So there.*

This managed to cheer her. She laughed, pulling the bulk of the knapsack closer to her chest. Cool air wafted from a sidewalk grate; she paused there and caught sight of herself in a vacant storefront window. Her hair was disheveled, her posture slumped, her smile taut and

119

deranged. She tried to hold herself straighter and strode on.

What did the girls at Banderhock say when they wanted to show they didn't care about something? *Screw that. I don't give a rat's ass.* Or they tried it in French: *Je m'en fiche; je m'en fou.* Sometimes they tried to outdo each other. *I don't give a flying fuck.* What did that even mean? They said it primly or boldly and laughed. One time someone had said it while hurling an open stick of deodorant at the locker room door. The veins in her neck throbbing. A white sticky splotch smacked on the door. Pluta asked herself if she even knew any curses in her own language. Had twelve been too young to pick that up? Or had she just not had the right friends for it? Had she lived for so long in a bubble? Her parents would have filled her ears with cotton, or let her grow up beneath an enormous overturned glass jar. She pictured a tattooed back, an older version of her own, squished beneath a glass cake cover, thick black lines curving against irritated, orange-red skin.

Heading north through a more respectable-seeming neighborhood brought a simultaneous feeling of safety and doubt. It seemed as if the people who looked at her knew what had happened—knew she was strange, dirty, bad. Knew why she was not in school in the middle of the day, and why her back was now aflame: permanent evidence of her badness. Didn't they say you couldn't be buried in a Jewish cemetery with a tattoo? What happened to those bodies, then? Were there special outcast cemeteries where no one came to visit?

No one, anyway, would ever visit her corpse. What would Isabel, the Professor, or Lolo say if they saw her walk into a drugstore to buy eyeliner, shadow, mascara, lipstick, concealer, face powder? (The wrong tint, it turned out, but she liked this mistake; it gave her a sense of clownishness, a wrongness like a mask, something her mother would find vulgar.) Anti-itch cream for her back (extra-maximum strength). And, in a secondhand shop next door, red-framed sunglasses and a black, wide-brimmed hat. She'd never bought so many things for herself. It felt liberating to think: *I want this; I will have it; it's mine.* She migrated toward the rumble of downtown Brooklyn, where the traffic's gear-grinds and honks helped to drown out the internal whistling.

In the bathroom at Kennedy Fried Chicken she rearranged her hair, dabbed on the new makeup, and smoothed out the wrinkles in her dress. All with cold intensity, in quick, staccato movements. This, too, brought back some semblance of internal silence.

One time last summer, she and Casey had wandered down a country road into town and loitered in the cosmetics aisle of the pharmacy. Casey, high on Pop Rocks and Pixy Stix, blurted opinions swiped from the magazines they both read: *your coloring is really dramatic, this foundation will even out your sallow tone, this eyeshadow will complement your deep-set eyes.* They pooled their money to buy one complete set of "essential" makeup to share, following the magazine's instructions for a "glamorous evening look," and blinked against the sticky layers of mascara that clumped their eyelashes together before smearing it all off with cold cream before dinner. Casey had suggested they pluck each other's eyebrows, but Pluta had said, "Pluck your own."

On Fulton Street, in a store whose racks suffocated with clothes and whose hangers screeched as she shoved them aside, she bought herself a new black shirtdress, almost identical to the one she wore. She imagined her mother chiding her for buying nearly the same dress and laughed. One day she would have a closet full of them. Because-I-Can was a good game to play. In the dressing room, she counted her cash and decided that, for now, this would be the end of the shopping spree.

Out of the shop, she ambled further, passing large, old, stone buildings—courts and government buildings surrounding a treeless red-brick plaza. Here the sun beat hot. It was early afternoon, one o'clock. She went beyond the plaza and down into the shade of a leafy commercial street, Montague. She scanned storefronts for Help Wanted signs. At a coffee shop, the woman behind the counter eyed her with a wary, gelid gaze and said the position had been filled. At a card shop she was handed an application, but when she left address and phone number and experience blank, the cashier expelled a sigh and said, grimly, "Good luck." At a large, bustling restaurant she was waved away, told her little arms couldn't possibly wash dishes fast enough to keep up with the lunch rush.

"Let me at least try," she said. The manager said he must be desperate for a dishwasher, because he was giving her one hour to show him how fast she could work. He gave her a white apron and yellow rubber gloves and said, "And don't leave any suds on the dishes, they'll give our customers the shits."

There was something soothing about blasting the food crust off the pots and dishes, something soothing in the rush of scalding water. She tried to get into a rhythm—squirt, scrub, blast-rinse—but plastic bins of dishes kept filling up with a steady clatter. "Gotta work faster than that," the manager said, hovering over her shoulder. She worked in a frenzy, her arms already beginning to ache, beads of sweat puddling along her brow. She was afraid to waste a precious second wiping away the sweat, so her vision blurred and her eyes stung. At the end of the hour, the manager said she wasn't great but did all right, counted out three dollars and ten cents, and said she could come back if she brought the right paperwork: proof of age, permission to work, etc. She gazed at the small sum in her palm and held back the urge to spit, or cry. The air outside, though hot, was a relief from that kitchen steam.

In the distance the river glinted. At the end of Montague Street, which led toward it, commerce dropped off. When she arrived at the same promenade Bobby had taken her to, she sprawled on a bench and baked in the sun. The occasional river breeze cooled the air. Traffic sped down the expressway beneath the promenade, winding to and from the Brooklyn Bridge. To the east, beneath a swath of brown haze, the Manhattan skyline shimmered. To the south, also beneath the haze, her unlit giraffes wavered vermilion. In the daylight they did not seem to reach as high.

The townhouses with their backs to the promenade, some covered in wisteria-heaped trellises, reminded her of Belgrano. She swung her legs up onto the bench. Except, in Belgrano, the nice places to live were not anywhere near the water. The water was for the shantytown. *Villa miseria.* Of course, that was probably because the water stank. Isabel didn't like it when the Professor referred to the shantytown. It's not nice, she said. Why speak of it? There were many things that were not nice and not to be spoken of. The Professor would heave an irritated sigh. What would he say to Isabel's destruction of his library? Of course *that* was not nice and not to be spoken of.

How was it that Pluta had never confronted her mother about it? Something surged up in her; she felt a power now that she didn't have then. Pure, hot anger: a fury to match her mother's. In strength if not strategy. Her mother's anger was strategic. In her mother's presence she wouldn't know how to wield her anger. She might try to lunge at her mother, smack and scratch her, and she was afraid of this because clearly she was capable, at least, of other things. But if he found out—about the library, that is—that would be the end of everything. (Then again, hadn't everything already ended?) The heat drained from her and her eyes went soft. The city was across the water; she saw it but didn't see it. What to do?

After a time, Pluta leaned forward and stretched. Cricks and cracks popped along her spine. She sighed. She had to find a better sleeping solution. There'd been a building, a YWCA, somewhere downtown that had a sign about rooms. But she worried. What if it cost too much? What if they wanted identification? What if they called her mother? No, she wasn't willing to risk it. The weather was warm. She could find a nook somewhere. Cushion it well with her dirty clothes and whatever else she could find. It wouldn't be so bad.

In the distance, a policeman in a dark-blue uniform patrolled the promenade. Her fingers curled into her palms, remembered the squeeze of Daniel's hand at the fairground. The last moment—why doesn't anyone tell you what the last moment will be? She walked, without rushing, off the promenade and into brownstone-lined streets with thirst-inducing names: Pineapple, Orange, Cranberry. The ghost of her father's hand hovered on hers.

Beyond the brownstones she was back downtown, the end-of-the-day bustle rising as clerical workers streamed out of courts, municipal buildings, offices. Gray suits and ruffled, high-collared blouses. Traffic on Court Street rushed, then congealed and blared.

On a corner, through the triangle formed by the metal chains of a sidewalk fruit vendor's scale, Pluta spied the small, wrinkled head of a bird-boned elderly woman, crowned with a fur cap. The woman perched on the rectangle of grass nearest the fruit vendor. She wore a red fox-fur coat that matched her cap and hid her legs. Both cap and coat were missing patches of fur. Dandelions poked out from under her and her small brown eyes gazed unfocused across the plaza, vacant yet glimmering; her small, wrinkled hands were folded delicately in her lap.

To Pluta, she looked like a queen. Pluta crouched by this woman and felt enveloped in a bubble separate from the rush and bustle around them. The woman did not react but instead continued to sit, staring, with calm repose. Plucking yellow and white-globed dandelions from around the queen, Pluta fashioned a small bouquet. Presented them.

"You are a queen," she said with reverence.

The woman turned and looked at Pluta, accepting the bouquet with a wry smile.

"You can eat these, you know," she said to Pluta. She plucked off the yellow dandelion heads, laughing softly, and pocketed them. Then she blew out the white orbs so that the seeds scattered. Perhaps she would take the yellow dandelion heads to some secret home vat where they would float and ferment. Like Lolo's odd garden clippings. Home remedies and medicinal vapors, bubbling potions. The woman handed Pluta the green leaves. "See? There's a water fountain in the little park across the street. You can wash off the dog and squirrel particles. Bring them back to me."

"Yes, ma'am."

It seemed that every place had its secret resources. You just had to know about them. Pluta brought back the washed bunch of greens. The woman put them in her other pocket.

"Thank you, dear."

Pluta glanced up at the fruit vendor, who stood with his hands in his pockets, watching office workers stream by. Then she handed her new friend a ten-dollar bill. The woman clucked her tongue, cooed, and asked her, please, to buy a bunch of bananas and a bunch of grapes. Pluta did so and returned with warm, heavy fruit that she placed in the woman's hands.

In front of the downtown shops by Fulton Street, Pluta gathered a few discarded, collapsed boxes. Isabel had pointed out once, back in Buenos Aires, that *cartoneros* were breaking the law; she'd bristled at the sight of them picking at garbage. Pluta didn't know exactly why they did what they did but guessed it had to do with survival. Now, she felt resourceful. Also: cautious, furtive.

She carried the boxes under her arm all the way back to Gowanus. Hauling the boxes, even if they were flattened, lengthened the journey. Fleeing Bobby had compelled her north, but she had to push herself back south to the playground on Third Avenue, because she knew the playground and did not want to wander in the darkness looking for something better that might not come. That evening, with the red sun still inching down toward the horizon, she cast off her previous fear of sleeping in the hedges and fashioned a hidden nest where they were a bit thicker and abutted the building next door.

Before she resigned herself to sleeping there, though, she made her way back to Bobby's one last time. Hesitant, she paced in front of his building, thinking of what to say. *I'm sorry.* Or: *What did I do? Are you still mad? I can pay some rent.* Her body jerked, as if to say: *No more hesitation.* Mrs. Hoffman's clucking reprise: *Play it or don't play it,* she'd say, her blue-shadowed eyelids lowered in mock disgust, *but don't loiter between notes. No more hesitation!* The Corrections Officer across the street looked out from the billboard with reassuring eyes. He seemed to say: *Go on.* The entrance was not locked. She ascended the six flights. Held her breath and knocked on the door. The knocks sounded hollow in the empty hall.

She stood there a long time; no one answered. Had she gotten the apartment wrong? Was he ignoring her? She didn't think that was it. She listened for movement inside, but there was none. And she didn't want to sit listlessly in the hall. Like a *lump,* her father might say. He could never know—would never know—what had happened, what was happening. The hall, with all the closed doors, the broken bottle still there from two nights ago, the buzzing, flickering light, was not somewhere she wished to linger. Shuffling back downstairs, she returned to her hidden nest in the hedges. Careful not to let anyone see her, she crawled inside the cool shrub tunnel, belly churning, and searched her mind for ways forward.

That night, through a small gap in the hedges, she watched the playground. Glimpsed a flash of neon orange: a wig that gleamed. A neon-pink tube top hugging pendulous breasts. A man approached. The wigged head cocked to the side, coquettish. Words were exchanged— she couldn't hear what. Then, arms interlocked, they strolled away from the park. How easy it seemed.

In the hedge-nest she felt herself more cunning animal

than girl. Sniffing out her survival strategy, her next steps. But there also was curiosity. About edges, about how far. Bobby, Leonard. Rustles in the woods near Banderhock. The possibilities of the body, of what it could do. Why people did what they did, why she did what she did. And maybe that wasn't entirely animal, or at least, maybe the animal in question was human; thinking this she felt very mature, as if she had made a major discovery. About her own resources, how far they could go. The orange-wigged one confirmed her suspicion that costumes made it easier. Perhaps made everything easier. She clutched her new glasses, her wide-brimmed hat. Armor, in a sense. *Play it or don't play it.* She would. Yes.

Orange Wig intimidated her the most, had a brusqueness with the other women as if she had some authority over them, and so waiting until she'd gone felt like the right choice. Pluta slipped out of the bushes and stood on the sidewalk, not knowing what to do with her arms. Glanced around the empty street. No one came. Across the street, a one-story concrete warehouse with rusted wire cages on its windows took up the whole block: The News Brooklyn Garage. A woman on that side of the park, impossibly tall and with a prominent chin, gave her a dismissive once-over. Strutted; got into a car that had purred to the curb. Pluta had also watched this tall one from the hedges, studied the theater of her, the poses, and realized how awkward her own gangly limbs were. The theater teacher used to say: *Put energy in those bones!* She put energy into them—a languid energy. She posed.

The first man who came took her into a wood-paneled station wagon with powder-blue seats and made his request in a manner that seemed so often practiced the words had lost their meaning. "I need your mouth, honey."

She wasn't sure what he meant until he unzipped. She hesitated. He put his hand on her head and gently pushed. *So people pay for this too*, she thought. And why wouldn't they? If some of the girls from school had giggled about it in the locker room, if she hadn't quite known what it was, then, well, now she did. The matter of payment hadn't been settled, so she calculated as she worked, completely unsure of what she was doing, checking her suppressed gags against his facial expressions, his (thankfully closed) eyes.

Who had the upper hand in this situation? "Watch the teeth," he grimaced, eyes scrunched. Maybe she did. He seemed uncomfortable, with his face screwed up like that. But he didn't necessarily seem uncomfortable because of the teeth; maybe it was more because he realized how new she was at this. Then again, that seemed to excite him, too.

It was all over quickly: salty milk, a weird glue. She didn't know what to do, so she swallowed; the heat in her belly smoldered; she wanted to break something—panes of glass, television sets, it didn't matter—into billions of minuscule pieces. She wiped her mouth with her hand. She gave him a price, twenty-five, and he counted out the cash, pointing out somewhat smugly that it was unwise to wait until afterward to ask for payment. Before she snatched the money and crawled out of the station wagon, he kissed her on the cheek. A wet smack of a kiss.

In a sense, it was remarkably easy, at least as far as obtaining transactions. The playground was a place that people knew to go to, a marketplace, and she realized in retrospect that Leonard had assumed she already was one. And then she became one. She didn't know what she would do if she met Leonard again, or Bobby—meet them, perhaps, with that indignant hauteur—or was it really indifference that she pictured, and not a cold indignation? Maybe she would pretend not to recognize them. *Oh, hello,* she'd say, a glaze over her eyes. *Have we met before?*

Her new way of dressing, conspicuously incognito beneath the wide-brimmed hat and red-rimmed sunglasses, increased her confidence. There was something thrilling in all this: seeing the others' costumes—wigs, boots, oddities of bright short dresses or negligees and heels; the theater of looking brightly vacant or downright cunning; being out in the night in the city, earning money. There were other places to go, like beneath the Gowanus Expressway along Second Avenue, but there was something *too* sinister about that, too unknown, too many shadows. The playground had a more out-in-the-open feeling to it. She had her youth; she had her deranged smile; she had her Because-I-Can. She had customers.

A week passed like this, then two. Breakfast at a diner on Fourth Avenue or, if she was lower on cash, at a gas-station convenience store on Third. Then she'd sleep through the height of the day, slipping into the nest when no one was around. (Children, she learned, did not frequent the playground. The occasional mother passed with a child asking to play, whining or skipping breathlessly, and the occasional mother yanked the child away, refusing. She wondered, then, whether her own mother would be back now, across the river, whether she'd have the school comb the forests of Connecticut, whether she felt some secret relief at becoming, finally, the true

130

center of her own world. Whether she missed Daniel as much as Pluta did, whether something like that could even be compared.) Starting at dusk, she'd pace. Smile with wide eyes, tense cheeks. Then get into a car, usually, but sometimes creak up the stairs to an apartment. (Though the stairs were not wooden but concrete, did not creak; it was a sound she imagined—she altered the spaces with her mind. Another game she played. Cars were sailboats. Tenements castle spires. Cellars submarines.) Then: money. Then: crouch like a bullfrog or go belly up like a gasping fish. Then: repeat. Unlike the others, she did not wear heels. She wore ratty sneakers. It didn't matter. It seemed a mark of differentiation. A niche.

Up close, Orange Wig's wig was stringy. She had the opportunity to notice this when Orange Wig told her to keep her skinny assthefuckoff the playground. She didn't understand the exact words at first, but she understood the sentiment. After that she kept clear of Orange Wig and anyone else who seemed hostile.

The evening after the encounter with Orange Wig, she moved her nest to another park several blocks away on Fourth Avenue, halfway between the playground and the spot under the Gowanus Expressway. It was slightly larger, with more hedges, wilder hedges. At first it seemed emptier. An old stone house sat at one side, along Fifth Avenue. It seemed much older than any of the other buildings, made of real stones piled one on top of the other, and quite wide. An anomaly. But it also seemed locked up and abandoned. An old farmhouse left a long time ago to rot, the farm ripped out and covered over with concrete. Her father might have had something to say about that—patterns of history, settling the land—but she didn't know what he would say about the other things she saw, the silhouettes of people sprawled against its stone walls or shimmying in and out of a broken window. In the morning they'd be gone, strange detritus strewn behind—baggies and needles shining in the light.

She poked at the detritus with the tip of her sneaker. She wanted to examine the residue inside. Smear it on the concrete, on fallen green leaves, see if it changed color, see what it smelled like, what it did. But it didn't compel her like the bug from Lolo's garden. She didn't want to risk convulsions again or stagger and sprawl the way the silhouettes did, heads nodding off, tired bobble heads, half-open mouths. She wasn't going to be here forever, she told herself, and it seemed that whatever went up those people's arms sucked them down to somewhere sticky, somewhere she didn't need to be.

There was a public gymnasium on Fourth Avenue with showers. It had once been a public bath, a grand turn-of-the-century structure embellished with columns, seashells, and tritons, but they were obscured by a ring of scaffolds. Behind the scaffolds, she supposed, must be bearded sea gods and starfish-crusted mermaids. For one dollar she could borrow a towel (small, thin, ragged), a lock, and a locker, and use the shower. In the middle of the day, few women were there; there was one regular, an old woman without teeth slumped in the sauna, large belly resting over her slight, warming bones. Pluta defecated, bathed; she seldom eyed, in the mirror, the mess on her back. She was afraid of finding there some festering, primordial chaos. It had been a nasty itch. With customers, the dress stayed on.

In the middle of the second week, she caught a glimpse in a mirror while she dressed. It seemed the ridges of scars were forming. She looked away. The itch, however, seemed to weaken. She was becoming accustomed to her new routine, and the itch was less often in her mind. She guessed it would get easier, the routine, but she also knew it would falter when the weather turned; she could not sleep in that nest for long. The experiment should wind down in advance of autumn. Best to squirrel away some cash and figure out the next step, how to get back on track, how to make a real life for herself.

In the third week, she remembered the old woman in the fur cap living on fruit and dandelion leaves. She had seemed cool in her fur coat, not red-faced. It had been very warm that day, and now the temperature only rose, becoming as suffocating as any summer day in Buenos Aires. There were not many trees in the area to cool the streets. But she had her cool tunnel of hedges in the park, and she refreshed her cardboard roof when it soaked in summer rain. She imagined the old woman lived in an elegant old hotel, marble-halled and gilt-mirrored, but chose to sit out on that corner because she liked the names of the streets, Montague and Court. Maybe that was so.

One afternoon in the shower, as she turned off the shower knobs, the old pipes screeched and rattled in the effort to halt the flow of water. She fiddled with the knobs until the noise calmed and then arched backwards in a stretch. Drops of water bubbled on the sea-foam-tiled wall. In arching her back she sensed something swollen. As if lumps on her shoulder blades were rubbing against one another. Turning her head as far as she could over one shoulder, then the other, she glimpsed them in snatches. Hurried, dripping water all about, to a full-length mirror. Still, she had to twist to see them— the protrusions, the fleshy nubs.

The wet slapping of flip-flops on tile forced her to cover up. But beneath the thin towel the unsightly lumps rubbed and almost, it seemed, squeaked, that faint squeak of those odd little cheese lumps she'd eaten with Casey in Vermont, curds. She wanted and didn't want to look at them, to acknowledge their existence and try to understand just what they could be: tumors, infection, or what? She remembered all the times she'd averted her gaze from unsightly lumps atop heads or protruding from necks. Goiters, bulging with the skin taut over them or receding and leaving behind loose, wrinkled, discolored skin, darkened with blood. Her stomach somersaulted. A wave of heat spread from it. Quickly she dressed, shuddering. Her knees felt loose and shaky, as if the bony caps could slip out and clunk on the wet tile, just like that. *Clack. Clack.*

The cover of clothes helped, if only slightly. Clasps, buttons, and laces held her together. She contemplated whether a cape would be useful, but decided its eccentricity would detract from business. Anyway, she would make a poor superhero. What would be her secret weapon? Revulsion?

Indeed, even the thought of the nubs began to detract from business. She managed, from time to time, the practiced, deranged smile, with eyes popping wide. But surely the more discriminating customers noticed the outline of the lumps and did not care for them. She thought of the bright-orange, bold-text "Manager's Special" stickers on discounted meat at the Payle$$ Mart where she bought ten-cent bottles of green or blue fruit drink.

She lowered her prices. To an extent, this worked, but it meant she had to work more. With increasing frequency, she would vomit after dinner. She called it the nausea diet plan. Not that she had been gaining weight to begin with, although the food she'd been eating (hot dogs, microwave burritos, scrambled eggs) had started to give her a certain bloat and sheen. Her period faltered, was late, but it came.

Casey had told her about purposeful vomiting (in the context of who, at Banderhock, engaged in it) and how all that stomach acid would erode the teeth, how it made the girls' periods irregular. Pluta knew her vomiting wasn't voluntary, but she did wonder whether it was, somehow, purposeful. As if her body *knew* the lumps didn't belong and would continue this purge with regularity until she lost so much of herself that the lumps would diminish and finally disappear. Despite the bloating, her ribs, by late July, gained prominence. She told herself there was a certain elegance to this.

In early August Pluta returned to the playground, where it was easier to find clients. Orange Wig had been gone for a week; she wasn't sure what had happened to Orange Wig. She was too afraid to ask the others; she'd barely spoken a word to them as it was. For the sake of harmony, to prevent hostility, it seemed safest if Pluta remained farther inside the playground and didn't compete for the most visible, coveted positions.

She sat on a bench and began reading a book that she'd found on a sunny stoop: *The Happy Hooker.* There was a whole other stratosphere of what she was doing— safer and with more money. How quickly she could be living indoors, how quickly she could even save up and get back to Buenos Aires! The author's name, Xaviera Hollander, had a certain regality to it, and Pluta wondered if she too had made up a new name for herself. (Just how many people out there did the same?) Though it was getting dark, she kept on her hat and sunglasses, reading over the frames.

As evening fell, a sockless, penny-loafered man strolled into the playground. He wore an untucked pink button-up shirt and stuffed his hands in denim pockets. The women shouldered forward as he eyed them. His hair appeared colorless, neither gray nor white nor brown nor blond but somehow all of those shades, and had the rumpled look of a coiffure normally well-ordered but today, a Saturday, left to a feigned dishevelment. He laughed when they called to him; he swaggered from corner to corner, looking one up, one down.

The man approached Pluta. He was tall, looking down with small eyes that also seemed colorless: light gray and watering, sucked into a doughy face creased with crow's feet. Despite its doughiness, his face also had a flatness to it that reminded Pluta of the Gingerbread Man.

"Can you read in this light?" Pluta removed her sunglasses and bit the tip of one temple, looking up at him through her lashes. It was a new pose she'd practiced, remembered from an old movie whose title eluded her; in her idle moments she dwelt often on these old movie images. "Ha-ha, I sound just like my father." His small eyes glittered. A gold-plated watch flashed in the evening's last pink rays. His wrist was fat and his forearm absent of hair. He sat beside her.

"That's a good one," he said, nodding at the book. "Planning for your ascension? Greener pastures?"

"I've only just begun."

"I see that, I see that. So . . . I'm a visitor to this area, per se. Would you care to escort me on a tour of the neighborhood? You seem—" he craned his neck as he searched for the adjective "—classy." He took out a wad of cash. "How much?" Pluta cited an hourly rate. He wedged enough in her fist for a half-hour. "Half now, half later. We'll take a walk."

She bristled, wary of the giddiness he seemed to be trying to suppress. But went.

Down Third Avenue, the yellow spotlights revealed the empty streets and shuttered warehouses that had begun to feel almost safe in their familiarity. They crossed the canal at the Third Street Bridge. In the near distance, six blocks away, the train trestle soared over black water and the silhouettes of industrial plants along the canal. Behind the station, the red, backward letters of KENTILE FLOORS glowed. In the foliage of a stray locust tree along the bank of the canal, something rustled, squeaked, and flapped.

What had started as a linear walk began to meander through the smaller streets on the other side of the canal. Left on Bond, up Fourth Street, left again on Hoyt, up Fifth Street. Here the zigzags slowed. The man stopped at a tall fence encompassing an overgrown vacant lot that took up the length of the block, neighbor only to the darkened edifice of a cement factory. A hole at the bottom of the chain-link fence appeared to have grown larger as people tugged it up to slip into the wilderness on the other side. Olde English bottles, vials, pantyhose, and junk-food wrappers (Cherry Pie, Nutter Butters, Zebra Cakes) lay strewn about in the tall grasses poking from either side of the fence.

"The Public Place," said the man, standing beside the gaping hole. "Have you been?" He said this with low-lidded, high-chinned boredom.

"No," said Pluta.

She hadn't known vacant lots had names. But appreciated the fact. It reminded her of the unnumbered, stilted country homes in the Tres Bocas area of the Delta del

Paraná, or the names of English manors in novels. And yet this was utterly different. How could this lot—with its high, barbed-wire fences—be public?

"*Après vous*," said the man. Pluta crouched and wriggled beneath the fence, wary of catching a hidden shard of glass in her knees or the heels of her hands.

The grass, in places, grew waist-high. Dry stalks of Queen Anne's lace swayed in a slight breeze beside the orange mouths of tiger lilies speckled vermilion. Short, craggy locust trees dotted the place, seeming to form a ring that shrouded some inner sanctum. The trees had the slender, twisted trunks and far-reaching leaves of unchecked weeds, the kind of trees that could sprout untended, be chopped down, and yet sprout quickly again from between the concrete slabs. They had a faint rotten-egg smell. Crickets hidden in the greenery rubbed their song and a single cicada whirred. Pluta thought this place would be a better spot for her nest, were it not for the man scrambling in under the fence beside her. A heavy moon, the color of *calabaza* flesh, hung low and full above the craggy trees. A pumpkin moon. It seemed to rub its cheeks against the trees' uppermost branches. The man moved ahead, indicating she should follow him down a narrow path beyond the grove.

In a clearing, there was the inner circle, formed from the ruins of whatever had been the prior industry. Its slabs of concrete were spray-painted with bubbled orange, purple, blue, and black letters. Black barrels, upright or overturned, were scattered inside, smelling of char and kerosene. There was a heap of rags, the kerosene tins, more empty bottles, wrappers, a syringe, a doll with an eye scratched out, a gray-white baby shoe; red bricks and gray cinderblocks scattered among the tamped-down grass.

The man slapped at his thighs. "No one's home." Then he laughed. "Party for two then?"

Pluta put on her clown face. "Sure."

Beneath a craggy tree, shaded from the moon, atop a heap of flattened cardboard, they did the thing.

After, panting, he slid off and propped his head on one arm. Huffed out a manic, triumphant laugh. "In the Public Place," he said, "everything is possible." They sat up. Encircling her nape with one hand he said, "You have such a small, such a little neck." His hand brushed down her back, accidentally grazed the nubs. "What—" She flinched away. He pushed down and said, "Stay still, you freak. What the fuck kind of disgusting thing is on your back?"

She scooted away. "It's nothing." She wanted him to pay and she wanted to go. She rose and smoothed her dress. From where he lay, he reached up, tugged at her skirt, guffawed. A fat black fly, glinting blue-green, buzzed between them, flew in a languorous drunken sway, grazed her arm with its plump tiny body. Her skin prickled. She slapped at it, slapped at him. Laughing, he hauled himself up and slapped back, at her mouth, hard.

She knew she should retreat, but something inside bubbled up, rooted her to the ground, made her whole body rigid. He lunged forward, still laughing and snorting. He seemed now a bone-and-gristle-crunching ogre. She shuffled backwards into the clearing of the inner circle. Lumbering after her, he sneered and shouted obscenities. Glommed together in a thunderous slurry:

Howdyoulikearatupyourcuntstupidnastylittletwat; thatlleatyourdisease.

He pushed her to the ground, a knee in her back, and her face churned on grit and pebbles. The soil smelled of gas; as she struggled for air, grains of dirt snorted up her nose. A liquid redness seeped into her vision. Her hearing seemed to fail as his slurred threat echoed inside her head (*RAT up WHERE?*), mixed with her own stream of threats to herself: *you're going to die like this do you want to die like this oh god don't die like this—fight*. She clawed at the dirt, flailed arms and legs. At this flailing he laughed and grunted, digging his knee further into her pelvis and kidneys, his palm mashing her face harder against the ground.

Then he rose, squeezing the back of her neck with one hand, and yanked her up to stand. *Oh god.* Her vertebrae stretched apart. *Where is this going?* Prying her arm back with his other hand, he shoved her forward, toward the cover of the trees.

That crackling ball of belly-heat, the one that had smoldered in her so long, grew hotter and expanded—a blue heat—and pressed against a brittle coldness in her chest, pressed against the impulse to go limp, to yield. *Die like this. Or fight.*

At a concrete slab she managed to swing out a leg and push against it, push back against him. She tried, with her elbow, to wind him. He expelled a breath but laughed. Their limbs slipped about, slapped in the confused struggle. She'd come to learn about men's vulnerability, how the graze of a tooth was enough to elicit a grimace; she tried to grab between his legs. Use what nails she had, dig in, and squeeze, twist quickly and with as much force as possible. Until it felt liquid. This gave him pause. *Aha.*

Still twisting hard as she could, she cast about for more solutions. She spied a brick on the ground. Heat on her cheeks, blood and grit in her eye, she scooped up the brick and in a clean, graceful arc, with momentum both merciful and merciless, with a mind that had gone momentarily, peacefully blank, she swung up at his nose, a cry bursting from her throat.

He'd already been stooped forward and now, with a wet, gurgling moan, he fell in a heap on the dirt. Still clutching the brick, still feeling the momentum of the swing, buoyed still with the blue heat, she launched the brick hard at the exposed side of his face. With a dull crack, deep red seeped out. With a quiet thud, the brick slid to the ground. His body twitched. It lay on the edge of the circle.

Fuck. A deep shudder shook through her. With chattering teeth she gathered rags and kerosene. Stuck his reddened mouth with a soaked rag, sprinkled his body. Haphazardly, she flung the remaining kerosene among the grasses at his feet, among the wildflowers and the trees. They'll grow again, she thought. From her pocket she extracted a book of matches.

Bless you, she thought, lighting the match. Bless me.

Dropped the blue-lit match at his feet.

A plume of orange-black flame rose up. *Whoomph.* Noxious smoke unfurled beneath the silhouettes of tree leaves, beneath faint stars; it stung her eyes and curled in her nostrils. For a moment she watched as the fire licked branches, ignited and crackled grass. For a moment, she thought she too should burn.

But from the quickening fire she ran, slipping out from under the fence, remembering at the last moment to snatch her knapsack. Hat and glasses melted behind her. She crossed the street, the pain making her run more of a lollop, skidded around the corner, and from Smith Street watched the fire spread and flicker. Would it consume the whole neighborhood? She held her bag close, first running down a small side street and then, realizing she'd entered a residential area, turning

sharply down another small street where she forced herself to walk calmly. As she walked, teeth still clanking
against each other, she tried to assess the seriousness of
the hurt. Cuts and bruises on arms and legs. A trickle of
blood down her cheek. Blurred vision. Eyebrows singed.
She felt the crisp hairs with dirt-crusted fingers. From
time to time, she spotted a person in the distance and
crossed to the other side of the street. She took a cir-
cuitous route back toward the train station, a large U,
though the station was only two blocks away from the
burning Public Place.

Behind the glass of the token booth, the vendor
dozed. Pluta stumbled into the station restroom. Brown
rings coated the sink and ancient scum clouded the mirror. She washed the dirt from her hands, gently splashed
water over the scratches on her face. The whites of her
eyes were bright red. Her stomach seized; she leaned
against the sink, gasping out a dry heave. Then she
rinsed blood and dirt out of her mouth and nostrils and
forced herself to drink some water.

Outside, a garbled announcement blared over the
loudspeaker. Pulling at her earlobes as if to pry open her
hearing, which still felt somehow altered, she popped
her eardrums and tried to decipher a tone of alarm in
the announcement, any mention of nearby fire. But she
understood nothing.

She poked her head out of the bathroom. The man
in the booth had woken up and was wandering out of
the station to see about the fire. Ducking beneath the
turnstile, she moved as swiftly as she could up the long
escalators. From a distance came the growing whine of
sirens. Pluta went up to the Manhattan-bound platform,
to a spot where the station wall gave way to a view of the
city. Below, the blaze whipped and crackled. Her fingers

laced through the chain-link fence as she caught her breath and gaped. *I did that.* The flames had rushed to the edges of the lot, flickering over and through the high fence, and had leapt up onto the roof of the neighboring factory, closer to the station. Through the upper windows of the factory, shadow and flame danced, and the pressure of heat burst the top windows to shards. Glass rained on the sidewalk.

Even from above, Pluta could feel the heat on her cheeks and shrank back behind the station wall, watching with one eye as her heart pounded harder. She clenched the fence. *I can't believe I fucking did that.*

Two fire trucks and a police car arrived. Firemen scurried to nearby hydrants and blasted water into the lot and the factory. Blue and red lights swirled. The station worker stood across the street from the conflagration, watching with crossed arms. Another police car pulled up to the curb, and more sirens screamed in the distance.

Pluta decided it was unwise to board a train in her state—anyone who saw her might be compelled to ask questions—but she wasn't sure how to escape, where to go. Both platforms were still empty. Across the way, there was an unassuming door; the silver knob caught her eye first, distinct from the murky green of the door, which blended with the station wall. There. She could rest while she hid.

She craned her head each way down the tracks. Seeing no train lights, hearing no distant rumbling, she jumped down off the platform, feeling for a moment a soaring sensation—a moment of exhilaration, a moment of fear and time extended, a moment in which, she thought, she could hang suspended. Her feet slammed into the wooden tracks, jolting her bruises, but she tore across despite the pain and leapt over the electrified third rail. Her hearing seemed to sharpen now; she thought she heard the distant pulse of radio communication. Rough static, orders, beeps.

She hauled herself up to the opposite platform. Clambered for the door, fearing it would be locked, but it wasn't. Pluta slipped inside and shut the door behind her. Wherever she was, it was dark and musty. Grit scratched under her shoes. She waited for her eyes to adjust, clinging to the doorknob behind her with a sweaty palm. Her heart knocked against her throat. She groped at the air, but nothing met her hand. Slid down and sat balled up against the door.

The air stifled, thick with mildew and sawdust.

At last she could see that she was facing a staircase. Near her feet there was an old work lamp. She fumbled for it and switched it on. The door behind her didn't seem to have a lock, but a plank of wood lay on the ground; she wedged it beneath the knob and hoped it would do. The plank fit so well there, she hoped no one else used this place for refuge. A faint light seeped from a room above. She shuffled upstairs, her legs gelatinous.

The room at the top was also entirely concrete. No heaps of clothes, no food wrappers, nothing indicating anyone used the space, though there was a grimy slop sink. Exhaling, she leaned one shoulder against the wall, leaned her head against the wall, but they both felt tender and she wished for a soft mattress to sink into, or a cool mound of grass.

Three stained-glass windows along one wall glinted in the lamplight. Two were bricked up from the outside; the third had a jagged hole as if a large rock had been thrown in. Hot wind whistled through. The remaining shards of glass gleamed ruby and sapphire.

A white puff, a fuzzy new feather, floated in on the breeze, and Pluta tried to catch it; it slipped through her fingers and wobbled about the concrete room, in and out of the soft, yellow light.

She lowered the work lamp and went to the broken window. It would have been impossible for someone to throw a rock this high. On the north side of the street below, a white building, perhaps a large warehouse, hulked above the shorter buildings, streetlights giving its pale bricks a sulfurous glow. Pigeons roosted in the station's ledges. It wasn't possible to see the street directly below the station, or the canal intersecting it. The roar of the fire and rush of the water hoses persisted outside, but they seemed to be growing fainter.

Thankful the fire was being contained, that it had not consumed more than it had, and thankful for a quiet place to hide and rest, Pluta sank to the ground. She sat atop some of the old clothes from her bag, leaning the back of her head against the wall. Afraid her eyes would crust over, she kept them open and sat upright, trying to be ready for anything, but this concentration became too much; she dozed.

When she awoke a strange, gauzy light streamed through the jagged stained glass, throwing faint triangles of violet, rose, and goldenrod around the concrete room. Rising, she managed to stick her head through the window. Pigeons cooed in low, gravelly tones.

White flakes fluttered down from an overcast sky. She laughed. Snow in August? She put out her tongue and tasted ash.

In this light the white building across the street took on a bluish cast; she could only see two columns of windows from the station. Screwing up her eyes, she saw in the top corner window a red-haired man. Though not mustachioed, nor balding, he reminded her of her father. The man drank from a white coffee mug—she could almost hear him slurp—and seemed to be looking directly at her. Glaring. She drew her head back inside, careful of the sharp triangles.

She awoke again to the rustle of pigeons, the whistles and trills of sparrows. She'd slept with one arm against the floor and now the arm tingled. Her entire body ached. Parts of her had begun to swell. Though the room was concrete and should've been cool, she felt hot. The slop-sink faucet shuddered when she turned the knob; she tilted her head toward lukewarm water.

Outside it still appeared to be gray dawn, as if not much time had passed since she'd poked her head outside and seen the red-haired man in the window, and yet her body's tingling suggested that much more time had passed. Her dress, filthy with dirt, dried sweat, and dried blood, chafed against her skin. A single dress, not fresh but not filthy, remained in her bag. Slowly, she unbuttoned the shirt dress. Every so often she winced.

As it slipped off her back, the dress seemed to catch on something. Those nubs. They seemed larger, when she had already thought them enormous. She had the sensation that they were, in fact, no longer nubs, but something balled up, little fists, ready now to open. She rifled through her bag for a mirrored compact. It was difficult to get a glimpse of her back. She shifted, trying to use the corners of her eyes.

Finally, she set the mirror down and reached back. With her fingers she caressed one ridge, then the other, and was surprised to feel her own hands on these smooth protrusions: she'd expected them to not be a part

146

of her, or to at least be numb. But it seemed her nerves went into them.

She felt how she could *unroll* them, and extend them, folds unsticking from themselves. Slightly rubbery. Slightly sticky with moisture.

What were these things?

Her heart pounded.

What *were* they?

Thin, webbed skin.

She stretched them further and swallowed.

Thin, webbed wings.

8. *Manaus, Brazil*
July 1978

THEY BROUGHT THE GIRL tea, toast, and fruit. The doctor had said not to let her loll about in bed, that it would only make her weak. Children needed to play when they had energy. Isabel sat beside her until she finished each bite. Lolo hovered in the doorway.

"Are you feeling better?" asked Isabel.

Pluta nodded and cleared her throat. "I slept a lot. But I still feel tired."

Isabel touched her forehead. "You don't feel feverish. Why don't you get out of bed and at least go sit in the garden, get some fresh air?"

Pluta shook her head. "That's where the bug came from."

"Ah, right. We don't want that, no. But sit up, sit up, get out of bed." Isabel flung back the bedsheets. Pluta shivered despite the warmth of the day. Isabel pursed her lips. "You are fine. Don't pretend to be sick. It's not nice." She helped Pluta put on a light sweater. "At least go watch television."

Lolo helped Isabel look up Banderhock and make some phone calls.

* * *

For two days after this, Pluta lounged watching game shows she did not understand or read from the crumbling library. Something bubbled between her aunt and her mother, but she assumed it was the usual strain of their relationship, since they had barely seen one another in so many years. Lolo's clucking was preferable to Isabel's sternness. There was an odd jealousy between them: the more Lolo doted, the sterner Isabel got. Lolo would bring Pluta a blanket and a ginger soda. Shortly after, Isabel would come in with a chalky pill and yank the blanket away, saying *don't sleep, get up—sleeping so much will only make you more tired.* When Isabel finished her nagging and stalked off downtown to make her important business calls (she said calling from outside the house was less expensive), Lolo would creep in again with another treat, more honey cake, a caress on the forehead.

On the third day, Isabel walked in front of the television and switched it off mid-applause. She sat beside Pluta.

"I see you're feeling much better," she said. "Maybe later you can go to the beach with Lolo. But first—" here she paused, as if the harshness of necessity and authority might dampen Pluta's supposed recovery or the empty suggestion of the beach "—we need to talk. In a little while, we're going to pack our things. You've had a nice little vacation and it's time to go back to school."

Pluta perked up. "We're going home?"

"No." She exhaled through her nostrils. "I'm afraid we can't go home yet. You're going to the school your uncle went to. Banderhock. Near New York."

The room narrowed, darkened.

"Why?" The sounds of those place names at the back of her mother's throat were harsh and awkward.

150

"You can't ask why, Pluta. Things are very difficult now. It's better for everyone if we go there. And you'll get a good education. You'll meet nice people, make friends. It will be good for you, for your future."

"Does Papi know where we're going?"

Isabel's eyes darted. She hadn't expected resistance, but she realized now how unrealistic that was. Pluta was getting to that age. She could not feed her sugar-crusted lies anymore. She should, she thought, say something of the truth. But looking at the girl's wet, reddening eyes and pulsing throat, she faltered. "Yes. He does. He wants us to go. I was able to call him in Tierra del Fuego while you slept." Inside, she cringed, but her face remained placid. What would she need to say in the future? He'd been lost in that wilderness?

Pluta snuffled; her throat convulsed. "I don't want to go."

"You don't have a choice."

"I'll stay here with Lolo."

Isabel fidgeted as her daughter whimpered. "She doesn't want you. She can't take care of you. You know she isn't all right in there." She tapped a finger to her head and then glanced over her shoulder, but Lolo, as Isabel already knew, was in the library.

"I hate you." Pluta looked feral: fists clenched, nostrils flared, eyes sharpened, as if she were ready to lunge at her mother and bite her wrist or her jugular.

"No, you don't. I know you don't." Isabel rose. "You'll regret later that you've said that. We'll talk again when you're calm." She hesitated before the television, thinking to switch it back on and then deciding against it. She closed the door behind her. A muffled cry seeped through it, a cry which grew to a full-throated bawl. Isabel waited for the noise to diminish and then, relieved that the outburst had been short-lived, walked on. In the library she asked Lolo for directions to a travel agency and went downtown to make the arrangements.

Lolo creaked into the television room and handed Pluta a handkerchief. Together they went to the sitting room, to the table behind the beaded curtain. Lolo lit some candles and they held hands over the cool marble.

"Close your eyes," she said. Pluta sniffled but obeyed. "Are you here?" She lowered her voice. "He's here. What do you want to know?"

Pluta squeezed Lolo's hands. The words barely came out, a sputtered whisper. "Where's my father?" The table trembled. Lolo sucked her tongue.

"He says . . . a foreign beach." She leaned forward, squeezed her eyelids together, and listened. "That is all he can say about that."

"Can he see the future?" Pluta opened her eyes a crack and watched the candles flicker. Lolo squeezed her hands and Pluta closed her eyes again.

Lolo clicked her tongue. "Yes, but—" She spoke not to Pluta but to the rubber baron. "Are you sure?" A door slammed shut and they jumped in their seats. "He says you will be fine." Lolo blew out the candles and pulled Pluta up out of the seat. But it wasn't Isabel returning earlier than expected who'd slammed the door, only a rare Amazonian breeze.

They were to leave the next week. Hectic packing subsumed hesitant packing; Lolo helped where she could. When Pluta looked lost, Lolo's chest imploded. She wanted to reassure her, give her strength. Sometimes she would go to her, embrace her, and Pluta would give in to this embrace, as if Lolo had the power to create

152

a protective bubble around her. But sometimes, afraid these shows of affection would make departure more painful, Lolo abstained.

On their last day together in Manaus, as they sat one last time on the red velvet couch, Lolo gave Pluta some tattered English books for the long plane ride, tied together with a bit of twine: *Travels with My Aunt, A Tree Grows in Brooklyn,* and a pocket dictionary. She admitted to Pluta that she hadn't read these books thoroughly, but she hoped Pluta would enjoy them and perhaps learn from them, and write to her and tell her what she thought.

"Wouldn't it be nice to exchange letters?"

Pluta nodded.

Isabel eyed the titles of the books and seemed calm, relieved for a moment, before her nerves set in again and they had to hurry to the airport.

At the gate, Lolo hugged Pluta for a long while, enveloping her in warmth. Pluta stuck her nose between Lolo's neck and curls and sniffed; her nape smelled like perspiration and jasmine. Isabel touched Lolo on the shoulder and Lolo reciprocated. They offered each other enigmatic half-smiles of strength or reconciliation or resignation.

"Be well," said Isabel, finally.

"You too," said Lolo.

After they boarded, Lolo watched the plane push back from the gate and taxi up the runway. Sighing, she watched its miraculous rise, up, up into the air, until it receded to a speck in the sky. She hoped Pluta would be all right. She did. But the rubber baron had told her otherwise.

9. Brooklyn and Manhattan
August 1980

GRAY DAWN PINKED. At last the patch of sky visible through the jagged stained glass turned pale blue. A triangle of light warmed the concrete on which Pluta sat grasping her knees, afraid to reach back again and feel the wings with her fingers and have them feel her fingers back. But the wings kept twitching, and though the twitching at first seemed involuntary, at last she tried to *flap* them. Concentrated, tried to isolate muscles, nerves. A vague tremor, nervous energy, whirred through her brain, mouth, chest, belly, calves, toes. When one wing flapped—just a tiny movement, really—she let out a yelp, then clamped her hands on her mouth.

Her aching knees crackled as she stood, liquid pressure filling in the bruises about her face until she was fully upright. She paced. Bit back the yelping. Whatever happened, she must not be found out. She'd killed a man; she'd set a fire. She'd never thought: *when I grow up, I want to be an arsonist; when I grow up, I want to be a murderer.* Her wings twitched now of their own volition. But did their twitching agree or disagree with her thoughts, or did it mean nothing? Were the wings

155

separate from her, "given" to her, or were they of her own making? Would they gain strength and carry her away? How to flex them, control them?

The red-haired man in the window—he seemed to have seen her, seemed to know something, with a glare whose heat she could feel, even from across the street. Her hearing had sharpened while crossing the tracks, and though her vision hadn't, her *sense* of things, other objects around her and in relation to her, seemed sharper. The man probably smelled the char in the air, probably saw the plume of smoke over the train trestle. But the man looking at her, that was a dream, she'd thought. Wasn't it? She imagined what he might have seen. The fire in the dead of night and, in the early morning, a girl poking her head out the window above the train station, licking at falling ash. Any half-wit could put the two together. Her pacing quickened. No, she couldn't be sure of anything anymore. The wings flapped once, as if in agreement. Even if he was real, there was no reason why the two must go together, fire and girl. Or was it the girl's fire that had summoned the man? No—ridiculous—forget the man in the window. Focus on the wings. She paced. Maybe she had to use them to understand. She continued her attempts to control their jerky movements.

As the sun moved higher in the sky, a yolk-light seeped into the room. Pluta dressed again and took one of the jars of *dulce de leche* from her bag. Praising herself for saving it so long, she unscrewed the cap with trembling fingers and scooped globs of it into her salivating mouth. Sucked on dark buttery sugar. Tried to slow herself but moved faster instead, caramel bits catching under her nails and at the corners of her mouth, until half the jar was gone and the sugar filled her whole being with expansive lightness. She forced herself to stop. It was an odd feeling of fullness that she knew would soon evaporate. But she wanted to stay in this perch above the station as long as she could. A day, perhaps. Then slip out at a time when no one would see her.

Beneath the black cloth of her dress, the wings warmed. They seemed able to furl back upon themselves, resuming their old lumped forms. With concentration she managed to unfurl them. It felt like loosening the grip of a fist. She smiled at the roosting pigeons outside the window. *I am like you now,* the smile tried to say. They looked back with small, wet, red-ringed eyes. Puffed out their feathery chests and cocked their little heads.

Beyond the white building and the rowhouses snaked the Gowanus Expressway. Upon it, evening traffic shimmered. Beyond it there were more industrial buildings, then came the cranes and the water. Then Manhattan. The glass of Manhattan's towers flashed orange-pink. The concrete room had stayed cool through most of the day, but warm wind whipped in through the broken window.

The sun, brilliant red and radiating fuchsia, sank beyond the expressway, leaving streaks of faint green in its wake, above which hovered a deepening cerulean. A single cold, white star pierced the darkest part of the blue. Not the green star she had dreamed, low and smoldering and pulsating, but something far more distant and aloof, something far lonelier.

Pluta remembered there would be commuters trickling off the Coney Island–bound trains until late in the night. She focused her concentration on the frequency with which the station rumbled. The rumblings had increased in frequency before the sun began its descent and now decreased. Regardless of when she emerged, she supposed there was always the chance of someone on either platform spying her. She continued pacing and sitting, stretching and twitching, yawning and repressing violent hiccups. To quell the hiccups, to quench her thirst, she drank from the shuddering sink, but only when the trains arrived, lest the banging pipes call attention to her.

The wind turned cooler. Pluta decided to wait until three A.M., an hour at which the station would most likely be deserted. At once, time slowed. Undressing again, she played with the work lamp, throwing the shadows of her wings onto the wall. Light shone through the translucent, pink-hued webbing. The wings furled and unfurled with a faint, rubbery squeak.

Why had this happened to her? Did it have to do with her dreams of stars? She grew lightheaded; her thoughts turned to useless tufts of cotton. When she left the concrete box, then would she be able to understand?

At the appointed hour she dressed, gathered her things, and crept with shaking legs down the stairs. She removed the plank of wood from under the doorknob and slipped out, trying to appear as if she'd been waiting on the platform just like anyone else. Both platforms were empty. Once, she'd seen teenage boys slide down the escalator railings with giddy abandon, but the nervous energy whirring in her did not quite have that quality—she thought that if she tried it in her present state, she'd skid off the rubber and break her neck or get shredded in the grate at the bottom of the escalator. She felt on the edge of catastrophe.

Catastrophe, or revelation.

Down the street, yellow tape ringed the blackened Public Place, fluttering in the breeze. Its wild vegetation razed. Just a charred, empty lot. Puddles rippling on the sidewalk, in the gutter. No matter how badly she wanted to get closer, to see what had become of it, to run her hands through warm heaps of ash and feel what she had done, she turned away, south on Ninth Street. The farther she got from the Public Place, she thought, the safer she'd be.

Several blocks down, outside a shuttered store whose sign simply read HOT DOGS in shiny green letters, her stomach growled. She scavenged the dumpster. Bags of old buns and packages of expired hot dogs lay among strands of sauerkraut, rotten onions, and tomatoes spotted with white and blue fuzz. She scooped out the still-sealed food, shaking off the loose detritus, and closed the dumpster lid. A light in an upstairs window switched on; someone shouted down through an open window to stay out of the trash. Down a block and around a corner, she tore into the packaging, inspected the food, and sniffed it before gobbling it up. She ate three hot dogs, wet beneath the plastic and still misshapen into rectangular pink rods, the processed flesh salty, faintly sweet and faintly tangy; they were warm from sitting in the metal dumpster.

Back on Ninth Street, workshops slowly opened. The metal shutter of Gabriel's Iron Works was raised. Inside, wrought-iron rods, straight or twisted into curlicues, lined the walls. Above them, on a row of hooks, hung welding masks. A man in a black apron and an upraised mask moved with slow, deliberate steps, setting up his shop for the day. Pluta watched him until he sensed he was being watched and rose to attention, holding the first glowing iron rod of the morning in a stance that seemed calm, collected, and yet alert to threat. He squinted—it was not yet dawn, and light from the shop spilled onto the sidewalk. She stood at the edge of the light, by a row of garbage cans; his eyes screwed up in confusion. Was it her slight hunchback or her battered look or some other part of her strangeness that caused his disquiet? She didn't want to be seen. Backing away, she crashed into the metal garbage cans behind her before fleeing.

She continued straight along Ninth, advancing through and out of Gowanus and past stately brownstone houses until she hit the verdant park, the one she had skirted in her first wander through Brooklyn. This time she entered. In the still-dark, birds cheep-chirruped. She slumped beneath a tall oak. Dew gathered on her skin, cooling and soothing it; she hadn't until then realized the pained heat of her skin.

In the coolness her father came to her, and her mother. How would she ever explain? *Dear parents, this is what I've become.* No: she wouldn't. The Professor might have attempted an explanation: tumors or mutation or evolution. Isabel would turn away in revulsion. She'd already been repulsed by her daughter *before* all this; now she would be utterly revolted. Pluta's stomach twisted. She bit the inside of her cheek.

What if. What if on top of this, of all things, she'd become pregnant. She imagined a tiny pink squiggle in her belly, tiny nubs upon its back. Even if she somehow removed her wings, perhaps this was something inherited. Did Isabel, too, have wings, tightly hidden away? She couldn't imagine that; it just didn't seem possible. So. She must be some sort of mutant. Her belly rumbled. She couldn't yet distinguish between stomach and womb. She flung herself belly-down on the wet grass, lying across her arms. Rubbed her cheek and snuffled.

As blades of grass broke beneath her, their green scent enveloped her; she wondered about animals that ate their young. Hamsters, lions, guppies, polar bears. Wolf spiders. Burying beetles. Casey had a special interest in the subject. She'd memorized a growing list, having decided to become a zoologist after watching one classroom guppy devour another, its own offspring. Did they devour one another with blank-eyed, pointless ferocity? Or did they do it with intention—to assert their power, to right some wrong with the breed?

A flock of small flying animals shrilled. They didn't sound like birds. More like bats. Pluta propped herself up on her elbows to watch them and the bruises in her face pulsed; the animals swooped in arcs across the indigo sky. If it were a question of hiding things or exposing them, maybe she would need to *expose* the wings to use them, to understand them. After all, she couldn't use them if she scrunched them up. So what if Isabel would be repulsed. So flying-fucking what. She heaved herself up, following the swooping flock. Now she *hoped* Isabel would be revolted if she found out. Pluta's stomach, lumpy with old hot dogs, gurgled. When the bats moved on to roost in other trees, so did she.

Across a long green meadow, the morning gray burned off to light blue. A dirt path on which a few joggers panted circled the meadow; she avoided this path, cutting across the damp grass. She passed a pond where large dogs—German Shepherds and Great Danes and tiger-patterned mutts—played, wagging their tails and splashing in the water as their owners waited patiently with leashes in hand. Beyond this lay a narrow strip of woodland. She crossed over a small meandering creek and through more parkland until she reached the western edge of the park.

At this gate, several large boulevards intersected. Across the street, several elderly ladies dressed all in white—white pillbox hats and white suits and white orthopedic shoes—held a banner advertising a church while a minister, also robed in white, preached through a megaphone that garbled his words in static. The group appeared to be handing out miniature Bibles from a Cookies Department Store bag to commuters streaming toward the nearby subway entrance.

She dug into her pockets for change and descended with the morning throng, taking the D train to Manhattan. In the subway car, bodies pressed against her, backs against her back, shoulders swaying with and bumping against hers. She clung to a metal pole alongside dozens of other hands, the sweat of palms microscopic on the metal. Hot breath gusted on her neck or wheezed above her ears. She had been in desolate Gowanus in its off hours long enough to nearly forget what a city crowd could be. But because it was anonymous, because everyone in the swaying car was engrossed in something else—a newspaper, a makeup compact, a paperback, the tunnel wall rushing by—the crowd didn't feel too imposing.

If she were to expose the wings eventually, she supposed, she would need to be among others. But when or how this operation would occur, she had no idea. Pluta observed the crowd of totally normal people in light blazers or shirtsleeves, in flouncy summer dresses or, occasionally, shorts and tank tops. The air conditioning was on full blast, their faces content.

Then she noticed her. One woman, particularly engrossed in her something else, muttered feverishly; dirt was smeared across her sunburned face and streaked through her short, coppery hair; a dusty pea coat opened to a black bra beneath. Her watery eyes, lined with thick black smudges, roved about the car as she muttered, until they settled on Pluta and seemed to crackle. As the train slid into Grand Army Plaza, the woman rose but kept her eyes fixed on Pluta, who thought she probably shouldn't maintain the eye contact but also, maybe, she should. Before the doors hissed open, the woman said to Pluta, "I'm onto you." Then she stepped off the train with a jaunty gait. Someone hiding behind a newspaper whistled and laughed, with a conspiratorial glance at Pluta. But when this passenger took in Pluta's own disheveled state, she quickly returned to the safety of her newspaper.

The headline: "FIVE-ALARM FIRE IN GOWANUS." A grainy photo showed the cement factory burning, arcs of water puny against the flames. Pluta's body stiffened. Her heart thrummed in her ears, as loudly as when the ogre's hand had grabbed her throat. What she could see of the article was only a couple paragraphs; clearly there were few details. She wanted to see what the paper said, to know what they knew. But she also needed to get away, quickly. She squeezed toward one of the doors and pressed her face to its window, anxious for the next station.

The train flew over the Manhattan Bridge. The grand old warehouses of Vinegar Hill receded beneath it. At least one of the warehouses was a roofless ruin; her heart thumped. She thought of the destruction she'd left behind her, the factory beside the Public Place a new ruin, and of the hot green star she'd reached for that first night dozing in the playground in Gowanus. She thought of the abandoned houses in Manaus that Lolo had shown her, which in her memory were covered over in thick green moss, and somehow this soothed the thumping in her chest. She closed her eyes and wondered what Lolo would say.

Well, my dear, there's nothing to do but fly.

She imagined trying to take off over the East River. Water splashing in the wake of her fall.

On the other side of the river, they roared past Chinatown's squeezed tenements and its balconied towers dotted with laundry and potted ferns. Pluta got off at the first stop in Manhattan.

Upstairs was a small, cobblestone plaza with a statue at its center splattered in pigeon excrement. Down a narrow street, a man in a white undershirt stood with arms crossed next to something burning in a black barrel. Sleek young eggplants in light and dark hues of purple were piled outside a grocery; Pluta ran her hands over them as she passed but stopped short of caressing the wet fish that lay on crushed iced at the next stall, their scales silver and eyes glassy. Her hand plunged into an open crate of dried mushrooms. An old woman clutching a rolled-up newspaper came out of the store. The paper was in Chinese; Pluta could not, in that brief moment, make out any pictures of the fire. She let the mushrooms drop back into the crate before the woman could chase her away.

Scrounging for courage, she followed winding streets with names that rolled in the mouth: Mulberry, Worth, Pearl. Ducking under the curved ramps ascending the Brooklyn Bridge, she walked the pedestrian Rose Street, which beyond the bridge became Gold. From a large industrial warehouse came a heavy smell of rotting fish. She passed the fish market where burly men in blood-spotted aprons hauled bags of ice.

Two police officers patrolled the piers. They approached a man in a bloodied apron, twenty feet away from Pluta. While one questioned him, the other glanced at her. Her skin prickled. A voice scratched out of his walkie talkie. Affecting calm, she turned a corner, then fled.

A grimy barber pole swirled outside the entrance to a subway station. A haircut, a change in appearance—yes. She followed the signs down to the first underground level and entered the small, stifling shop wedged between a cobbler and a shuttered newsstand. A fan with thick clumps of dust caught in its grill buzzed near the entrance, pushing out gusts of hot air. The barber, in a white, high-collared shirt, was sweeping the floor.

"How much to chop it all off?" she asked.

The barber flicked his fingers through her greasy hair. He had a gaunt face and deeply wrinkled cheeks. Iron-gray hair neatly greased to the side.

"Shampoo too?"

"No, just to take it off."

He inspected a few more moments, eyes narrowed as if in search of lice. "For you? Dollar fifty."

Pluta flopped into the chair. "Do it," she said. She looked down, avoiding her reflection in the mirror.

"Okay, girlie."

The barber tied a smock around her. A few deft moves and all her smooth black locks fell to the tiles. The barber turned away to slip the shears into a glass jar of cobalt sanitizing liquid. Pluta ran her hands over her freshly shorn hair, enjoying its lightness. Flinging off the smock, she dug in her bag for a crumpled dollar and change and smacked it on the counter beside the jar. The bell on the door jingled behind her.

Downstairs, on the station platform, the morning rush had waned. Midday commuters looked deep into the tunnel as if to beckon the train with impatient eyes. Water dripped from a small white stalactite. A puddle formed beneath the dripping.

Pluta opened her mouth and let a cool drop of bitter

stalactite water fall on her tongue. Beside her, a buxom woman in a dress spotted with enormous bright flowers edged away. Pluta closed her mouth, scanning the crowd for police. The A train whooshed into the station in a draft of grit, cheap perfume, and body odor.

On the air-conditioned car, Pluta's sweat dried. Her shorn head felt cold first and then the rest of her shivered, but her back, with its lumps tightly crammed beneath her backpack, stayed hot. The train sped past lonely local stops; its speed gave Pluta's heart a pleasant thrum. *Away, away,* the train sped. *Forward, forward.* At 34th Street, a man boarded dragging a garbage bag. Bulges in the bag writhed. He held out a rubber duck as he walked through the car, squeezing and squeaking its yellow-orange body in quick triplets. "Toys!" he shouted, at intervals. No one bought his wares and he moved on through the door at the end of the car. Pluta gasped, thinking that as the train jerked he would be thrown into the tunnel, but with light, sure steps he disappeared into the next car.

At 42nd Street, two police officers boarded the train. She gulped. Slipped through the closing doors. Outside, the temperature had risen. Sunlight seared her skin. Air so thick it clung to her like an extra layer of clothes. Flushed crowds streamed on the hot sidewalk. The neon lights of theaters and a nickel-and-dime Peep-O-Rama pulsed anemically in the sunlight. Further on, past a row of fast-food restaurants, she found an indoor bazaar, a relief from the sun. Fluorescent lights buzzed over tube socks, imitation designer purses, bags, and watches. One vendor sold bikinis, wrap-around skirts, and flip-flops; she fondled a red-and-white polka-dot halter top that she thought would suit her new look. Bought it for $2.75.

Toward the back of the bazaar hung a sign for a restroom. She moved toward it, seeking a splash of water, a cool drink, a place to change. Behind the vendors' stalls she found a row of white, unmarked doors. The first one was locked; the second led to a janitor's closet. Door three was also locked, but door four opened to another door, a heavier, metallic door painted forest green. She slipped through.

On the other side yawned the musty shell of an abandoned theater.

It was terribly quiet. Pluta stood at the orchestra level. Faint light crept in from high windows with curtains askew; it was a pleasant thing to adjust back to this dimness. As she grew accustomed to the hush, her ears began to welcome it too. She could hide here a minute. Collect herself. Her eyes watered.

Some of the rows of seats had been ripped out. On others chunks of plaster had fallen, white dust speckling ochre velvet. From the corner of her eye, she caught a slight figure on the stage. She turned; there was no one there. But she had the sense that an elderly woman had been standing there, watching, stern like Mrs. Hoffman but skinnier. Old floorboards creaked beneath threadbare carpet as Pluta moved to the center aisle for a better view of the mezzanine and balconies. Chipped gilt scrolls embellished Corinthian columns. Gilded plaster scalloped the arched ceiling, from which a chandelier hung, dulled by a layer of dust. On a side balcony, the blurred silhouette of another figure crept into view, but again, when she looked directly at it, the figure was gone.

A distinct sense formed: this was her stage. This was where she was to try out her new apparatus. She nodded to herself, searching for more ghostly figures, wondering if there were people hidden behind curtains, inside balconies, beneath trap doors. Ascend, she commanded herself. By the curtain levers, she changed into the new halter top and an old school-uniform skirt. Set her bag down. Dank air trickled on her back. She walked solemnly to center stage before jumping up and clicking her heels once in the air. Swung her body around to face the audience, eyes glistening, forcing a smile. *Fake it till you make it, honey,* a tall woman back at the playground had told her once.

"*Mimimimimi!*" It was important to warm up the voice. Exceedingly important. She closed her eyes and concentrated. She imagined a packed house, full of glittery sequins and extravagant feather boas quivering in the drafty theater. Lolo was there, her wild hair wrangled into a messy updo. Isabel smoked nervously, afraid for her daughter's life, afraid for her reputation. *Can she do it, ladies and gentlemen?* The Professor stood quietly in the back of the theater, the gleam of candlelight reflected in his glasses, obscuring his eyes.

Yes, candlelight: they'd shut off the electricity. Wax dripped off thousands of candelabra.

Her torso ached as she leapt across the stage; she ignored this, leapt despite the pain. She tried to unfurl the wings and catch the air, but all that practice up in the train station had not been enough. Leaping and flapping at once seemed impossible. She stood at the center again, gathering repose. Tried to flick the wings, twitch them, stretch them out. She pulled at their tips with finger and thumb.

Shuddered at the still-odd sensation of stretching new skin. Crouched down instead, curled into a tight ball on the dusty floor. As the Maenads beheaded Orpheus in Manaus, the thud of brick hitting the ogre's face erupted in her skull. The deformity she'd wrought, the fire she started—at every turn were two police officers, one who'd caused her father to squeeze her hand and disappear, and another one coming for her.

She made herself smaller. Saw herself floating down a white swirl of a building. Her toes dragged lightly along the floor as she passed curving walls. She wore an old school uniform, the kind of plain smock worn at some schools in Buenos Aires, but she'd dyed it bright orange and lined her eyes with a smoky green shadow, the color of her dream star.

Perhaps the floating in this vision was achieved through rapid fluttering, like that of a hummingbird. She didn't have the proportions of a hummingbird. Thus her toes dragged.

The white swirl: the Guggenheim. They'd gone there on a field trip with Banderhock in her first year. *That* was a stage. But this empty, rotting shell—it was good for practice. Running forward, she leapt into the orchestra pit. She thought for a moment that she'd caught some air, but she landed with a heavy thud and a wince, a shock to the ankles. Nevertheless she repeated this exercise a few more times.

In her peripheral vision, the slight elderly woman who'd been on the stage gave an approving nod. She swiveled to catch her, but again, no one was there. Goose pimples skittered up her arms. She rubbed them vigorously. A passing shadow in the side balcony propelled her toward her backpack. She put it on, readjusting the straps so that her wings were hidden. As she reentered the bazaar, she heard the faint echo of four hands clapping.

Further uptown, the shade of Central Park eased the heat. Humidity released the green scent of chlorophyll. She plucked fan-shaped gingko leaves from trees and dabbed at the sweat on her forehead, pressed them to her cheeks in an attempt to cool her face. At a drinking fountain, children filled up plastic containers and hurled water at each other, squealing and hooting. When Pluta walked toward them they stared before trotting away, toward a playground across the dirt path. She dipped her face in the trickling stream and wet the hot skin of her scalp. Groaned and moved on. Further north loomed her curved theater.

The woman at the ticket counter checked her watch and studied Pluta carefully as she smoothed out the dollar bills for admission. For a moment Pluta stood at the center of the lobby, tracing the swirling ramp leading up to a bright apex, a corona. A fountain gurgled with gallery visitors' echoed murmurings.

The elevator brought her to the top. She gazed down over the white, waist-high barrier, slinging her backpack across her front to free the wings. White-sneakered and khaki-shorted tourists meandered between paintings and sculptures—obsessive black-and-white stripes and crosshatches, striated circles of floating color, double rows of corroded metallic rods. A few museum-goers, scattered about the higher levels of the ramp, peered down to the lower levels and the clear blue, rippling fountain. She, too, stared into the white-ringed abyss, contemplating the heave over the barrier and the fall.

"Miss." Cold, dry fingers tapped her shoulder. "Miss, don't lean so far like that." She glanced over her a shoulder at a security guard who shook his head in a *tsk-tsk*. "It's dangerous."

She slunk away, dragging her hand along the barrier, and tried to find a spot away from the guards' prying eyes, but her head swam; she was not committed to the performance. On one of the lower levels, across the swirl, she spotted him again. A red-haired man. *The* red-haired man? Who'd stood in the window after the fire? He'd glared at her then, but in the glare was there an understanding?

The man didn't seem to be loafing about the museum to take in the art but walked with purpose down the ramp, lugging a briefcase and a box. She screwed up her eyes, trying to confirm that it was him. She loosened her grip on the barrier. His purposefulness comforted her; she wanted to latch onto it.

She hurried down the ramp and followed him out of the museum.

10. *New York and Rome*
Autumn 1978–Summer 1980

PLUTA HAD BEEN SWINGING her feet and biting her nails; Isabel touched her shoulder and this was enough to stop her. Now the girl leaned her head against the window. Outside, rosy light slashed the horizon, hues of blue above and dark clouds below. Isabel closed her eyes against the hum and shudder of the plane.

She told herself again and again: this is the only way, the best way. Lolo might be crazy, but Isabel had to agree that going farther away felt safer. It seemed as if everywhere there were lunatics. It didn't make sense—perhaps it would never make sense. This is what Daniel would have wanted, if he had known. Now she was sure of it. Who does such things? What else had he encountered? What *had* he known? She squeezed her eyes and dug through her purse for another Valium.

They would start afresh. It wasn't impossible. People all around the world encountered horrors and started afresh. Didn't they? She bit the inside of her cheek. Nothing else to do about it at this point. Medicine would help. Travel. Perhaps one day she could be glad of a new life. Horrible turn of thought! No, she was not glad for

173

this, never glad. What sort of person could think that way? She chewed on the Valium. The chalky crumble on her tongue helped calm a tremor in her gut.

Daniel hadn't been a suitable husband. If he had, this wouldn't have happened. He would've taken care, he would've been strong, he would've been cautious. This had been a thought she'd held at bay for a long time; she didn't want to think it now, but there it was in plain words. She resisted the urge to beat her head against something hard. There was nothing hard around, only the chair in front of her, the awkward tray table.

Isabel grew drowsy but did not sleep. Her half-closed eyelids made a pink blur of her daughter, balled up against the window in fitful sleep. Boarding school would make her strong, independent. What other decision was there?

What if she hadn't married a professor, an Ashkenazi, another Jew? What if she had married a lawyer, a doctor, a businessman? What if she had married a military man? Her head lolled to the other side. Most of the passengers who spoke did so in whispers to avoid disturbing those who were sleeping. But two old men in the back carried on a loud, friendly argument. She craned her head into the aisle; they were smiling at each other while nearly shouting. She flung her head back into the chair and tried to shut them out, wishing she'd brought cotton for her ears.

What would life have been like without the child? She couldn't quite fathom—and yet, she could. She opened her empty palms. The responsibility would always be there.

She had looked at that wrinkled newborn and felt something inside herself crumble. Her lack of the expected joy made everything worse. All around her people cooed; she cracked a tired grin. Newborns were ugly, they were known to be ugly. Her mother reassured her: *ugly little babies grow up beautiful—you know the story of the ugly duckling well enough.*

Then her mother had died, before the red wrinkles smoothed, before the black umbilical cord fell. It pained Isabel how ugly the child still was. But now was the awkward age; everything could change. Perhaps she'd emerge from the school a lady. One could hope.

Thirty-eight. She could still have another one, if she desired. Her own mother had had her late. Can you will a child in the womb to be beautiful? Weren't children supposed to be beautiful? Daniel had said once that children were programmed by evolution to look a certain way—eyes large in proportion to little chubby faces—so that adults would feel an urge to care for and protect them. So what of little eyes in gaunt faces?

Isabel wanted sleep so desperately that her eyes burned.

Pluta had wanted a view of the vast, deep ocean, but they were on the wrong side of the plane for that. Below them, gaps in the clouds showed forest and farmland reddened beneath the evening sun. The flight would never end. Isabel said they would change planes in Miami and have a chance to stretch their legs. Pluta kicked off her shoes and pulled her knees to her chest, making herself a tight ball. Tried to count to one hundred. Along the way, somewhere close to seventy, she forgot herself, leaning her temple against the cold, humming window.

I sway on a cold, windy threshold and something nudges me from behind, disturbing my sense of balance so I fall into the black of night, down and down and down, plunging into the sea. I grow fins, and my gills reemerge, and I see green-gilled mermaids with pearls tangled in their red hair, lips mouthing, "Jump, jump, little bird." Bubbles burbling up in the silvery-black water. I leap out of the water into the vast pulsing darkness, the stars shivering in the sky, and my fins are transformed into wings. And I land on the shores of Uruguay.

A sensation of water rushing through Pluta's chest wrenched her awake. The back of her neck was damp. She clutched her armrest until the plane's wheels roared against the tarmac in Miami.

Mid-morning they arrived in New York. Outside, the air stifled, and the city's haze lay thick as any Buenos Aires summer smog. A yellow cab rushed them away with a familiar zest for speed. They spent a week in a small Midtown hotel room, sharing one double bed; at night the air conditioner gurgled and dripped, and they slept fitfully back to back. For a few days they attempted to sightsee, and they spent an afternoon buying Pluta school supplies and weekend clothes. School was to begin a week after their arrival. They would take a northbound train from Grand Central. Isabel would return and find a modest studio in the city. She didn't really know what was next, exactly.

They ate raw oysters in a dark restaurant at the train station. Pluta slid the sleek gray mollusks around in their shells.

"Eat it, it's delicious," said Isabel. Her white wine was so cold it frosted the glass.

They ate rare steak. "It will put the blood in your cheeks," said Isabel. She tried to sound hopeful.

Then it was time to board the train. Isabel had bought Pluta a new suitcase, taupe with a hard shell. The old one

176

had seemed shabby. A redcap heaved the bag onto the train; Pluta hugged her knapsack in her lap, filled with books from home and from Lolo's, though Isabel had forced her to leave some behind. She would have plenty of books at school.

At the station in Connecticut, a blond woman greeted them. Her broad smile revealed crowded little teeth. To make conversation, Isabel told the woman how Pluta's uncle had attended the school a long time ago; the woman beamed and rambled on about tradition.

At the door to Pluta's room, when she'd set down her suitcase, Isabel said, "Hug your mother goodbye." Pluta went to Isabel and pressed an ear to her ribcage, as if listening to the slow thump beneath. In the hallway was a pay phone, to be shared by the students on the dormitory floor. Isabel kissed Pluta's head, told her to use the phone when she wished, be nice to the other girls, smile at them. Smiles were expected.

Isabel left Pluta standing alone in her room, arms dangling at her sides. She stood a moment at the end of the hall. A shaft of sunlight spilled from the open door to Pluta's room. Just then another girl arrived, wearing a plaid skirt and white blouse and swinging a satchel. She entered the same room. Pluta's roommate.

"Hi, I'm Suzanne," Isabel heard her say. Voice like a bell.

"I am Tatiana," her daughter said.

Isabel descended the staircase, its old cherry-wood banister warmed in the sunlight streaming through the mullioned windows. Outside, a maple tree reached thick branches to a clear sky. Something about broad green leaves against a cloudless sky reassured Isabel. A wood pigeon on a lower branch fluttered its light-brown wings, sunk its head into its puffed chest, and cooed. At the train station, she filled her lungs with several deep, cleansing breaths, as if to carry the fresh air back with her to New York.

She found a studio in Carnegie Hill. She sublet it from a woman who lived in New Mexico. It was well decorated—not too sparse, not too gaudy—and the couch opened up for when Pluta visited during holidays. Lolo wired money even though Isabel said it wasn't necessary. *You have expensive taste in an expensive city*, Lolo said. Isabel guessed her sister was trying to make up for lost time. She was glad Lolo had the sense to chide her spending habits instead of destroying her with: *Can you manage? Are you all right? What will you do now?*

The woman from whom she sublet the studio had some Modigliani prints on the walls. When Isabel couldn't think of what to do with herself she wandered between them, staring at each one. It was odd that the women in them did not have eyes. Or, they had eyes but they were hollow, they had no real color, no pupils. She spent whole days pacing, not going out, nibbling on dry toast and sipping half-cups of strong black tea. Pluta (or could she finally begin calling her Tatiana again?) called her collect every day in the first week of school, each phone call stabbed with silences; it seemed the girl wanted to speak yet had nothing to say. They were ten-minute phone calls with perhaps two minutes of conversation (led by Isabel's questions) and a few gulping sighs. Then she must have gotten busy with assignments, for the calls slowed to twice a week, once a week. Once a month.

Isabel, too, needed to occupy herself. After she learned her immediate surroundings, she took out her address book and wrote letters to friends. She kept them brief.

Some of their responses took a long time to arrive and were equally brief: mild surprise at her move, best wishes for her time abroad. Other letters went unanswered, and still others were sent back looking tampered with: the envelopes opened and resealed, the corners of the paper crumpled, stray marks of black ink in the margins. She wrote longer letters, speaking of her anxieties about being away, asking friends to stop and look in at her house, but she stuck these in a drawer. She didn't want to cause trouble for her friends if receiving letters could be a cause for trouble. She got into a habit of this, writing letters she never sent, about what people might be saying of her abrupt departure, about her husband's disappearance and his possible association with those other disappearances, but these letters, even sitting in the drawer, began to make her nervous, so that one day she ripped them up into tiny little pieces and watched them flutter into the darkness of the trash chute.

She spent a week spraying perfume at Bloomingdale's. At first she thought she would enjoy the atmosphere, being surrounded by the pleasant buzz of people who liked quality things, but she grew to hate standing all day and being refused. She felt ridiculous. The job was better suited to young girls.

She looked for *porteños* wherever she went. How would she build a society for herself? She wanted it and didn't want it. There were no real cafés to frequent. There were coffee shops and delis not suited for lingering conversation. On walks in the city she passed tall townhouses in which, she assumed, society gathered, safe behind private limestone walls.

In that first month, Isabel passed a large public library that had a bulletin board outside. The board advertised free conversation classes that met one evening a week.

She attended the first evening; it was run by a woman with sleek dark hair and pearl earrings. Both Isabel and the teacher wore black turtlenecks that night, and Isabel immediately liked her, the way her skin was like porcelain and her face stern and composed. The rest of the students were a motley bunch whom Isabel eyed with suspicion. The teacher told one of them not to talk with her hand in front of her mouth; the student could not stop her nervous giggling. There was such a range of ability that Isabel lost patience after the second meeting. But the teacher had used a strange verb, *to fritter*, and Isabel held onto it even after she gave up the class. *To fritter* her time away. It seemed appropriate for this period in her life. She spent time with the dictionary, thinking more of Pluta's schoolwork than Lolo's bizarre hobby. *To fritter, to flail, to flagellate.*

Pluta came home for the winter vacation. At the train station, Isabel spotted her first, hesitated in calling out to her, whether to say Pluta or Tatiana; instead, she strode to the girl, clasped her shoulders, and kissed her forehead. A light snow flurry swirled about them. If speaking to each other had been difficult before, the long time away had created a larger wedge between them. They left their wet shoes by the front door of Isabel's studio and sat in their stocking feet at the small kitchen table. Snow melted in their hair and dripped down their ears.

"You have to tell me all about school," said Isabel. Her voice sounded funny in the room. A dull echo. She lit a cigarette and turned on the loud, whirring exhaust fan.

Pluta shrugged. "It's okay."

"Did you make any friends yet?"

Pluta shrugged again.

"Are you tired?"

Pluta nodded. She used fatigue as an excuse to sleep through much of the break. But Isabel did get her outside a few times. They crunched on fresh snow in Central Park, well-bundled against a cold wind. They stood before a thinly frozen pond and watched more flakes wobble down from the sky and dust the ice with more white.

On Christmas night, they dined at a Turkish restaurant and Isabel found her stomach squirming with nostalgia and dread and unease. The waiters happily served them, almost doted on them; the restaurant was not very large and hardly full. Pluta nudged her food around her plate, having never eaten stuffed grape leaves before. She dragged her fork against the dark green wrapping, shredding it open and eating only the ground beef and rice. She spent most of the dinner gazing at the red tablecloth and drinking ice water from a glass which was swiftly refilled.

"Clean your plate," Isabel commanded. The empty grape leaves sat there, an affront.

Pluta dragged her eyes upward and kept a steady gaze on her mother as she munched on the greens.

It was a relief for both of them when Pluta got back on the train at the end of the week, even though she did not want to return to the school, even though Isabel sensed this.

During the gray slush of February, Pluta called. She'd made a friend named Casey. Magnolias budded in late March; she called again. Casey had invited her to spend the summer in the Vermont countryside. At first Isabel thought: *Why wouldn't she spend the summer with her mother?* A moment of indignation seized her. Then she relaxed and smiled into the receiver. "Of course you may," she said. "That is a wonderful opportunity." It was good that Pluta had a friend, and Isabel would be free to do what she liked. Pluta gave Isabel the names of Casey's parents and their phone number. Casey's parents, Larry and Julia, threw in a half-hearted invitation for Isabel as well.

"Come for a week or a weekend, or even the season; whatever you like. We don't want you to broil alone in the city. There's plenty of room." Isabel at first entertained the notion, then bristled at it.

"Thank you, that's very kind," she said. "I actually have plans to go abroad."

"Oh, yes, I see," said Larry. "I understand. Tatiana is in good hands."

"Yes. Thank you." She was grateful that his discretion did not allow for probing questions.

On a whim, she went to Rome. She'd always had a soft spot for Rome, and now the idea of strolling ancient streets and soaking up the Mediterranean sun appealed to her more than ever. So while Pluta ate ice cream in Vermont, Isabel licked gelato. She read bits of international news when she could bring herself to touch a newspaper. She told herself she wasn't looking for news about Argentina, but she was. She knew vaguely that *las Locas* had been to Brazil, had been to Rome, had seen the Pope, the Italian president; she understood that abroad they weren't called *las Locas*, these women in white bonnets.

She had a tiny hotel room on a fashionable boulevard near Piazza Barberini; the fumes of heavy traffic competed with greenery from the Borghese gardens across the way. Some mornings, she stood with closed eyes by the window and tried to discern the smells: heavy, light, dirty, clean.

When she wandered the city and the sun became too hot on her head, she ducked into churches, took in random masterworks. At the Church of San Pietro in Vincoli, she found Michelangelo's statue of Moses, seated, his muscular, veined fingers thoughtfully entwined in a long, curling beard. He seemed to have nubs of horn atop his head. Isabel rifled through her guidebook, the thin paper beginning to wrinkle and spot from her sweaty fingertips. A man nearby saved her from rifling.

"*Luce, luce*," he said, radiating his fingertips from his forehead.

"Ah, *luz*," she said. Light.

In the Borghese gardens, she strolled by groves of elm trees and down an *allée* of potted bitter-orange trees. The *melangoli*, her guidebook explained, were purely ornamental and not meant for eating. In some corner of her mind, Daniel laughed, both amused and irritated at the idea of ornamental fruit. Isabel was curious just how bitter the oranges were, but she walked on and found an aviary topped with an elaborate wire dome. Inside, the walls were frescoed with rare birds that used to live there in the time of the Borghese family. A warm breeze wafted through the wire dome. As Isabel bent to sniff a fuchsia orchid, a butterfly perched on her forearm. Its light touch shocked her, but she managed to be still and to let it be. Its delicate wings, deep brown streaked with murky cream, moved in slow, unsteady flicks while it rested. Then, as suddenly as it had landed, it pushed off, fluttering deeper into the sun-filled hall.

Rome calmed her. Italian made more sense than English, and the city's heat was more satisfying than that of New

York. Being addressed as *bella* here and there did not bother her; though she never responded beyond a cold nod, it made existence in this third place more pleasant. If she could return the following summer, she decided, that would be a good thing. Upon leaving the hotel she grabbed a handful of brochures for fanciful excursions out of the city: the canals of Venice, the island of Capri, the strange blue grotto. After so much baking in the sun, this last destination seemed right: to board a small boat and slip through a tiny entrance into an enormous aquatic cave, to bathe in the glow of oceanic light, and perhaps to hear the boat-guide's echoing song.

In the autumn a friend mailed her a bumper sticker that had circulated throughout Buenos Aires, littering the streets like confetti. It was a heart with the blue-and-white stripes of the Argentine flag, and upon the three stripes it carried the message *Los Argentinos Somos Derechos y Humanos*, We Argentines Are Right and Human. The friend offered no explanation, only wrote that they were being circulated, that people were circulating them. It seemed a salve against the piece of news she both wanted and didn't want to encounter: that some international commission had denounced the Argentine government. But that sticker, which part of her wanted to cling to as a talisman, only made her old anger more confusing, only made it feel as if the ball of a mace—cold, heavy, and spiked—rolled in the pit of her stomach.

She contrived for Pluta to return to Casey's the following summer. Larry and Julia graciously agreed.

"One day you'll all be welcome to visit us in Buenos Aires," said Isabel. "We have a large, beautiful house sitting alone down there, all locked up."

184

As soon as she set her bag down in the hotel room, she set out again to revisit the Roman streets. It was early evening: the twilit hour at which everyone strolled. Few people were out alone. Strolling was an activity done in groups, between setting sun and brightening moon, chatting and nibbling gelato. She headed toward the Colosseum.

On the plane she'd glanced through a newspaper. There was a small bit about *las Locas*. A grainy photo cropped closely around a woman in the now internationally recognizable white bonnet. They had an official name: Association of Mothers of the Disappeared. The article mentioned seven thousand unexplained disappearances and said the Mothers were clamoring for explanations. Said there might be more unaccounted for. Isabel tore out the article and put it inside her purse, yet she had no idea what to do with it. She'd left the blue-and-white sticker back in New York, in a drawer, just as Daniel had pushed the Ministry of Education pamphlet to the back of his desk. Now the clipping seemed to weigh down her purse as she walked.

A boutique window displayed gold sandals, red flats, pumps in all colors.

"*Prego*," said the salesman in a crisp white shirt open at the collar. His dark eyes glimmered as he ushered Isabel toward a chair. He fetched her an array of shoes. Not the gold, she urged, but muted blacks and deep reds. His approval of her taste was attractive.

When she had first seen Daniel he was comical, less a man than a strange animal, his plastic face full of silly expressions, his mustache used as a prop. *Funny little monkey!* she'd thought. At this, she cringed.

185

The salesman presented maroon pumps with tiny bows. He slid one foot inside, but it looked wrong against her tan skin.

But Daniel's eyes had softened the moment he saw her; his eyes moistened and his lips parted in awe. There was something pathetic but also endearing about it. She'd wanted to touch his lips to press them shut; she'd wanted him to play the game, show less obvious adoration.

The salesman's hand lingered on her ankle. She pursed her lips in disapproval at taupe heels.

And then Daniel courted her, indulging her every whim. He didn't tease her with backhanded insults, the way some macho men won less esteemed women. No, he treated her as the lady she was, his queen, putting her before everything else.

She pointed at black peep-toes. Their eyes met as her red-polished toe slipped into place. A tiny thrill.

"*Perfetto*," she said.

He helped her up. Isabel paraded up and down the store, glancing in the mirrors. Growing up, she'd often assumed she'd marry someone in "business," whatever that was—so when Daniel came along, there was something exciting about her life taking an unexpected turn. Later he grew more ambitious in his career, just to show her he could, staying later at the university to write articles and prepare for conferences and do whatever it was that he did there. (And maybe that led to the problem— although *problem* was entirely the wrong word, wasn't it?)

At the cash register the man asked in Italian, "Are you going to dinner with a friend?" His eyes glimmered, hopefully, it seemed. A lone foreign woman in his city. She was still wearing the new shoes. She thought of the thrill of their eye contact, she thought of obliterating her grief, forgetting herself. But she shook her head. No, to his question. No, to his invitation.

From afar, the Colosseum rose up like a jagged yellow tooth.

She couldn't have changed Daniel's path; he wasn't going to leave all that for her family business, for something he knew nothing about, even though she thought now that that would've been a safer path. So after he won her, she was locked in, in a way. Certainly once the child was born. And they'd been comfortable, hadn't they? They didn't need him to earn money for the girl, not really, not even for the private schools. It had been a better match socially, if not economically, than her sister's. At least he was an appropriate age. This is what she imagined had passed between her parents, but had never been uttered to her. She wondered what they would think of all this now. There was solace in their not being here to see it.

The Imperial Forum was lit up for the night, bits of ruin, broken columns, all scattered on an empty field of dirt, gravel, grass; she headed down Via dei Fori Imperiali back toward the hotel. The new shoes hurt. She grimaced, intent on breaking them in. What would it be like to crush another man with her beauty? To be someone else's queen? Gravel crunched beneath her feet as she turned to take in the Colosseum one last time for the night. It no longer seemed like a jagged yellow tooth but something grand, ineffable.

As a child, Isabel had often imagined what it would be like to rule as a great empress, the world at her feet.

11. Brooklyn
August 1980

A HONEY LIGHT SPILLED over the white building in the late afternoon. Even from the outside, the place smelled of cinnamon and licorice. The train overhead darkened the street, rumbled and clanked. But in the honey light Pluta found something like peace. She had followed the red-haired man all the way back from the Guggenheim: she was convinced now that the key to everything lay with this man and shoved off her initial doubt, her instinct to forget him and focus solely on the working of the wings. The conviction hooked her gut and pulled her forward. Seeing him in two different places—here and the museum—it seemed like magic.

At the Lexington Avenue station, a t-shirted boy with knobby elbows had put his lips on a token slot and sucked. He smiled up at her, the retrieved token shining between his clenched teeth. The red-haired man passed through a squeaking meat-grinder gate, was on the other side, descending to the level below. She doubled up with the boy through another meat-grinder. Pluta and the boy tittered, warmth between them in the tight space. The red-haired man descended another level to the express platform. She went after him. The boy grasped her wrist, said he was going local, didn't she want to go too? She patted his cheek playfully but twisted her wrist away from him, galloping down the stairs, ignoring the throb of pain that came with each step.

She spotted Red. The train pulled into the station with a rush of air that cooled her skin. She slipped into the same car as he did. Afternoon crowds on the subway were not so dense that she could lose track of him and not so sparse that he should notice her. She tried to keep some distance, sitting across the car and to the side, and pretended to study the thick layer of dirt under her fingernails, only sensing him in the periphery of her vision. She rocked with the train's movement, giddy. Only a few stations later, he hopped off and she followed.

In a long subterranean passage between train lines, its dim lights kelp-hued, a cellist played a song with somber, gorgeous longing. Pluta caught herself—one twirl, only one, feeling her skirt fly up, soft cloth grazing her palms—then continued her pursuit before Red could turn any number of corners, board any number of trains, and vanish.

The second leg of the trip, on the Culver Local, lasted far longer. She bit her nails and tried to decipher graffiti squiggles so inky they seemed to still drip. Always she kept the red hair in the corner of her eye. When the train finally burst out of the tunnel atop the elevated tracks in Brooklyn and Red rose to debark at the station where she'd first spotted him, her giddiness turned to exaltation. She hadn't assumed that he would be returning to that place, and now that she saw he might, she felt as if this return to Gowanus was fated, as if what she had dismissed before as ridiculous might have a spark of something to it after all. As if he, on the other side of the tracks from the Public Place, might offer an antidote to the ogre, the fire, the mutation, the hollow in her gut. She darted from the train at the last minute, her skirt catching in the closing doors. She yanked it out and hurried down the long escalator with knees nearly buckling, her eyes on the back of the man's ruddy head. The hair didn't quite bob in tufts the way *his* did, but it was the right red, the right red.

Red crossed the street and rounded a corner into an Italian deli. Salamis and hams dangled in the window. She perched on a fire hydrant kitty-corner from the deli and waited. He reemerged, a loaf of bread poking out of a brown paper bag brimming with—what? She attempted nonchalance as she followed him back to the white building on Court Street, the same long street she had followed after Leonard, the one that went by the courthouses and the old woman in the fur coat with her bananas and grapes and dandelions.

As he entered without a glance over his shoulder, she stayed back, searching for her own way in. She couldn't very well tap him on the shoulder and ask to come inside with him. She hadn't figured out the next step, the step beyond following him here, seeing if he was *real*. She crossed the street for a better view of the rooftop terrace, but the angle was not as good as from up in the station.

A car sputtered to the curb. She felt adult eyes on her. She hadn't been thinking about how strange she must look, but now, subjected to a prolonged gaze, she grasped an inkling of the effect of her appearance. She dragged her eyes away from the honeyed white bricks against the sky.

Bobby. A rusty Datsun. His thievish forearm resting

on the open window. The hood of the car was mottled, discolored and mismatched. The engine rattled.

"Well, now," he said. "What happened to *you?*"

Did he recognize her, then, or was he attracted and appalled by a new monstrosity? Was he talking to a complete stranger or a faint acquaintance? What kind of greeting was this? She tried to gauge the expression in his eyes. Large and brown and mocking. She wanted to slap him. But she winced at this thought; after all that had unfolded this summer, he'd been the closest thing she had to a friend. And he did recognize her, it seemed. She softened.

"Give me a cigarette," she said, eyeing the building, afraid to miss her chance. The oil-in-the-creases hand gave her what she wanted and she puffed at it. He shut off the idling engine.

"Are you okay? I'd-a thought you'd-a gone back home to mommy and daddy. You seemed the type."

"The type?"

He sucked on his cigarette, exhaled. "Back there, with the school."

"Shows what you know," she said, glancing up at the terrace.

"What are you looking at?" He leaned out the window, heaving his torso halfway out of the car, and twisted to face the building behind. Light gleamed in the grease of his locks, now growing shaggy. Flecks of premature gray veined them. He seemed connected to the machine he drove. A mechanical centaur.

"Nothing," she said.

He untwisted, chucked the stub of his cigarette into the gutter, and smiled. His front tooth was chipped. She hadn't noticed that before. Was it new? She chided herself: *focus.*

On one side of the building there were rickety fire escapes. If she couldn't actually fly, she could climb. In the late afternoon, how many people would be inside the white building, what were the chances of being noticed? Could she, with her sore body, be swift? Would Bobby disappear if she went up the building? Would *he* disappear if she went with Bobby? But who said she would, or could, go with either of them? And to where? They were different paths. Bobby or magic.

She closed her eyes and focused on the hook in her gut. Red was more important. Was she following a ghost? And if he was one, did he know it? In some ways he seemed princely. A princely ghost. This didn't quite make sense. Her mind felt jumbled. She needed Bobby to leave and still he sat there. Was he smirking?

"Where'd you get that top?" he asked.

"Times Square."

"Huh."

Her mother's spears reared up in her eyes, aiming at his placid, bemused face. "Is that so strange?"

"No."

"Listen," she said. "I'm busy right now."

"Oh?"

"I can't tell you about it."

"You can't? Okay, okay." He put his hands up. "I've got to get to my own business, anyway." He restarted the ignition. "But I hope we run into each other again soon."

She flicked her cigarette onto the sidewalk. Focused on the flying ember, tried not to look pleased. Maybe he would take her in again, if she needed it. Maybe if she showed him how she couldn't go back. He drove slowly in the zebra light beneath the train tracks. The Datsun wobbled as it sputtered.

193

Across the street, beside the white building, she checked around the empty sidewalks. A closed-top dumpster sat beneath the fire escape. She hoisted herself up on it, knees knocking on metal fragrant with banana peels, chicken bones, sawdust, and curdled milk. Steeled herself; imagined a tight coil at her core about to spring. Then jumped to catch the lowest rung of the fire escape and hauled herself upward, clawing with shaking muscles, nearly slipping, fleshy lump-wings twitching beneath her knapsack, until she reached the first landing. As she ascended the iron steps she could only hope the noise would be dismissed as the work of fat squirrels. At last she lurched up onto the steaming blacktop of the roof.

White and purple pansies quivered in the breeze. Eggplants drooped from their stalks. Green and orange bell peppers gleamed in the evening sun. Potted tomato vines, lined up in neat rows, were the most populous plant in the garden, and the red fruit bulged. She plucked a tomato and ate it, ravenously, like an apple. It was sweet but its skin tasted of ash.

Red appeared at the windowed door to the terrace. Their eyes met, but the glare on the glass interfered. The hook was still in her gut. She plucked another tomato, devouring it. Seeds dribbled over her hand.

Red opened the door.

"How'd you get up here?" he asked. He gauged the distance from other rooftops, but this building took up a whole city block. The neighboring buildings across the street were of brick and ruddy stone, too low, too far. He crossed his arms. Far away, Manhattan twinkled in the sunset.

Pluta swallowed a large hunk of tomato and shrugged, plucking another.

"Those are my tomatoes you're decimating."

"They're very tasty."

He huffed. "Why don't you come inside?"

Pluta ate without responding. She hadn't thought he'd invite her inside. This was better than she'd expected: perhaps he'd been waiting for her. And now she was dawdling.

"They're good with a dash of salt," he added.

In three large bites she finished the tomato, its skin and juice warm from the August sun. She spat out the green stem. "Okay."

The man stepped aside, holding the door open. She grabbed a fourth tomato on her way in. A set of stairs illuminated by skylights led down into a dimmer, curving hall. The ceilings were high and the walls, gallery white, smelled of fresh paint.

Where the hall opened up, a bouquet of glass irises sat in a vase on a long glass table. The man gestured toward a white leather sofa; Pluta sank into the cushions. She set her knapsack down on the white floor. It looked filthy against this impeccable place, as if a rat could scamper out of it at any moment. She sat up so as not to smear dirt on the sofa.

"Do you eat meat?" Red asked from the kitchen that opened into the living area. Pluta nodded. A large triptych hung on the wall across from the sofa. Colorful squares, each with a single off-center dot: red dot in a blue sea, blue dot in a lavender sea, lavender dot disintegrating into a red sea. It reminded her of a monster with three lazy eyes. Red unsheathed a knife from a stand on the counter and sawed through a crusty loaf of bread. He brought her a salami sandwich.

"Marbod," he said as he sat in a clear plastic chair beside the sofa.

Benumbed, Pluta said nothing, just tore into the sandwich, stuffing her mouth with crust and fatty meat.

"Marbod. That's my name."

Pluta turned her back and jerked her thumb at her tattooed name. Very convenient, she thought as she chewed, not to have to interrupt eating to introduce herself.

"Ah. So we both have unusual names."

Whereas the ogre had poked at her wings and called her a freak, the prince made no comment, seemed to take them for granted, and she felt on the edge of something powerful, as in a lucid dream, realizing she could walk through mirrors and fly. This frightened her. She swallowed, tongued her gums for stuck remnants.

"What's yours mean?" she asked. Then she focused on chewing, because otherwise she might float up to the ceiling and not know how to come down.

"I understand it means 'he who walks at the bottom of the lake.' My mother was a fan of Robert Graves."

Mother. She winced. The name Graves was meaningless. Halfway through the sandwich now, she slowed, the heaviness of it mixing with the acid of the tomatoes. She turned her attention to his face, spattered with a galaxy of fine freckles. Her lips, she found, were mumbling. *Marbod, Marbod.* It was an ugly name. *He who walks at the bottom of the lake.* The *boto* were river creatures. Then there were the mermaids of her dream, on the shores of Uruguay.

Marbod was sitting upright in the chair, fingers loosely interlaced in his lap; his fingers, long and tapered, were also freckled. His eyes green. Guarded. Curious but impatient. But what color had the Professor's eyes been? And how could this now be a question? Had they been light brown, with large green flecks? Or pale green, speckled amber? She wanted to shake herself. Alone at Banderhock she would bang her head against the wall; she had banged this detail out of it. She was ready to dissolve, lavender dot in the triptych; she trembled and sniffled. *He who walks at the bottom of the lake.*

"Why does it smell like licorice in here?" she asked, suddenly.

Marbod grinned. "This used to be a candy factory. They made striped mints and candy canes. Taffy too, I think. Big sticky tubs pulling at sugar used to be right where you're sitting."

It felt so good to eat. Salt, fat, and spice coated her insides, dulled the feeling that her molecules might fly apart, allowed her to stay longer in this place that was beginning to trouble her with its sweetness and light. Within minutes the sandwich was gone.

"Another?"

After the second sandwich, Marbod produced a five-layer cake. Dark chocolate cemented with unctuous *dulce de leche*. He lifted off a heavy glass cake cover in the shape of a bell.

Agog, Pluta glided to the counter separating the kitchen from the rest of the space. Marbod let her run her finger over the steel knife after he cut the cake to catch the errant crumbs. She licked them off her finger. Could plop her face right into the gooey center of the cake, balloon each cheek with sweetness. But one large wedge did the trick, clung to her insides, pleasant mortar, pleasant insulation. Her stomach burbled with satisfaction.

"Tea?" She nodded.

He opened a glass cabinet. Emanating from it was a distinct smell she had not encountered in two years. Herbal, almost like eucalyptus, but metallic and fishy.

Why couldn't she place it? A green scent. She sniffed again. Maté? Pale green, speckled amber. He who walks at the bottom of the lake. "Wait." She slid off the stool and tottered. "Where am I?"

"What do you mean?"

It could not be, this place, this candy-factory loft with impossible food. If she stayed, her molecules wouldn't know how to cohere—they *would* fly apart.

Pluta grabbed her bag and ran for the front door of the loft, seeing two places at once—this one where she physically existed and another that held her former existences. The door chirred behind her. She followed a winding gray hall whose walls seemed haphazard and hastily built to a steep and uneven staircase that listed to one side.

Launched herself down, two steps at a time, gulping for air, wings flicking. Wanting, now, to scream.

Outside it was still Gowanus. Hot air clung to her skin. Saliva rattled in her throat. Down the street, a man in rubber boots and coveralls blasted the sidewalk with a high-pressure hose. Industrial chemicals in the air stung her eyes and nose, overpowering any lingering scents of cinnamon or licorice.

Cloud tufts foamed blue-gray, almost like sea-froth; the air tensed; a storm threatened to overwhelm the canal. She crossed beneath the train trestle, past the corrugated tin fence of a scrap metal collector. Through a crack in the fence she glimpsed Bobby's Datsun awaiting cannibalization with other cars lined up for the same fate. A heap of twisted metal loomed behind them. It was the same heap she had spotted from the other side of the canal at the start of the summer. She kept going. *He who walks at the bottom of the lake.* She would go to the bottom, then, yes. The sky seemed to lower and growl.

Behind her Bobby shouted. *Hey.* But she was shifting into another place, that second place, and kept going. Footsteps behind her. *Hey.*

In a poorly fenced lot beside the canal towered a structure, not quite as tall as the train trestle but with latticework easily scaled. It seemed to be some sort of car elevator—on top sat the rusted metal husk of an automobile—but the mechanics had long since abandoned it. Between the elevator and the trestle, the backwards red letters of KENTILE FLOORS did not yet glow.

Still ignoring Bobby, Pluta climbed the elevator. Below, the canal glinted; across the water to the north lay the charred remains of the Public Place. When she reached the top she gasped, losing steam. The car door whined as she pulled it open and flopped into the driver's seat, sending up a dust cloud. The sound of panting, at first faint, grew louder below her; Bobby struggled up to the platform and toppled into the passenger seat.

"What the fuck." He struggled to catch his breath.

Stone-eyed, she surveyed the landscape ahead, the black steelwork of the trestle, dark netting drooping from its underside. An oblique view of the sunset behind Bobby, behind the soaring trestle. The sun a red pupil, the low clouds a thick eyelid. She thought, *we are inside the eye. Turn it inside out.*

"What are you doing up here?" He dropped a small black duffel bag at his feet. Tools clanged inside. Something liquid splashed in a metal container. When she didn't answer, he reached inside the bag for a flask and took a swig. Without turning toward him, she stuck her hand out. He let her drink.

After the burn slid down her throat, she said, "I have

199

this small problem. See?" She turned her back to him. Let the wings unfurl.

He snatched the flask back from her and drained it, bewildered.

"You can touch them, if you want," Pluta said. It came out accusatory, aggressive. She was going to use them. Dive. See if they really worked, let them fail, the end. But first she would let him see.

Reluctantly, he skimmed one wing with a fingertip, then poked it. The skin indented and popped back to its natural curve, like ear cartilage. She faced the windshield of the vehicle again.

"Where've you been?" he asked. "What happened to you?" His eyes skittered over her scalp and bruises. He seemed to avert his gaze from the wings.

"What do you mean? You kicked me out."

"Yeah, but—geez." He ran his fingers through his hair so it stood up with its grease. "That problem is way beyond me."

She sprang up. "This is all *your* fault. All of it. *All of it.*" She swung the car door open and stuck a foot out.

"*Hoooold* on a sec. Let's come down from here and talk about this."

The water glimmered with promise. The promise was in there because there were two places. Maybe more. Simultaneous places. She was beginning to understand. Everything that had happened, starting with that day at La Rural, it would continue on a loop, it would continue until she made it stop. Red had given her the key, it was in the water.

"First, watch me fly," she said.

But Bobby grabbed her shoulder and pulled her away from the edge.

They climbed down the structure, one on either side.

His eyes riveted to her through the latticework as if his gaze would hold her, prevent a premature jump. Her legs shook, felt prickly. Back on the ground, they paced; gravel crunched. On this side of the canal, no fence blocked the water. Black gravel became neon-bright grass. She stood on the grass, bag at her feet, and hugged herself. A second set of arms, to wrap around the back, to clasp the wings and stop their twitching—that was what she wished for now. Water lapped against the canal wall. A light drizzle pattered; drops rippled the black water in overlapping circles.

He who walks at the bottom of the lake. The dive from above wasn't as important as simply the dive, the going beneath. Were they wings or were they fins? If the water didn't have the answer it would have silence, and that was almost good enough.

"So?" he asked.

"So this." She pointed down to the water. With a sharp intake of breath she plunged in. Eyes open to the opaque black. The water viscous. Arms outstretched, hands searching for the bottom. Shoulders pinned back as if they would lift off the spine, wings extended, taut. She bumped against shadowy forms, floating or sunken. The rubber of a car tire, the spongy remnants of a seat, a corroded chain. The water slowed the flap of her wing-fins; she plunged deeper. Her mind said: *latch on*—

—a *boto* a mermaid a manatee a fish a body a whale a drowned giant—

—then, the bottom: coarse, oily sand. Little rocks, little bones. As she ran her hands along the canal bed, a picture emerged: the bulging whites of enormous eyes. Chaotic hair against pitch-black nothing. Enormous, knobby hands; enormous, knobby limbs; a huge mouth open wide. The bloody stump of a body clutched in one hand. Saturn's blank-eyed, mad ferocity. Against her palms this sand burned. Lungs burned. Eyes burned. Her body—all of it—would burst.

She blew out a single air bubble that pushed against grit and sludge. Her body floated upward. Her fingers reached for the canal wall, the tied logs slippery with moss.

There was a pull at her wrists, under her arms. Gasping, skin slicked over with muck, she snorted out canal water.

The sound of the water clung to her ears—roared and deafened.

She tried to lay in a fetal position on the bright grass, coughing and spluttering, but Bobby dragged her up. All her mucous membranes felt seared. She tottered forward, Bobby guiding her. Rain slid over the muck. There were clanging tools; there was the hard rush of cold water. Both of them knelt on concrete; he'd yanked open a fire hydrant to full blast. They flushed off what they could. She coughed and hacked.

And then he led her into a car. They drove, they stopped somewhere, he disappeared, he came back and threw a towel at her. She wrapped it around herself, not seeing, and then he sped on. She sank into the seat, crushing the wings and feeling pushed with the car's speed. On and on they drove. The memory of him shouting at her revolved upon itself. The dive into the canal, bumping against things, water filling in the gaps, the gaping holes, open mouths, and missing pieces, reaching out of the canal, him shouting through the watery noise: *you're batshit crazy, lady.*

He led her by the elbow to the entrance of a hospital. Everything was dark around her, tunnel vision leading to the cold brightness of the hospital's halls. Ambulances screamed. She wrapped the towel around herself to swaddle the wings.

In the waiting room there was a seat and a clipboard and a pen that eluded her. It shook in her grasp and turned her words into squiggles. Across from her a man clutched his belly and moaned. A woman in a housecoat patted his hand and said *there, there*; she also tried not to stare at Pluta but failed.

Pluta didn't know where Bobby had gone. She didn't think he'd left. He'd set her down and given her the clipboard and sternly said not to move, and she felt so exhausted now that it wouldn't be possible to move a centimeter. A millimeter, even. The pen fell onto the floor. She let it sit there a while before trying to pick it up. Water gurgled in her ear. The woman in the housecoat still stared but wouldn't come near her to help with the pen. She could probably smell the canal stench from where she sat, Pluta thought, sniffing at herself. She stared back at the woman, gently knocking at her ear with the heel of her hand.

Bobby came back with a Styrofoam cup of hot, brown coffee-water.

"Drink this," he said. His voice was muffled, as if damp felt wrapped his vocal cords.

She cupped both hands around the coffee, steadying it with her knees between sips. Sour liquid. Almost as vile as what she'd swum in. He glowered at the squiggles on the intake form. Got the pen off the floor and then went for her bag. Stuck his arms inside and rifled through it.

"We're gonna do this right," he muttered.

The water still roared in Pluta's ears. She picked at

the squeaky styrofoam and flicked loose pieces to the ground. From the bottom of her knapsack Bobby extracted her stained and wrinkled passport, found the page with her name, and put pen to form.

"Hey," she whispered. She tried to send him a withering glare. Wanted to say that she wasn't Tatiana anymore, she was Pluta. But she wouldn't say this here, across from the belly-moaner and the starer. Orderlies in sneakers squeaked down the hall.

Bobby handed her the clipboard. "Maybe you can handle this part," he said, referring to the section on family medical history. His eyes kept sliding around the room. Wary. She thought about scratching out her name. But that would raise suspicions.

Family medical history was a checklist. She could leave a simple scratch mark as needed. She tried to snap together, stop the internal sinking. But she didn't know what half the items on the checklist meant and didn't know about the rest anyway. Isabel had told her once when she was very little that her grandfather had died after eating too much spicy food. No item on the list seemed to correspond to that.

Bobby sprang from his seat again and paced, pausing to read a bulletin board by the entrance. Struck by something he read there, he borrowed a pen from the triage desk and scratched a note on his hand. Pluta struggled with the checklist, leaving it mostly blank. She could feel his tiger-pacing. A gaggle of white-coated men pushed past, shoes clopping on the hard floor.

Bobby had left the reason-for-visit line on the form blank. She grasped the pen in her fist. Seemed to have more control of it this way. She bit the push button. Then she wrote: "remove back-lumps." Bobby's pacing brought him back to the rows of seats.

"You done?" She handed him the clipboard. He took it away. They waited. The belly-moan man was called in first. A young boy with bloodied paper towels wrapped around his hand came in and was called next. An hour became two, three. Bobby drifted in and out of the room; each time she thought he wouldn't come back, but he did.

A nurse finally stood at the edge of the empty waiting room. "Spektor?" Pluta twitched up, as if ruffling feathers. The nurse eyed her, quizzical. They went to a ring of blue-curtained cubicles. Bobby followed to the edge of the curtain.

"I'll just be outside," he said. Pluta nodded. Nice of him to stay. She didn't know what she would have done if he'd left her there. Under the bright hospital lights her giddy resolve started to crumble. She'd run away from Red, she'd run away into the water, but she hadn't gotten anywhere. Through the dark surface, through the viscous liquid, her hands had bumped against things, and the wings had stretched out. Remembering exhausted her. If she lay down, she might not get up. Maybe there was a chance—if Bobby stayed, she could stay with him. But she didn't like that he'd gone through her bag, used her passport name. She didn't like that at all. And now he had her bag, too, she realized.

The nurse didn't shut the curtain. "On summer break?" she asked. Her smile forced.

Pluta nodded. The nurse stuck a thermometer under her tongue, wrapped a black band around her arm and pumped it tight, calculating her blood pressure. The thing released, hissed. The nurse jotted down figures on a clipboard.

"Blood pressure's a little high. Excited about something?"

Pluta glared.

"The doctor will be here in a little while—sit tight!"

The metal rungs of the curtain scraped on the rod. Now Pluta was alone in the blue box.

She swung her legs; the table, made of cheap, hollow metal, jiggled beneath her. She hopped off, peeked through the curtain. Bobby sat at the end of a row of chairs; his head rested against the wall. He swallowed, Adam's apple bobbing. Her bag sat at his feet. She shut the curtain. The nurse returned.

"We're moving to a little room down the hall. Not admitting you, dear, just putting you in a room with a door, okay?"

Pluta didn't know what she meant by *admitting*. She made a quick detour to Bobby, snatching back her bag. He was halfway through a nod when she turned. Down the hall, away from the ring of cubicles, the nurse led her to the new room and closed the door.

Shiny metal instruments lay out on a tray. A small radio beside the tray crackled static at a low volume. She slid off the exam table and fiddled with the knobs.

"And now for some velvet fog," an announcer purred.

This was intriguing, but when the music played, the smoothness of the singing voice irked her. She fiddled more but only found hissing, snaps, and white noise. Settling back on the only working station with the volume low, she slumped onto the table. Its cushion sighed beneath her.

Perhaps the whole removal process would be swift. Quick snips and everything back to normal. She hoped it wouldn't hurt. Perhaps the nerves in the wings were not yet fully developed; perhaps the wings were just flab, excess skin. They quivered at this, quivered and flapped in rebuke. Sharp, almost like a sail's snap. She hadn't expected this: she thought their erratic movement was done. She wanted it done—she'd gone in the water and touched something and seen something, and she still didn't understand. Only hurt more.

She lunged back on the exam table, on top of them, tried to flatten them into stillness. The waxy paper beneath her rustled, the rustling growing louder as the wings fought her crush. Suppressing a yelp, clasping for her hair and only finding scalp, she hunched her back and tensed her fingers, felt cracks in the residue coating them. Springing upright again, she pounded her fists once against the waxy paper, tightening her core to suppress a caterwaul. The wings calmed.

She leaned against the table, head in her folded arms. She sniffled. No more Gowanus. She nodded to herself. Blamed her mutation on that place—that's the rational explanation, isn't it? Too much poison. Isabel would hardly withhold her revulsion; *nice people do not mutate*; *couldn't you at least have grown some pretty white wings?* Bat girl. White—they would've quickly grown filthy anyway. Isabel would never know; she would never see *Isabel* again: It felt good to refer to her mother this way, just as it had felt better to refer to her father as the Professor. Maybe not good, but comfortable, stronger. Yes, if she were never to see the Professor again, she would also never see Isabel. She tried to make her face stony. There would be no return to Banderhock. She would keep wandering. Forever? That was the only thing that seemed plausible. Bobby was a wanderer. At least he wasn't tied to Gowanus, she hoped. Maybe this time he wouldn't abandon her, maybe instead they could stick together and flit from place to place. Her mouth felt dry.

The door opened. Pluta stood up. A white-coated woman with hair pulled tightly back entered, studying a clipboard. Large, red-framed bifocals slipped down her button nose. She pushed them up.

"Miss . . . Spektor?"

Pluta nodded. The doctor washed her hands in the sink and gave Pluta's filthy hand a quick shake. Her cold fingers were long and skinny; they had Isabel's elegance but seemed somehow crueler in their boniness.

"Let's take a look at those growths." The exam table had a donut-like cushion at its head. The doctor draped the donut with large paper towels and told Pluta to rest her face in its hole. She pulled at Pluta's halter top a little. "Convenient top, eh? Very thoughtful." Pluta attempted polite laughter—she needed this woman to help her, she reminded herself—and lay down. Resting her face against the donut made the bruises ache. Her eyes felt glassy.

Latex gloves snapped on. The doctor poked Pluta's back. She seemed to be playing with the wings, unfurling them and letting them flop closed. Despite all the quivering and involuntary flapping that had occurred before the doctor's arrival, they seemed to have slackened now into dead things.

The wings made a faintly wet noise as they flopped. *Clllop. Clllop.* Like curling parchment but cold, and damp. The doctor unfurled them more times than seemed necessary, to the point where Pluta wanted to raise her head and say: *look, they aren't toys.* But she held her tongue.

"How long did you say you've had these 'back-lumps'?" The doctor held one wing taut and shone a light through the skin.

Pluta wondered if it was possible to decipher tattoo ink in the delicately veined, pale pink flesh. "I didn't." She thought a moment. "A month? They grew over a month."

"Mmhmmm. And do they hurt?" The doctor's voice was much too bright and chirpy. Did she wish for them to hurt?

"No. They itched. Then they stopped itching." But maybe they *had* hurt. Everything had hurt. It was relative. There were bruises on her face, everywhere, but the doctor had not said a thing about it. As if what had happened only two, three days ago hadn't happened at all. Everything started to blur. It took a lot of concentration to focus. Pluta felt a third eye rattling around in her brain, remembered the monster she'd seen in the three paintings, in the white building.

"Well," the doctor said, finally releasing the wing she'd held taut, "we can probably lop these off."

Pluta raised her head to look at the doctor. *Lop* was an unknown word but it sounded wrong.

The doctor smiled. "You didn't indicate an insurance company. Are you paying cash?"

At the bottom of Pluta's knapsack were some wrinkled traveler's checks that had been useless in Gowanus. Isabel had given them to her for emergencies. She sat up. "Do you take traveler's checks?"

The doctor rolled her eyes and let out a hearty belly-to-throat laugh that bounced off the white walls. The medical instruments gave the echo a tinny quality. Pluta wasn't sure why she laughed. Had she been teasing her? Why wasn't she concerned by the wings? The filth? The bruises?

"I'm sorry. I didn't mean to laugh." She shined the pen light in each of Pluta's eyes and spoke to her forehead. "Looks like you're all scraped up," she said.

Ah, thought Pluta. "Yes. A little." The doctor set down her flashlight.

"What happened?"

209

The "velvet fog" still played low in the room. The doctor switched off the radio. The quiet unsettled. The doctor's eyes became earnest, but it seemed false somehow. Pluta shook her head, shrugged. "Nothing."

"Nothing."

"Nothing. Fell down in the playground. Nothing."

The doctor pressed her lips together, waiting. Finally, she said, "Please wait here a little longer. I'll be back."

Two orderlies stood outside, as if at attention. Pluta thought she heard the doctor say something to them as she passed—*watch this door*, something like that. She hopped off the table and paced the room. The sweat and hydrant water had dried a while ago and now she shivered in the air conditioning.

In the mirror above the sink, her lips were blue-purple; she forced a grin, scrutinizing discolored, uneven teeth. One eye puffed more than the other, the flesh blue and yellow and green. The reddish-brown hatch marks of her abrasions were no longer quite as raw.

She rummaged through her bag for makeup and ran thick black eyeliner around her eyes the way she had seen some women do it, the copper-haired woman and women on the subway in leather jackets and studded belts. It caked at her eyelashes and clumped at the inner corners of her eyes. She dampened her index finger and ran it around each eye so that the caking smudged. It didn't hide the monstrosity—it enhanced it.

The black smear on the pad of her finger triggered something else. She rubbed her thumb over it, circular movements of rumination. The viscous dive—the break of the surface—what she had touched with her hands. That picture of Saturn that she'd remembered. Where had she seen it first?

In a big, glossy book.

Was it with Daniel? Was it on his shelf with the myths?

Saturno devorando a su hijo, just this gigantic cannibal taking up the page, his mouth open to his child against pitch-black space. What had Daniel muttered when they turned to that page? Something about its tragic relevance.

She was certain that her wing-fins had, beneath the water, *flown*.

12. Rome and New York
Summer 1980

"SIGNORA," said the concierge as Isabel stepped in from her night stroll. He leaned forward, brass buttons knocking against the ebony counter. "A message for you."

Isabel glided to him in the dreamy haze induced by her long, solitary amble, but her steps clacked loudly on the marble floor of the lobby and punctured the bubble of the dream. He handed her a heavy sheet of cream-colored stationery, folded crisply in half. There was something in his ardent leaning that caused her stomach to flutter. The message gave only an international number and a directive: "Please call immediately." She scanned the careful black cursive a few times before recognizing the number from Banderhock.

"The phone, please," said Isabel, riveted to the cream-colored paper.

"*Prego.*" His voice steady and somber.

The cord of the black rotary phone stretched over the counter to a column alongside the front desk. The dark, prickly leaves of a potted shrub brushed against her leg. She dialed, wound the black coil around her hand, and tried to breathe steadily through her nostrils. As the phone rang, she calmed, remembering that it must be early afternoon there; perhaps there had not been some urgent off-hours catastrophe, but some need for mild admonishment, nothing more. The word *immediately* grew damp in her sweaty fingers.

The line crackled.

"Mrs. Spektor," breathed the Banderhock secretary. "We're so glad you called." She connected Isabel to the headmistress, Dr. Tran. A distant hiss on the line: the weight of the ocean.

"Mrs. Spektor. I'm sorry to say it." Dr. Tran cleared her throat twice. "Your daughter has disappeared."

Isabel's chest contracted, the wind sucked out of her. Her jaw and knees slackened. She stepped back to the edge of the front desk, propping herself up on an elbow.

"We've notified the police and they are already working hard, but we suggest you come back at once, if you can."

The stationery crumpled in Isabel's fist. She locked her knees as she stammered, "Of course. Of course I'll come back. My god. How did this happen? How *could* this happen?"

"I know it's distressing. The police are at work, and we can put you in touch with excellent private detectives. My assistant is drawing up a select list. Your daughter seems to have slipped away during the study hour before dinner."

It took a moment of calculation; the disorientation of travel and separation deepened. "Yesterday?"

"Yes. Of course we wanted to be absolutely certain, you understand. But we also don't want to lose time."

"Well, I'm coming, of course. Of course, I'll be there, I'll take the next flight." Her heart pounded in her throat, knocked against her brain. Her eyes bulged, straining out of the sockets; she closed them. On the insides of her eyelids she saw the shimmering light of the blue grotto. She hadn't gone there yet; she'd only seen a program about it on television. Her eyes wrenched open.

"Mrs. Spektor, wait," said Dr. Tran. "Is there any place she could have gone? Did she talk of wanting to go some place, some place she wasn't allowed? We can give the police this information while you travel. It could save time."

Isabel rubbed her nose. "I want to say Buenos Aires. Or Manaus. But that is ridiculous. She couldn't get that far. Have they checked the airports?"

"I'm not certain, but I will check. Is there any place else?"

"No. No, I can't think of anything else."

"Thank you, Mrs. Spektor. Whatever information we can get will help. We can have someone pick you up from the airport. Just tell us the information when you have it."

"Thank you." She hung up. Before going upstairs, she leaned against the column, cool marble against her hot cheek.

Outside Banderhock, a morning breeze stirred a grove of oak trees. Wrens chirped; white pebbles clicked beneath Isabel's weary steps. The halls were already empty of children, as the school year had ended the day before. The car service driver carried her luggage into the vestibule of Dr. Tran's office. A glass case of medals and awards towered over a brown leather sofa. The secretary brought Isabel coffee on a lacquered tray and said Dr. Tran was in an early board meeting but would be with her right away. With calm efficiency, the secretary moved on to another room; only the quick swish of her pantyhose seemed to betray anxiety. Isabel caught a glimpse of a small woman presiding over a long table and supposed the board was meeting about her catastrophe, their catastrophe. Isabel sipped black coffee from bone china. She cradled the delicate porcelain in her palms as if it were the head of a newborn baby. She finished the small pot while waiting.

Dr. Tran burst out of the meeting room, five feet tall but commanding the space as if she were twice that. A heavy scent of coffee and tobacco clung to her. Isabel rose; Dr. Tran took both of Isabel's hands in hers.

"Mrs. Spektor." Her address a susurrus. She led Isabel into her office.

Men and women in somber suits filed out of the meeting room; some regarded Isabel as they passed while others walked as if in a dark tunnel.

Isabel and Dr. Tran settled in across the desk from one another. Dr. Tran rifled in a drawer for a clean ashtray and new pack of cigarettes and called for her assistant to take away another ashtray piled high with ash and stubs. Isabel's eyes darted about the room as the caffeine began its work, thumping against the weariness of the transatlantic flight. Leatherbound books lined one wall of the office; diplomas tiled another. There seemed to be a degree of every sort: a Radcliffe BA, a Barnard MA, a Yale MBA, and a Harvard EdD. Orbiting this quartet were various certificates of appreciation, commendation, and recognition. Isabel wondered why Dr. Tran hadn't gone ahead with law school and medical school and perhaps an art degree to round things out. On further inspection she found a Juris Doctor tucked away in a corner of the wall, almost as an afterthought. She found this woman both admirable and repellent.

"Mrs. Spektor," began Dr. Tran, as if saying her name

again would buy time to think of what else to say. "I know this is difficult." She offered a cigarette and Isabel accepted. Both puffed quickly. "I have a list of three vetted private detectives. You should meet with the sheriff first, though, and then once you choose your detective they will work together. The board would like to help pay for the detective."

Isabel murmured a perfunctory *thank you*.

"Fortunately, we had a class portrait we could give to the police, but if you have other recent photos, I think that could help."

Isabel dabbed at perspiration above her lip. Recent photos? She hadn't bothered to bring a camera when they'd left. Who would want to preserve—

The class picture would have to do.

Dr. Tran handed her the information about the detectives and said someone had arranged for a ride to the local sheriff. In the meantime, Isabel was invited to look around her daughter's room in the dormitory; Dr. Tran accompanied her across the long green lawn. Isabel was surprised, thought the assistant would have accompanied her instead. Perhaps Dr. Tran was afraid, wanted to mend the damage as much as possible. Spume of old anger: Pluta's strange, stubborn badness. But this idea gave her pause, a twinge in the gut, as she remembered her own teenage reign of terror. Perhaps her parents would have sent her away to school too, if they'd had the opportunity. The school was negligent. Of course the school was in the wrong. She had trusted them. What was the phrase they'd used in the brochure? *In loco parentis*? Still. Dr. Tran waited patiently outside the open door.

Pluta's roommate had already stripped her side of the room clean. On Pluta's side, there wasn't much to see: rumpled sheets on a narrow bed, strewn with red-and-gold candy wrappers; a stack of textbooks shoved in a corner on the floor. Isabel leafed through a spiral notebook on the desk. Sparse class notes on geometry, the French Revolution, the digestive system, all mingled together, all decorated with drawings: obsessive patterns of stars (pentagrams, Stars of David, asterisks); long-lashed eyes floating on the page, unconnected to faces; crude renditions of wings. No strange messages; no forlorn poetry. An empty cardboard box sat beneath the wooden chair. Isabel crouched to it. The return address was Lolo's. She hadn't even known her sister had sent gifts. Slowly she rose, feeling lightheaded.

Sheriff Strawbridge didn't have much to say. Isabel's head swam, so it would have been difficult to take in more information even if he had it. But she tried. The little class photo, Pluta's tiny face in a group of twenty students, would be blown up and distributed to other police stations and post offices around Connecticut and beyond. When the sheriff asked about other photos she squeezed the handles of her purse. How could she say they'd left in a hurry without arousing suspicion? What did he know? How did he sympathize? Lolo's hiss, *governments cooperate*, sprang into her mind. A crazy thought. All of them? Ridiculous. How had her sister infected her with this thought? And yet, how could she tell this man, from the beginning, what had happened, when she didn't understand it herself? How could she show she was not some negligent monster?

"I'm sorry," she said finally. "I just don't have other photos. Not as recent as that." He could help, she thought. He could help. He doesn't have to know everything.

The sheriff nodded. "That's fine, that's all right. Go

home and rest. Stay close to the phone. If you think of anything, call."

She settled on a detective in Midtown Manhattan. His brochure had boasted about state-of-the-art technology and some sort of interstate network of detectives. The next afternoon, she entered the tall, boxy building, the cool lobby a relief from the sun beating down on her head. On the thirty-seventh floor, enormous fans whirred at either end of the stifling hall. She patted down loose hairs whipped up by the wind and found the detective's suite.

A woman at the front desk clacked at a typewriter. Through an open door beside the receptionist, Isabel could see the detective, a tall man in a cream-colored suit, leaning forward over a roll of paper that spilled out of a screeching telefax machine. The receptionist stopped typing.

"Isabel Spektor?"

"Yes."

She granted the receptionist foreknowledge and not presumption. She'd decided that, if she approved of this detective (the upkeep of the building left something to be desired), she would have to be more candid with him than with the sheriff; he would be doing most of the work, so he would need more information. And the privateness of his venture suggested more discretion. His white seersucker suit was immaculate; this mitigated for Isabel the hot dustiness of the building.

"Jack Fraser. Pleased to meet you, Mrs. Spektor," he said. They shook hands. Despite the heat, his palms were dry. He had thick black hair combed almost into a pompadour, but it wasn't so large as to be ridiculous. He spoke with a mellow voice, a classic radio voice.

"Please call me Isabel." She'd had enough of *Mrs. Spektor* over the last two days.

"I'm sorry, Isabel, that you're going through this. Annie will give you a written questionnaire—it's rather extensive. Then we'll talk and find out as much as we can."

In a quiet corner of the office, beside drawn blinds, Isabel scribbled on a clipboard. Given name (Tatiana), name she went by (Pluta), date of birth, height, weight, eye color (here, rather than a blank, a checklist: brown, hazel, green, blue, blue-gray, gray, sapphire), hair color, complexion, facial structure (including, to her surprise, nose shape—more like Daniel's than hers; she'd lamented this, the wrong kind of nose, but never let the thought slip), body type (skinny, mild case of scoliosis), distinct markings (none), friends' names and contact information (only Casey; she gave the number in Vermont), disposition (morose, given to unexpected outbursts), any recent disputes (the instructions suggested use of the blank side of the page as needed).

Annie photocopied the completed questionnaire and fetched Isabel ice water. She assured her that everything but "recent disputes" would be shared with out-of-state detectives, should they run across a girl of that description. The last section was confidential, for Jack Fraser's use only. Isabel breathed easier, relieved by the tactfulness. Even if she hadn't written anything there. She preferred to speak with the man directly, not wanting to create too many written records.

Fraser leafed through the questionnaire and invited Isabel into his office. Isabel pulled Pluta's notebook from her handbag and slid it across the desk.

"I didn't find anything in here, but since you are the expert, perhaps you can find clues."

Fraser opened the front cover, flipped through some pages. "Yes, thank you. Anything you can think of or bring in is potentially useful." A small black box at the corner of his desk crackled and spoke. "Excuse me." He picked it up, pressed a button at the side of the box, and mumbled code words. Turning back to Isabel, he said, "As you can see, I am connected. When I'm out on the street, moving from clue to clue, I can still be in touch with the police—and with you. Just call Annie, and she can reach me."

"Thank you very much, Detective."

"Jack will do."

"Jack."

She returned to Carnegie Hill and waited by the phone. She didn't know if perhaps to comb the streets herself would be a good idea. But then, she'd be away from the phone. If it had been two days, how far could the child have gotten? Could she really have found her way onto a flight? Perhaps as a stowaway? Little girl huddled among the baggage. *Why* had she thought it a good idea to go again to Rome? Would this have happened if she hadn't? But—no. She shouldn't do this to herself, couldn't question every single choice she had made. She had trusted the school. And Pluta—Tatiana, she desperately wanted her to be Tatiana again, hoped she could see her again and call her that and it would feel natural even after all the years of another name—would have developed her friendship with Casey if she had simply done what she had said she would do. Isabel pushed back her shoulders and gulped at her drink. She called Lolo and spoke with no greeting.

"What do you know of this?"

"Of what?" Groggy-voiced. "Isabel?"

"Pluta's gone. What do you know?"

"Gone! What do you mean, gone?"

"Run away." Isabel clutched the receiver, wanted to shout. "What do you know?"

"Nothing, I know nothing. Oh, god." The sound of cloth fanning, flapping against hot damp skin. Isabel pictured goose-pimpled, aging flesh dripping from the neck. A squawk in Lolo's distant garden passed through the receiver.

"If she calls you, if she comes to you—"

"*Comes* to me? Isabel, how could she do this? Well, of course I will call, I will let you know, of course. What—"

Isabel hung up on her sister. In the kitchen, she opened the freezer, letting cold air coil and cloud about her. The refrigerator groaned. Blue plastic trays were stacked inside the freezer beneath a heavy layer of frost. She took out the trays and twisted each, shaking a cascade of ice cubes into a large glass bowl. Her face sank down, huffing into the pile of frozen shards.

13. New York
August 1980

A MONTH OF THIS: never knowing whether it was safe to leave the apartment, step outside a moment, buy groceries, feel something other than the four walls around her. Always afraid she might miss the all-important call. Isabel paid a neighbor to go out and purchase an answering machine, then figure out how to set it up. A heavy, clunky thing. They couldn't figure it out. A defunct metal box. The detective got her an answering service. Still. The immediacy of receiving the call herself had become important. There was little sleep and lots of restless napping. The detective would call weekly with nothing of substance to report. She grew to hate these nothing-reports.

In July she grew suspicious. If Pluta had somehow made it back to Lolo, would Lolo hide it from her? Was such a thing possible? How would she find out? She didn't want to waste energy calling Lolo all the time, trying to catch her off guard. Nevertheless she called Lolo. She called Lolo to listen to her voice, to see if any hint of something hid there.

"Isabel! Have you found her?"

"No. Not yet."

"Ach." A plastic stretching sound, the coiled telephone cord.

"You haven't heard from her?"

"No, not at all. I would tell you immediately, immediately I would tell you. Do you—would you like me to—"

"What?"

"Would you like me to see if I can—no, you wouldn't want it. I know you don't like it."

"What? Spit it out."

"I could try to contact the spirits. See what they know."

"Oh, please."

"Don't you want to try anything, everything?"

Isabel stood very close to the window. She let her forehead drop to it. Her breath clouded moisture upon the glass, upon her own face. "Fine," she muttered. "Do it."

Lolo said she would put the receiver on the table. Rustling, footsteps, the drag of the line. A quick, rough, sweeping sound, a crackle—the striking of a match. She picked up the phone. "Just a moment now. Just a moment." The phone clattered on the marble table. Lolo mumbled incomprehensibly.

Isabel stood against the window, holding her breath. Out on the street, a truck honked, a cacophonous two-toned blast. Black clouds of diesel smoke puffed as it idled behind a double-parked car.

On the phone line, in Brazil, three bangs on the marble. Lolo's voice returned to the line. "Isabel, did you hear that, Isabel?"

"Yes?"

"The instruments are clogged. I can't get through. I will keep trying. I'll call you."

Isabel wanted to say, "Don't bother." She hung up instead.

A hot August day suffocated her out of the little apartment. She had to get out. She had to. Zigzagging, she went down Lexington Avenue and then across 96th Street, down Park Avenue and then across 95th. Of course she loved Madison Avenue, and she walked a long stretch of it. The streets had emptied out for the summer. Early afternoon: the sun blazed and bits of grit drifted on humid air. Patches of the asphalt seemed to melt. She ducked into a café for iced tea. Condensation bubbled on the glass. She felt swollen from the heat.

She would go to a museum, she decided. She would distract herself for a little while and come back to the vigil renewed. One side of her hesitated: surely this was the wrong thing to do. Another side of her said: what, then? Sit in that hell-prison with nothing to do but broil?

She felt herself nearly floating, buoyed by the hot, thick air. What would this solitary life be like, prolonged? What would she do if this were the end? If she encountered tragedy yet again, mourned still longer, and then, and then . . . lived an independent life? Would she stay here in New York? Would she try, somehow, to live in Rome? Or would Rome be tainted for her? How would she live? What kind of callousness would she have to cultivate? What kind of self-preservation?

On Fifth Avenue she spotted the Guggenheim, poking out from among the classic apartment houses and mansions that calmed her so. She didn't have much of an opinion about modern art. It never made any sense to her. But the building had a sleekness to it, a kind of chic. She would give it a chance. Cool off and come back home with a steadier head. It was only two blocks away.

Hot air shimmered in the distance, a brown haze along the skyline. There were more people out on Fifth than on deserted Madison. Tourists streamed in and out of the Guggenheim.

A block away, she stopped in her tracks. *Tourists.* What was she doing? Any minute she could get a call. It was madness, complete and utter madness. The guilt she had felt before, back in Buenos Aires, shopping for the right thing to persuade the right bureaucrats and officers and gatekeepers—that seemed like nothing in comparison to what she was doing now. She ought to be ripped limb from limb. Like the characters in those horrible myths Daniel had kept on the shelves. Laid out on a table for stretching or for chopping. A vulture devouring her transgressor's liver, infinitely.

She turned back north under the hot glare of the sun. How could someone experience this twice in a lifetime? She tried not to think about that first fruitless search, how her pushing and asking seemed to lead directly to that horrific delivery. But had she pushed too much, or had she waited too long and not pushed hard enough? Things were different here—they had to be. The cause was different; therefore the outcome would be different. Such words reminded her of Daniel, even if the logic was wrongheaded. She surprised herself, having the presence of mind to recognize that. Her hands trembled. Stopping on the steaming sidewalk, she crossed her arms, trying to quell the tremors that grew more violent. Damp, hot, shaking bone.

Perspiration streamed down her face. Should she comb each street herself? She had rejected the idea before. It seemed idiotic—there would be thousands of streets to walk. But what else was there to do? What else? She was walking again. She was nearly hit by a car.

The car honked; she stumbled. She didn't know where to go. Blindly she continued, arms crossed, hands squeezed under her armpits. But then, there she was in front of the apartment building. Mechanically unlocking the front door, mechanically riding the elevator, mechanically back inside the broiling studio. In the heated box, the tremors slowly stopped.

She dialed the detective, fingers tripping in the rotary. Annie said he was in. She was transferred.

"*Anything?*" she asked, almost shouting.

"Mrs. Spektor?"

"*Anything?*"

"We're still looking. I know this is painful. We've interviewed her friend again. She still claims to know nothing. But you know we'll let you know and you know you can call anytime. Even at my home."

Isabel clutched the business card with his home phone number scrawled on the back. "Yes. I know."

After hanging up she flung herself on the couch with a long, bellowing shout. She wanted to tear up the cushions. She writhed, got up again, paced the room. In the fridge there was a cold bottle of Chablis: dinner. She yanked the cork out of the bottle, threw herself back on the couch, and drank. She lurched up again, holding the bottle, cool at her chest. Drank. Pink-hued light glowed from the windows. She switched on all the lights to drown it out. Drank. Returned to the couch. Let out one sob. Drank. Choked on more wine with another sob and coughed the wine up; it splattered on the floor, curled with thin wisps of stomach acid. She set the empty bottle down, gasping, her throat contracting. Buried her head in her hands. Curled up on the couch, tightly, tightly, tightly. And slowly, clenching her whole body, fell into a doze.

As she drifted in and out of sleep the coil of her body loosened. She dreamed something vague: comforting a faceless, nameless cousin, caressing her shoulder, her arm, some cousin she hadn't seen in years. Only one side of her visible. A purple sleeve. A jawline. As she couldn't see her face, she couldn't gauge an expression. And she couldn't hear her murmurs. Isabel could only caress her shoulder and arm, an ineffectual salve. What had happened to that cousin?

The telephone shrilled. She bolted up, knocking the wine bottle onto its side. Her bare foot surprised by the lukewarm puddle she'd spit up earlier. All the lights in the apartment still shone. From the corner of her eye she caught something ghostly: her own pale face reflected in the darkened windowpane.

The ringing stopped. The green glass bottle, nudged by her big toe, rolled on the parquet. She had no idea what time it was, how late in the night. She swallowed, glanced at her watch—11:30. Not so late after all. She fetched a tea towel and wiped up the mess on the floor, then slumped onto the couch again. She hadn't been fast enough. Why wasn't she fast enough? What if it was the detective? Or—what if it was Pluta?

No sooner had Isabel rested her forehead in her palms than the phone rang again. She lunged at it.

"*Bueno*? Hello?" She clung to the cord's black coils.

"Mrs. Spektor?" A stranger's voice. Male. Noise in the background: voices and crackled announcements. A train station? An airport?

"Speaking."

"You have a daughter?"

"Yes?" She leaned forward to the edge of her seat. "Yes?"

"I found a bulletin about her. I found your number."

"Yes, *dale, dime*. Tell me!"

"Well, she's here in the hospital. I think—I think she's okay. But, she's here. You should come get her."

"Wait. *Wait.*" Isabel's voice thundered. She reached for a newspaper, disarrayed on the coffee table. She upturned clutter, rummaging for a pen. In the gray margins she scrawled the stranger's instructions, looping around the newsprint. The hospital was in Brooklyn. She didn't know where. Her hands shook. How long had she been there, only across the river? How dangerous was Brooklyn? Wasn't that where there'd been that big fire, that rash of looting, several years ago? No, that was the Bronx. All she could imagine: blight. Vast blocks of nothing but the darkened husks of derelict buildings. She hung up before she thought to ask: *and who are you?* His voice had a roughness to it, not a professional lacquer. An orderly?

She called the detective at his home.

"I'll come get you," he said. She heard the rumpling of sheets, the clink of a belt buckle, the murmur of a sleepy wife.

On the drive to the hospital in Brooklyn, she twisted a handkerchief. Did the man say he *thinks* he found her? What did he find that he couldn't be sure? He *thinks* she's okay? Shadows beneath the Manhattan Bridge flickered, long stripes moving across her hands. Releasing the handkerchief, she rested her head on the window. Bargained. A whole month of bargaining had gone like this: *If she is all right, I will try to be more kind. But first I will smack her.*

What could Pluta have been doing all this time? In this city? Isabel tried to calculate how much money she

229

could possibly have had (Lolo had sent money, but not much, mostly sweets). She tried to think of where the girl might sleep, then stopped herself.

She'd rarely prayed in her life; now, she prayed. To what or whom, she wasn't sure. Maybe wishing was a better word.

A life untethered: what she thought she'd created in Rome, with Pluta seemingly safe at Banderhock or at Casey's. A life untethered: if only her skin hardened further. A solitary, independent life . . . Isabel came back to herself. Had Lolo's instruments somehow guessed at her untethered thoughts and sought to punish her with more uncertainty, more waiting, more questioning?

She was really becoming good at paranoia. Daniel might have said to this séance business, *poppycock*. But did he ever say that word? Or was she only imagining it? He'd had a fondness for such words. *Chompers, poppycock*. He taught them to Pluta, flourishes for her English homework. Isabel smiled briefly before she felt her face break. She turned away from the detective and focused her gaze on the window crank. Had Pluta really run away because of all that? Was she all right? Would she be all right? Would they be able to live together? Isabel tried to calm her facial contortions.

Jack glanced in the rearview mirror and then at her, asked in his smooth voice how she was doing.

Gulping for air, she muttered, "I'll be all right."

The small hospital sat across the street from a dark, leafy park where oak, maple, and sycamore trees stretched their branches over an enclosing stone wall. Isabel, bleary-eyed, snatched a glance at the park, those grasping branches—it was the kind of park where bad people go in the night; every large city had them. In her mind's eye Pluta slipped out of its woods, leering.

Jack took Isabel's arm as she got out of the car. The red and blue lights of ambulances whirled, flashing on their skin. He opened a glass door and guided her through, steadying her by the elbow. A police siren bleeped, but its noise was soon swallowed by the steady hum of the hospital as Jack led Isabel down stark halls. She avoided the gowned patients marooned along the walls, reclining on beds with their jaundiced skin, ashen skin, slack purple mouths.

Two plainclothes police officers, a man and a woman with badges clipped to their shirt pockets, stood not outside a hospital room but near what looked like a small lounge with a groaning vending machine. The presence of the woman surprised Isabel—was she there for the girl's comfort? But which was Pluta: victim, or offender? The door stood partially ajar. Jack shook hands with the officers while Isabel shrank from their sympathetic masks—surely their gazes hid contempt. She wanted to slink away. She didn't want to have this problem. Her face burned.

The woman officer gently said: "She's inside. We'll leave you alone, but we'll be nearby."

If they said anything else to prepare Isabel for what she would see, she couldn't take it in. Nothing but quiet gibberish. After they left she held her breath at the threshold, afraid of what she would find. She gave the door a little push with her fingertips.

Inside the lounge, Pluta sat on a turquoise couch with her legs tucked under her like a mermaid on a rock. A mermaid with cropped hair in a garish polka-dot halter and plaid pleated skirt. And all scratched up and bruised. Why weren't the scratches slathered in ointment and wrapped in bandages? They had the appearance of old

231

scratches and old bruises: yellowing green, clouds of violet. She wanted to swaddle the girl in big rolls of sterile, white gauze, hold her together in the swaddling.

Stains of dark, unknown muck streaked her clothes. Wild animal loosed upon the world. Absentmindedly, the girl sipped at a can of grape soda. Isabel stared, unable to move, voice caught. Pluta's glazed eyes slid over and stared back, then contemplated something over Isabel's shoulder. Isabel turned.

A young man hovered nervously behind her. He had shaggy, greasy hair and ragged, simple clothes—a white t-shirt with sweat stains at the neck and underarms, ripped jeans. She wondered how old he could be. Nineteen? Twenty? He shifted weight from foot to foot and nestled one hand into the other and cracked his knuckles. Nausea washed over Isabel. The urge to vomit on him rose. She held a closed fist to her mouth, looked askance. The nausea subsided. She refocused her glare.

"Mrs. Spektor, I—" She eyed him up and down. Filth crusted his hands. Her eyelid twitched.

"Who are you?"

"I'm the one who called you."

"Oh." Her nostrils flared. "I see."

"Um." He scratched his head, which she surmised would be ridden with lice, and put out his hand in a feeble gesture, as if to bolster what he had to say. "Your daughter needs you."

She leaned back, blinked. Leaned forward, chin jutting. *"That's why I'm here. And who did you say you were?"*

"Bobby." He shifted weight again. Now he seemed eager to leave.

"Bobby . . . ?"

"Listen, she's in there. I saw her. I saw your sign about her missing. Listen, I found her." He kept gesturing in

Pluta's direction, pointing. Hadn't anyone taught him not to point? Of course not. "Don't you want to see her?"

She wagged her finger at him. "*Yes.*" Her finger felt loaded, as if a whip could spurt from her nail. "Don't you go anywhere." She tried to sear the image of his face in her memory, in case he slipped away. She spun around and slammed the door to the lounge behind her. She would deal with this Bobby later.

Under the bright hospital light, Pluta's mother glowered before she softened; she hovered by the door, leaned against it, as if the sight of Pluta made her legs weak. Stale air cooled Pluta's bare head. Dried sweat and dirt had tightened the scratches on her face. Her bruises pulsed. It felt as if one side of her body prickled green and the other smoldered purple, as if half her face had collapsed upon itself, as if her body had shriveled and was no longer Tatiana's body, no longer even Pluta's body, but a discarded husk. At the sight of her mother, she wanted to whimper.

Why couldn't she slip into that loop, she knew it was there—she'd been so close—why couldn't she slip into it and disrupt it, go further back in time, how many times had she thought, well, they might be wrong, well, she might yet rest her cheek on his arm again. How far away she'd gone from those thoughts! The hissing in her ears oceanic. Static was all there was, cold, echoing static, remnant of the rush of water.

The wings gave an involuntary flap and she sat back, crushing them into submission.

Unuttered, unutterable, their dialogue of glances went something like this:

What could we say to each other?

Why do we hesitate? Why don't we rush to each other immediately in motherly-daughterly embrace?

You look much the same.

You look terribly different.

Where have you *been*?

Where have *you* been?

What have you done?

What now?

What now?

Isabel broke the bubble, crossing the room to sit on the couch, afraid to touch her daughter, afraid to hurt her. Daniel would have scooped her up in his arms—or maybe she would be too big for his arms now, but he would find a blanket and cover her from the cold hospital air. Isabel worried that if she wrapped her in her arms she would squeeze too hard, she would be overwhelmed and nearly snap the girl in two, or worse, worse yet—because this was what she really felt—she wouldn't be able to embrace the girl with sufficient warmth. And though she knew, rationally, that she wouldn't do it, she was afraid of her impulse to punish, to smack. But how battered! Maybe she doesn't want to be touched. Daniel would know how to tread that line. Isabel didn't, but he would just *know*. Maybe he would kneel beside her, maybe take her hands in—

Isabel touched Pluta's wrist. She tried not to shake.

From the back of her daughter's throat came a gurgle. Isabel wanted to pass out at that unearthly, inhuman, infantile gurgle, a last-breath gurgle. The girl could sit up, so it was clearly not her last breath, despite everything, despite her battered look, despite whatever gutters she'd been traipsing through. She was sitting there, alive, and Isabel had touched her, and in response she'd made that involuntary noise, that muddled wolf-pup cry. Isabel held on, encircled the wrist with her fingers, gripped the couch cushion with her other hand, tried not to be overwhelmed by the stench—such an abominable *stench*—that emanated from her daughter. What on earth had she done?

"Do you want a blanket?" Isabel asked, so quietly she wasn't sure she'd uttered any words.

Pluta nodded yes.

Isabel roved around the small lounge, opening cabinets, but they were empty or else held paltry collections of brown swizzle sticks and pink sugar packets. She glanced into the hall—Bobby was gone and the detectives were still far off—and grabbed the attention of a passing nurse, demanding a blanket. Back in the lounge, she took away the empty can of soda and unfurled the bleached knit blanket, wrapping Pluta inside of it.

A gentle knock on the door opened a floodgate. Isabel consented to whatever barrage was necessary. There was a full medical examination. A social worker floated in, a psychiatrist. Because of the late hour, there would be certain things that needed doing in the morning. She peered up and down the hall; that Bobby person had not reappeared. She told the detective about him, described him, his shiftiness. The detective nodded, said he would look into it. Then she was swallowed in bureaucracy. After the examination, a doctor talked of excising growths. At first Isabel thought it was some sort of euphemism for a terrible disease, something Pluta contracted while doing bad things (they hadn't discussed it, mother and daughter, they'd barely exchanged words, words were impossible—perhaps the girl had said *mamá*, but perhaps Isabel had imagined it). She suspected and feared bad things and hoped she was wrong. She felt as if she were

235

underneath a dirty glass, nodding consent to things she couldn't stop if she wanted to. It would be a simple procedure, the doctor said calmly, without a hint of horror.

So Isabel said: "Whatever you can do now, do now." Then they would leave this place forever.

Now. This word opened a chasm for Pluta. Now. Not what had been, not what had happened, not what could possibly be understood let alone discovered; not what will be, how will things go, how will we live, will we live together, will we live together but apart, will we love or simply tolerate, will we even tolerate, will we hate, will we continue to hate if hating was ever part of it: simply now. Little steps in place, barely moving: blast and chisel the remaining dirt off, douse the flesh in rubbing alcohol, sanitize it (was it ever sane?), sterilize it, for it is now teeming with millions and billions of winged microbes. Now, little moments of eyes opening, sensing eyes, not blank eyes, not mad eyes; little moments of breathing out, breathing in; moments of fists grasping and slackening, wings curling in and cocooning. Now, cut them off or bind them tight. Now, growing skin, layer upon layer of skin, now a hardening, now a crusting, now a calcifying. She imagined exoskeletons for them both, mother and daughter, moving together at arm's length from one another. Arm's length was all that was possible, a careful dance. The Professor had been the most human among them, the balance in their awkward encounters, the warmth. So a new balance was needed for this dance, for claw touching claw, shells clacking, exoskeletons blindly scuttling together edgewise.

Two days after the maelstrom of official inquiry, Pluta, in a faded hospital gown, dozed in her room. The growths had been excised and she was neatly covered in sterile bandages, and they'd be leaving soon—in two or three days. A pang of hunger hit Isabel for the first time in a while, a painful growl. She went to the cafeteria and examined premade sandwiches wrapped in plastic. What should have been moist looked dry; what should have been crusty looked moist. Not a single morsel enticed. Empty-handed, Isabel wandered out of the cafeteria and into the small gift shop beside it. Lilies, carnations, and chrysanthemums sat in plastic buckets beside helium balloons that swayed beneath the air duct. Isabel had a lime-green ribbon strung around a bunch of chrysanthemums and stuck them in a cheap glass vase.

Late-summer sun streamed through the window by Pluta's bed, a goldenrod light. Isabel put the flowers on the nightstand in a sunbeam. Her stomach growled, which made her feel exposed. She drank a glass of water. Pluta rustled in the sheets, sat up and watched as Isabel pulled a chair closer to the bed. They were alone in the room. The nurse had already checked in. She wouldn't be back for a while; they knew the pattern now, generally. The noises in the hall seemed to mute.

Isabel caressed Pluta's shoulder. Pluta looked down at her hand. Isabel kept it there.

"So," Isabel said. She hadn't meant to ask her right then, but it came out of her mouth because she wanted to know, she had wanted to know for two days but hadn't been able to ask, and now they were finally alone, there was finally a quiet moment, a moment that didn't seem ripe for intrusion. Pluta hadn't told the social worker, hadn't told the psychiatrist. Maybe she would tell her mother. Maybe then they could move forward together, find a new way. "Who is he?"

Pluta looked away. Isabel saw how she tried to keep

237

her face blank but how her brow furrowed. So now Isabel rubbed her shoulder as if to encourage. She tried to invigorate her, tried to summon it out of her. "Who is he?"

Pluta seemed intent on staring at the floor.

The rub became brisker. Then she shook Pluta's shoulder, shook it just a little bit harder.

"Who is he? Who is he? Who is he?"

Epilogue
1984

THE WAR, as they'd begun to call it in the papers, had ended with another war. One internal, horrific; the other for show, and absurd. In April 1982, Argentina fought Great Britain for a sparsely populated archipelago called the Malvinas, or the Falklands. Perhaps the rationale was that it would be a source of national unity. Perhaps it was meant to distract from the mounting discontent. Almost everyone in Argentina, it seemed, knew of someone, had heard of someone who disappeared. But even if they hadn't, the rapid inflation, the layoffs, and the extreme uncertainty had made life difficult— nearly impossible. Briefly, the gambit seemed to work. *We're winning*, proclaimed the magazine *Gente*. But by June, Great Britain had retaken the disputed islands and declared the confrontation over. In 1983, the dictatorship dissolved.

Some of the people who had scattered around the world (Isabel still had trouble with the word *exile*) began returning. For a while, Isabel and Pluta had made a life in New York. They moved into a two-bedroom apartment in the same uptown area, and Pluta finished high school in the city, at an all-girls school a few blocks from the apartment. She hated the school. It was small enough that everyone there knew each other and seemed to have known each other since they'd learned the alphabet. But when she asked to go to the large public school twenty blocks away, a nice big school where she could hide comfortably in a crowd and more easily reinvent her past, Isabel gave a definitive no, and so Pluta discovered an easier path, the path of least resistance: an impassive exterior.

If she had trouble communicating before, in these years after her summer of wings it seemed even worse. She spoke to her mother even less; became, with her, willfully mute. She filled the silence between them with drawings. What started out as idle doodling, a way to bide her time while stuck at a school desk, became an active thing that took up all her attention, a constant effort to blot out the tea kettle, the static.

Casey sent Pluta a letter at the beginning of the school year. Two weeks later, Pluta finally opened it. It was a sweet, hesitant message: a hope that she was feeling better and that they would see each other again. Pluta wanted to write back, but her hands shook too much. Eventually she gave up; but she kept the letter in her school bag, rereading it on occasion.

Sometimes Pluta spoke with Lolo on the phone, no longer caring if it might make Isabel jealous that she spoke with her aunt and not her mother, for Lolo was, in a way, more of a mother, even though she'd never had children. Lolo never seemed to mind Pluta's sideways talking or her need to blot out static. *I think I know what you mean*, Lolo would say, and then send packages with books and tapes on Ladino and other rare languages.

Pluta took the sounds she heard and the alphabets she saw and fed them into her drawings.

She filled notebook upon notebook with charcoal or pencil or rich oil pastels, in indigos and violets, in incandescent greens and shades of rust, creating scratched, wiry outlines that recorded what she'd envisioned: the dark, watery viewpoint of crustaceans, the geodesic vision of slow-flying bugs, the feeling of hooks, the pulse-catching rush of a fall.

Isabel was content to have her retreat like this at the weekly drawing club at the school or in her room, as long as she knew where she was, and Isabel would occasionally and even not too reluctantly go downtown with her to the big art supply store on Canal Street, Pearl Paint. She didn't ask what Pluta and Lolo spoke about or ask to look at the drawings, but had Pluta offered to show them to her, she would have. Isabel had grown tired, and through being tired she'd grown. In her own Isabel-way, she was gentler.

Bobby had vanished. There was no trace of a young man named Bobby. The police asked if Isabel wanted to press charges, but she didn't know what charges to press. Pluta gave away nothing. Then Isabel decided: the less noise, the less scandal, the better.

Then came the day to return, to see what was what. Isabel and Pluta boarded a plane to Buenos Aires.

Isabel drank two glasses of wine in rapid succession. It didn't seem to matter whether she closed her eyes or opened them, which way she looked or didn't—a ghost with wooden hands knelt alone in their garden. She knew the ghost well. She saw him bumping around the house, fumbling into rooms, looking for books and papers long ago burned. The ashes surely remained where she'd left them. She pressed curled fingertips to her lips. How would they ever—they could never live there again.

What layers of dust. What moth-eaten heaps.

She would unlock the house, liquidate it as quickly as possible. She considered the possibility of never living in Buenos Aires, or even in Argentina, again.

But there would be some sort of commission to uncover the truth of the matter. She could add his name to a long, long list—some said twenty, maybe thirty thousand names. Maybe his bones would be found one day, identified. The ball of a mace in her gut resurged. A geneticist was involved in the whole thing. Pluta's blood could be taken. She could submit his dental record, if she could find it. She wasn't sure of his dental record. She wasn't sure about her daughter's blood, about whether it had become, in that terrible time, diseased. She didn't know if that part of the blood could somehow change. She didn't want to ask. The mace revolved upon itself, prickling.

Pluta sat beside her mother, looking out the window. The white noise of the plane overlaid the static that never quite left, only fluctuated in volume.

A man across the aisle asked if they were sisters. Isabel laughed before ordering another glass of wine. Pluta wondered if home would feel like home. She wanted it and dreaded it. Dreaded his absence in what should be a familiar place but might not be familiar any longer, or might be familiar, but too empty. What would it feel like, coming back to that? There was a hollow in her stomach but a tightness around the hollow, a tightness that intensified when she thought of the empty house.

She tried to sleep; she'd become very good at sleeping. In the last few years, sleeping felt most like home. Sleeping or drawing or sometimes talking to Lolo. Sometimes her back itched, a ghost itch, a quiver of nerves awakening and regenerating, and she arched her back as if to retract wings that weren't there and refocused on the task at hand, whatever it was, over the roar of water, the echo of an empty house. She closed her eyes against her mother's polite laughter and felt herself slipping.

There was a loud, drafty hum. He couldn't see. His wrists felt hot, his hands dead cold. He swayed on a bench, knocking against others swaying as if on a rapidly moving train, but it was not a train, it was a plane. They had been told the shot was a vaccination but it wasn't a vaccination. They'd been told they were being transferred, that they would be released, but he grasped now that it wasn't true even as he struggled with consciousness. Maybe the shot had not taken effect as it should, or maybe they intended his semiconsciousness, there was no way to know. His eyelids felt glued shut, he was blindfolded, he had been injected, fallen into a deep sleep, been shocked awake, heat in the wrists, he'd been tied too tightly, much too tightly. Something was very wrong about the pain in his wrists, very different from the bruises and the shocks. They weren't going to release them, he could sense this now, he was being yanked up to standing, he could hear tired huffs of breath, barefoot scuffles. He was barefoot on cold, corrugated metal. There was a draft, a horrible sway and a teeter and then as in a nightmare—maybe it was all an unstoppable nightmare—he plummeted from the not-train, cold air on his skin, the pressure of the fall beating against his bones, his back arched neck craned chin skyward as he reached his arms up from the dark water's approach and heard an echo of the mourner's kaddish—*Yitgadal veyitkadach shmé raba*—his daughter's voice—singing.

FINIS

Acknowledgments

Many kind, generous people helped me with this book and shaped the writer I am today. I would like to thank:

The early teachers who left a mark on me: James Shapiro for the Brothers Grimm; Michael Trano for Queen Mab; Georgia Scurletis for Raskolnikov's dreams; and John Faciano for *Invisible Man*.

My teachers at the University of Washington MFA program: David Bosworth, Jonathan Raban, Heather McHugh, Shawn Wong, Pimone Triplett, and especially Maya Sonenberg for sentence diagrams, fairy tales, and continued mentorship.

Chris Abani, for listening, encouraging my vision, and being such a strong source of support.

Writers who've helped me inch through early drafts, however inscrutable: in Montreal, Sean Michaels, Julian Smith, and Andrew Ladd; in New York, Helen Koh, Roohi Choudry, Laura Colby, Aharon Levy, and my fellow art-in-novels lover Kris Waldherr; and in Seattle all my UW MFA classmates, especially Lisa Nicholas-Ritscher, Ashley Herum, Sarah Erickson, Paige Eve Chant, and Kristen Millares Young.

Corinne Manning, for pep talks and violet tea. Karen Benezra, for scholarly insight and dumplings. Lisa Levine, for gummi bears and mermaids.

Eduardo, Jorge, Valeria, and Nora, for telling stories and fielding questions. And the librarians at the

Museum of the City of Buenos Aires, for handing me a pile of magazines from the 70s and 80s. And Eric Sadvari for serendipity.

The Vermont Studio Center and Centrum Foundation, where I made significant progress on this book.

Gar LaSalle, Artist Trust, Aaron Counts, Angela Fountas, and Sam Ligon, for the big vote of confidence via the Storyteller Award, which came when I thought I might throw in the towel. And Brian McGuigan, for myriad opportunities.

Peter Mountford, for loads of help and advice. And everyone at Richard Hugo House, for being such a tremendous community.

Christine Neulieb, for championing this novel and shepherding it out into the world with illuminating edits. And Amanda Thomas, Feliza Casano, and everyone at Lanternfish Press.

My family, without which I'd be nothing: my mother, Tania, for nurturing every pursuit, however improbable; my father, Gheorghe, for levity, jokes, warmth, and art; my brother, Victor, for imaginary spaceships; my grandmothers, Leni and Eva, for family stories of the Old World and survival. I love you all so much.

Michael, heart the size of Mars at least, for reading countless drafts and continually encouraging the weird; for making me laugh every day; for supporting this writing thing that I do; for travelling the world with me—thank you. I love you infinity to the power of infinity.

Photo credit: Sarah Salcedo
Courtesy of Tall Firs Productions

About the Author

ANCA L. SZILÁGYI grew up in Brooklyn. Her writing has appeared in the *Los Angeles Review of Books, Electric Literature, Gastronomica,* and *Fairy Tale Review,* among other publications. She is the recipient of the inaugural Artist Trust/Gar LaSalle Storyteller Award, a Made at Hugo House fellowship, and awards from the Vermont Studio Center, 4Culture, the Seattle Office of Arts & Culture, and the Jack Straw Cultural Center. *The Stranger* hailed Anca as one of the "fresh new faces in Seattle fiction." She lives in Seattle with her husband.

Follow her at ancawrites.com or on Twitter @ancawrites.